HARRY POTTER
AND THE DEATHLY HAIRBALLS

BY

TIMOTHY R. O'DONNELL

CHAPTER ILLUSTRATIONS BY:

GRIFFIN O'DONNELL

COVER ILLUSTRATION and

THREE BAD KITTEN ILLUSTRATIONS BY:

TIMOTHY R. O'DONNELL

Text copyright © 2011 by Timothy R. O'Donnell

Illustrations copyright © 2011 by Timothy R. O'Donnell

All rights reserved.

No part of this publication may be reproduced in whole or in part, or stored in a retrieval system, or transmitted in any form or by any means, electronic, mechanical, photocopying, recording, or otherwise, without the permission of the publisher.

ISBN 978-0-9825379-8-5

Published by

T.O.S.H. Publishing, LLC

(The Order of the Silver Hand)

www.TOSHpublishing.com

mail@TOSHpublishing.com

Printed in the U.S.A.

THIS BOOK IS DEDICATED TO

RILEY AND GRIFFIN.

IT'S THEIR STORY TOO.

Books by the author, Timothy R. O'Donnell:

Epic Fantasy

The Erthelba series:

Book 1 - Iibrahiim

Book 2 - Polydora

Book 3 - Hgia Lucii

Book 4 - Athandoros

The Hysterical Parodies:

Harry Putter and the Chamber of Cheesecakes

Harry Putter and the Deathly Hairballs

Contents

One
Memories are like Kittens,
Reality is like a Full Grown Cat * 9 *

Two
That really gets my goat! * 21 *

Three
Everything comes to a Boil * 27 *

Four
Where There's a Will * 39 *

Five
The Wedding Crashers * 51 *

Six
Grim Old Place * 57 *

Seven
The Most Exciting Monday Ever * 69 *

Eight
Aftermath * 79 *

Nine
Goldbrick Shallows * 87 *

Ten
A Surprise Christmas Visit * 97 *

Eleven
Christmas List * 109 *

Twelve
Silver and Goat * 115 *

Thirteen
The Three Bad Kittens * 127 *

Fourteen
Home is Where the Fart is * 153 *

Fifteen
Hoaxcrock Destroying Rampage * 163 *

Sixteen
All's Fair in Louvre and War * 171 *

Seventeen
The Holy Grail of Hoaxcrocks * 179 *

Eighteen
Irrational Treasure * 187 *

Nineteen
Calling Elvis * 203 *

Twenty
School of Hard Knocks * 219 *

Twenty-one
The Final Battle Rages On * 235 *

Twenty-two
The Deathly Hairballs * 249 *

Twenty-three
Epilogue: 19 Years Later * 261 *

HARRY PUTTER
AND THE DEATHLY HAIRBALLS

**Memories are Like Kittens,
Reality is Like a Full Grown Cat**

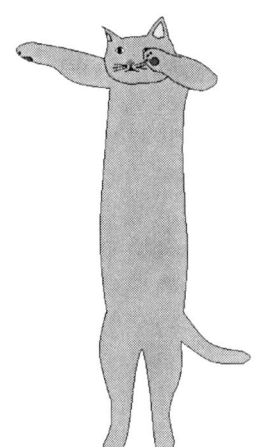

Chapter 1 – Memories are Like Kittens, Reality is Like a Full Grown Cat

Sure they were droplets of blood, but to Custodian Belch they were just another mess to clean up. He mumbled to himself, "Inconsiderate students. Just bleed anywhere. Do they clean up after themselves? Course not! All they've got to do is waive their magic wand and say the magic words, 'AAA drycleaners are the best.' But, no! They just bloody leave it."

He sighed as he bent down to wipe the small dark spot with a damp rag and walked in a crouch down the dimly lit dungeon corridor moving from drop to drop. When he stood up, the cumulative ache in his back made him groan. Even as he did, his squinting eyes automatically surveyed the stone floor for refuse or other aberrations. His eyes fell upon the next object of contempt.

He approached it with a scowl, wondering what was the disgusting thing lying in the darkness. He bent closer until he recognized it.

He mumbled, "Cursed hairball!"

But even as he uttered it aloud, his heart melted and his eyes became watery. He loved cats. As long as he could remember there was a cat in his life. Long ago there was Charles Bronson, Clint Eastwood, and Sly Stallone. And then there was his current one, Chuck Norris. Hairballs

Chapter 1

brought back sweet memories of the many cats from his life, especially of his first cat, Errol Flynn.

He stood there scowling at the hairball. His heart hardened once more as he reminded himself, "Memories are like kittens, reality is like a full grown cat. When you buy a kitten, no one can resist the cuddly, warm, cute and adorable creature. You don't think about the reality of the situation. That kitten is going to become a full grown cat. She's gonna claw your furniture, she's going to cack-up hairballs, she's going to spray her territory with urine, and she's going to leave decapitated mice and rats as her personal gift to you.

The reality is you'll spend more time feeding her and cleaning the litter box for that ungrateful feline than you will cuddling her. But when she's dead and gone, what do you remember? You'll fondly recall the cuddly, warm, cute and adorable creature and forget the disgusting, caterwauling, scratching, flea-bitten, pain-in-the-butt cat."

One thing he wasn't was squeamish. He picked up the hairball and he died. Ironically, his final words had been, "Cursed hairball."

Meanwhile, Harry Putter was dealing with a mess of his own. He was in his bedroom, the master bedroom of the Dirtley family home at 4 Privy Drive. He was almost seventeen, as his birthday was only two days away.

Harry was a thin teenager in regard to his arms and legs, however, he carried a somewhat protruding belly. He had neat black hair, which he wore in bangs to hide the L-shaped scar on his forehead. The hairs on his chin, cheeks, and upper lip were starting to come in now, but at the moment he was clean shaven.

He had a pronounced unibrow and refused to pluck the hairs between his eyes anymore. It hurt too much. He also gave up trying to shave the small spot between his eyes. The first time he had tried, it had been a fiasco. He made his eyebrows uneven to start, and in each of his attempts to correct the matter he overcompensated, making it even worse. Eventually, he had to shave them both entirely off. He got a lot of strange looks for his strange looks. However, since then, the singular eyebrow had grown back, hairier than ever.

Last year, he had gotten a new pair of glasses, but unfortunately had broken them already. He had placed them in his robe pocket and promptly sat down on them. The frame snapped at the bridge and he had makeshift-repaired them with masking tape.

He recently had lost five pounds because there wasn't anything left in the house to eat that was sufficiently fresh or wholesome. Mostly, that was due to the general lack of cleanliness of the Dirtley home. However, the real difference was the Dirtleys weren't around anymore, so no one had bought any food for a week now. Harry had not lost enough weight yet to get rid of his small protruding belly or to risk going outside.

Yet, the mess Harry was dealing with was not the Dirtley home. After so many years at school, he was finally cleaning out his school trunk. It was something he had never done before. He was no longer going to Hogwashes School for Wizards and Witches. He had dropped out recently.

There were good reasons why he wasn't going back to school this year. At the end of his sixth year in school, seventh if you count preschool, he had made a promise to the Headmaster, Elvis Grumblesnore. After Elvis had saved his life from the conspiracy to kill him, Harry said, "I'm sorry I ever considered not coming to school this year. I promise no matter what, no matter how many people want to kill me, I'll always trust you to protect me, and come here, where I belong."

He had not broken that promise. One of the reasons he wasn't returning was that Grumblesnore was no longer alive. It was quite a shock. Late spring, with the school year nearly over, the old headmaster had taken a tumble and it was a bad one. He accidentally fell down the extremely long spiral staircase to the Astronomy Tower, and that was a very tall tower. He was found at the bottom with nearly every bone in his body broken. And unfortunately, he was not found in time for Nurse Pomfrite to do anything about it, try as she did.

It was quite unusual. Everyone had gotten quite used to the school nurse performing the miraculous. Harry remembered many students dying during Defense Against the Fine Arts class only to be back in the swing of things the next day, thanks to Nurse Pomfrite.

And then there was Professor Carnivorous Ape. He had been killed in spectacular fashion. Harry remembered his gruesome demise. He had witnessed Ape's simian body as it was riddled with shot, seared with electricity, shriveled up in flames, and cursed to death. Yet even with

Chapter 1

most of his body destroyed, Nurse Pomfrite had managed to restore his head back to life. And while Ape no longer had a body, at least he was alive. His ape head was sustained in a large glass jar filled with some kind of liquid. He used a hoverboard to move around. He even had his wand and could hold it in his mouth, point it, and mumble the magic words to cast spells. The following year, Ape had resumed his teaching duties, and after Grumblesnore's Death, he had even been promoted to the position of Headmaster at Hogwashes. Yes, Ape's head was alive and well, thanks to the miraculous healing powers of Nurse Pomfrite.

And no one was happier than Harry that Ape was alive. He felt somewhat responsible for his teacher's death. After all, Ape died while trying to protect Harry. Afterward, Harry felt he owed it to the dead simian to take his difficult lessons to heart. Harry spent the ensuing summer trying very hard to maintain inner peace, obey rules and laws, and refrain from violence. It made him break out in a perpetual rash. He was so relieved when, the following autumn, he discovered Nurse Pomfrite had saved Ape's head in a jar. He promptly went back to being his old juvenile self.

Yet despite all her attempts, Elvis Grumblesnore somehow was beyond the school nurse's amazing magical healing powers. Ms. Pomfrite said she had tried everything without success. Perhaps his soul had traveled too far from his body, beyond the range she could call it back. Harry had attended his service and funeral as the revered headmaster's body had been laid to rest and sealed in a special tomb deep in the dungeon bowels of the school. Even Harry still had trouble believing his good friend and protector was truly gone.

More importantly, Harry was not going to school this year because he was on a mission to destroy his mortal nemesis, Lord Moldyfart. Nearly two years ago, Harry had learned about a sinister prophecy. An ominous prediction had been made before Harry was even born, back when the Fart Lord was a boy known by his given name, Tom Farisol Riddly. The troubled teenager had received a dire and ominous prediction, "Someone will steal your heart!"

The young man took the terrible harbinger of his doom quite seriously and literally. He believed a horrifying enemy was destined to rip his still

Memories are Like Kittens, Reality is Like a Full Grown Cat

beating heart from his very chest. And so the young Fart Lord took precautions just as any half-sane wizard would. His fear inspired him to become the most powerful and ruthless sorcerer the world had ever known. He made unholy pacts with demons, penguins, and llamas. And he had insidiously split his very soul, placing portions of it in repository objects, known as hoaxcrocks. If even one fragment of his soul remained intact, he could not be completely destroyed and could eventually recover. Several times, Harry had brought about severe setbacks to Moldyfart's nefarious plans. The last time Harry said the magic word, "Cripes," and Moldyfart changed into a groundysnout, a flying pig. However, He-Who-Must-Not-Be-Smelled had always sooner or later managed to regain his strength. He had done so once again. His disguise had been restored. He had regained his human form.

At first, Harry took the prediction seriously, too. He imagined some wise and profound seer was the source of the prophecy, and so he believed Moldyfart must surely have good reason to fear for his life. That is, until last year, when Harry found out from Professor Ape's head that the sinister and deadly harbinger of doom's source was a tiny slip of paper in a Chinese fortune cookie. Ape knew. He was with Tom Riddly at the Cho King Palace Chinese Restaurant that fateful day. He had read the fortune himself.

When Harry learned of it, he became incensed with burning rage and undying hatred for his archenemy. Moldyfart had murdered his parents over a stupid message from a fortune cookie! Harry had even tried to vent his rage upon the bearer of this news, his least favorite professor. However, Ape, the Poisons Class teacher, craftily escaped on hoverboard out the window to avoid Harry's wrath.

Harry was now obsessed with vengeance. He had given up yoga and his quest to find inner peace. He would find peace once his mortal enemy was obliterated. He was prepared to devote the rest of his life to destroying Moldyfart. He vowed one day to exact his revenge upon his nemesis, even if it was the last thing he ever did. And he often imagined the satisfaction he would derive by ripping the still beating heart from his enemy's chest. He could not think of a more fitting ending. However, his best friend Ron Cheesley always told him, "Right after, you should take a bite out of it. That would be bloody brilliant and savage cool!"

Chapter 1

Harry thought the idea was bloody gross.

And so, Harry was preparing for what was sure to become his greatest adventure to date, as Harry called it, *The Quest to Destroy Lord Moldyfart*. He felt quite sure that it would inevitably be turned into a best-selling book and a mega-movie blockbuster. He pictured Matt Damon or Brad Pitt playing his role in the latter.

But first things first, Harry had to confront Moldyfart and destroy him before the lucrative story rights would bring him riches. And so, he was preparing. Specifically, he was cleaning out the mess that was his school trunk. He was trying to sort the items within, particularly to find items he would need for his journey from the garbage that had accumulated inside. And there was quite a collection of trash from over the years, everything from wrappers from chocolate slugs bought while he was in preschool to his latest cell phone bill. It was seven years worth of litter.

However, among the refuse, there were saved items that brought back fond memories. These he meant to keep stowed away as cherished mementos. Going through the trunk was a bit like taking a trip back in time. The deeper he delved, the further back he traveled.

One of the first of such items he found was last year's Advanced Poisons class text. It was an old beaten up copy that had a former student's copious notes inside. The student had called himself "The 2/3rds Nigerian Prince" and he "needs your help transferring money into your country." The notes inside were from a true master of establishing email fraud schemes.

Harry had never studied school material with half the devotion he had given the profuse notes of the 2/3rds Nigerian Prince. In fact, he had neglected nearly all of his class work last year while establishing and running his very own email racket and in so doing, had made a killing. After all, he spent nearly his whole life breaking the rules, and after a summer of obeying them, he was ready to make up for lost time. Running email scams was such a natural extension of his conceited belief that the rules don't apply to him, that he felt no guilt for these minor transgressions. He justified his actions saying, "If someone is stupid enough and greedy enough to fall for it, they don't deserve to keep their cash."

Memories are Like Kittens, Reality is Like a Full Grown Cat

But the most shocking part was when it turned out Carnivorous Ape was the 2/3rds Nigerian Prince. Behind all of his big talk, advocating that laws should not be broken, the Headmaster of Hogwashes was the father of the email fraud scheme. Perhaps it was his own guilty past that drove him to preach to the students to obey the rules. Perhaps it was just a front operation to hide current nefarious scamming activities. Or perhaps he was just young and had not yet formed his convictions.

The next item Harry discovered in his very own personal dumpster dive was a paper napkin with the logo of "The Ambergris Grill." It was from his sixth year at Hogwashes, seventh if you counted preschool. He had saved it as a memento from the class trip to Atlantis. With the Chamber of Cheesecakes and the conspiracy to kill him, what an adventurous year that had been! Even the class trip had gotten off to a rocky start when the submarine was attacked by Ron's pet squid, Nemoy. Released by Ron in back of the school into the waters of Lake Iwannabealifeguard, the squid had grown to gigantic proportions. It had feasted upon mermaids and Gruntbelows, also known as undersea goblins, and had even eaten Gandulf the Off-White. The trip had been nearly ruined. However, Ron commanded Nemoy to release the sub and his ever faithful pet obediently complied. Thank goodness!

The whole trip to Atlantis had been wonderful. They stayed at the famous Parthan Hotel. They visited the Neptune Museum, the King's Palace, the Atlantic Aquarium, and the Coliseum. To top it all off, dinner was at the exquisite Ambergris Grill restaurant. After a year fraught with insane cravings for cheesecake, Harry had a harmless slice for desert and it was simply incredible.

Delving deeper into his trunk, Harry pulled forth the trophy from winning the Fry-Wizard Tournament. It was quite an accomplishment and had brought many followers into the Order of the Harry Putter Fan Club and a lucrative sponsorship from the Fry-Wizard company, makers of magical frying machines.

During the tournament, he competed with the best students from three schools. The first challenge was to fry eggs. The second challenge was to fry up fish and chips. The final and most difficult assignment was to

Chapter 1

navigate the Labyrinth of Death, past deadly blast-end toots and a ferocious minotaur, answer the Riddle of the Sphinx, and get to the trophy before their rival students.

Yet Harry's victory was so closely contested by another student, Cedric Biggleby, that they reached out and grabbed the trophy at the very same moment. However, it was all an elaborate trap. The trophy was really a bottle of port, and when the two grabbed the cup, it teleported them into the clutches of the Fungus Eaters. In order to restore their master, Lord Moldyfart to his full powers, the Fungus Eaters killed Cedric.

Afterward, Harry battled the Fart Lord. He was so nervous facing He-Who-Must-Not-Be-Smelled that his intestinal fortitude abandoned him. The noxious odors arising from the encounter rendered the nearby Fungus Eaters unconscious. In the end, Harry discovered when he needed to, he could match Lord Moldyfart, stench for stench.

Harry went on to win the tournament. However, the death of Biggleby cast a cloud of suspicion over the whole event. One had only to smell Harry to know that foul play was involved. The ensuing investigation into the matter eventually cleared Harry of wrongdoing. Harry felt terrible for his fellow student, Cedric, and his family, but not badly enough to give away the trophy.

Harry sighed and continued to pull trash from his trunk and fill up garbage bags. That is, until he came across a ticket stub from the circus. It was from when he tried to locate his uncle and godfather Serious Smack the Clown. Harry had very little family left and Aunt Hachooie was resentful and severe. She treated him so badly, he couldn't help but try to locate someone who might be more of a relative to him.

It was the second time the Fungus Eaters had set him up. They leaked information to Harry of the whereabouts of his uncle. Harry couldn't help falling into their trap. Finding his uncle was his vulnerability, and they took full advantage of it, setting a trap for when Harry arrived at the circus. If it weren't for all his good friends, he himself might not have survived.

As it turned out, his uncle wasn't so fortunate. Serious Smack died that day in a sudden and bizarre circus tragedy while trying to escape from Harry. It was all Harry's fault that his uncle was dead. If only he hadn't

Memories are Like Kittens, Reality is Like a Full Grown Cat

pushed, hadn't persistently kept trying to find him, the clown would still be alive today. While it certainly brought up a bad memory, at least he didn't get all choked up about it anymore.

The good news was that he found out soon afterward that Uncle Serious had a brother, named Regular Smack. Harry had another relative, another uncle – Regular Smack the Mime. Harry smiled. Sure, he knew a mime was one of the most evil kinds of magicians, so powerful they were able to discern objects that no one else could see or touch. Harry just knew he could overlook whatever peculiarities Uncle Regular possessed. The bad news was that his uncle's cell phone must be broken because every time Harry called, he picked up, but never answered. Harry was quite determined to find his missing uncle and make up for lost time. Only this time, he'd set up his own trap – an uncle trap. He'd capture Uncle Regular and force him to talk!

Harry sighed. It would have to wait. First he had to take care of Moldyfart.

The next object that provoked memories was the tattered remains of the Frozen Dairy Desert Cookbook. Sloberic Slipperin was the creator of the Chamber of Frozen Dairy Deserts and had left the cookbook to his heir as the key to the sinister chamber. Ron's sister, Ginny, had brought it in to Hogwashes. Shortly after, students and teachers and even Custodian Belch's cat were getting brain-freezed by tasting the ice cream novelties.

Meanwhile, Ginny became possessed by the persevering spirit of Tom Ridley, as he attempted to steal her body and regain his mortal form. Fortunately, Harry was able to defeat the giant mildew stain that guarded the Chamber of Frozen Dairy Deserts and destroy the cookbook, closing the chamber forever. Though he didn't realize it at the time, in doing so, Harry had destroyed one of Lord Moldyfart's hoaxcrocks.

Furthermore, he had rescued Ginny, and she had never been the same. She had fallen in love with her hero and savior, Harry Putter. She was constantly chasing him around, pulling him into closets to kiss him, and swearing to him of her undying love. Each Valentine's Day she made a foolish spectacle of herself with some elaborate display of her affection. Last year, she hired a mariachi band to serenade him with love songs. It was all very embarrassing, because for her own protection, Harry wasn't

Chapter 1

supposed to see her. It would be far too dangerous for her, since Lord Pull-My-Finger might kill her or worse in order to get to Harry.

Finally, when he closed the Chamber of Frozen Dairy Deserts, he saved Grumblesnore's job. The headmaster hadn't done anything to locate or close the sinister chamber, and so, was about to get the sack. Grumblesnore complained about it. He always said he was looking forward to an early retirement. Harry thought he knew Grumblesnore better than anyone. The teenager said, "Grumblesnore likes to grumble, but deep down, it's just his way of expressing how much he cares."

In reality, if it weren't for Harry, Grumblesnore would have loved to remain at Hogwashes. Harry had eventually irritated the headmaster to the point where he felt like killing the boy. Harry remained quite oblivious that Grumblesnore hated him. He even thought his attempts to choke the life out him were just good fun – playing around with his mentor. How he missed the good times with Grumblesnore now that the old wizard was gone.

Harry sighed again and was quite amazed at how many bags of garbage had been filled so far and there was likely to be a couple more. He continued his work, occasionally finding useful items that had been buried in trash. He found unused glue gum, silly string, dungbombs, butt-enlarging crackers, a ventrilo-whoopy cushion, anti-matter toothpaste, and even his dribble goblet of fire. He had forgotten all about that. He fired it up and was thrilled that it still shot forth flames large enough to singe someone's eyebrows off. He thought to himself, "I'll have to try it out on Mudley." Mudley Dirtley was his cousin.

Then he remembered that the Dirtleys, Aunt Hachooie, Uncle Vermin and Mudley had all been captured by Lord Moldyfart last week. It was likely by now they had been tortured to death for information about Harry. Harry sighed once more and wondered, "Who else can I fool with it?" Eventually he gave up thinking about it and set it aside to ponder about later.

After a few moments, he pulled forth an old library book, *The Cat in the Hat*. He said out loud to himself, "Wow, that must have been in there since first grade."

Memories are Like Kittens, Reality is Like a Full Grown Cat

He tried to remember if his Hogwashes library card had already been revoked by then. Perhaps this was the book Hermione took out for him that he never returned? She had complained about it for years. Then he sang out, "I know what somebody's getting for Christmas!"

Hidden at the bottom of his trunk, Harry discovered his dust bunny collection. It had been long forgotten. The last time he saw it was shortly after he brought it in to class on the second day of preschool for show and tell. Faco Maldoy, the Popular Rich Kid, asked with derision, "What's the matter with you, Putter? Don't you have any real toys?"

Of course not! He didn't have money, parents, or other relatives to give him toys. The closest thing he had was the Dirtleys, and they treated him like, well – dirt. Actually, they were kinder to dirt than to Harry. They ignored dirt, but they mistreated the weird little boy with the L-shaped scar on his forehead. Even on Christmas and on birthdays he received gifts like clothing, or a new broom and mop set to clean the kitchen floor.

For toys, Harry made due with dust bunnies collected from under beds and dressers. He even shaped them into bunnies, kittens, puppies, goats, and other animals. However, after Faco's remark, he buried the collection at the bottom of his trunk. This was the first time it had seen the light of day since. It made Harry smile to see his old childhood friends again and he spent several minutes trying to remember all of their names. Then he set them carefully aside in his small pile of saved mementos.

He glanced in the trunk to see if anything else was left. He spotted something dark in the nearest corner.

He asked out loud, "What's this? A hairball? Huh, how'd that get in here?"

He plucked it from its resting spot and tossed it in the garbage.

Chapter 1

Chapter 2 – That Really Gets my Goat!

Later that evening, numerous members of the Order of the Harry Putter Fan Club arrived at the Dirtley's house, 4 Privy Drive. There was old Mad Dog Hooty, Frommundigus Filcher, Wrestlemania Trunks, Fabulous Butterpants, Rhomulus Loopin, and Kingsley Shuckthecorn. They were an assorted group that had just one thing in common, – they were all diehard Harry Putter fans.

Two of Harry's former teachers were there, Cubious Hasbeen and Minerva McGooglesnot. Many of the older Cheesley children had come, including Bill, Greg, Marsha, Jan, Cindy, and the twins, Fred and George. Flour Delacour, Bill's fiancé, was there by his side. They were due to be married in a week.

The Cheesley's mother, Molly, and their father, Arthur, were waiting for everyone back at the Boil along with Ginny and little Suzanne. As usual, Perky Cheesley was missing, and since he was a stuck-up twit trying to brown-nose his way up the ladder at the Ministry of Magic, everyone was thankful for his absence.

Interspersed among them were Harry's many friends he had made among the students at Hogwashes including his two best friends, Ron Cheesley and Hermione Stranger. There was Neville Largebottom and his girlfriend, Looney Luvnoodle. And there was … oops, my mistake. That was all his friends, and really Neville and Looney weren't even close friends, they were more acquaintances who couldn't come up with a better excuse for not coming when put on the spot.

Chapter 2

Notably absent was Grumblesnore. The large group just wasn't the same without him. Harry would have felt a lot less nervous, too, if the crafty old wizard were there to protect him.

However, what made the gathering seem even larger than usual was the seven mannequins, all dressed up like Harry. In fact, most of his clothing wasn't packed in his suitcase, it was on the seven dummies, eight if you count Harry.

Their plan was ridiculous. There were probably a dozen more practical ways to get Harry safely from his residence; past his enemies, their spies, or whoever else may be watching; to the Cheesley home, known as the Boil. The easiest would be to use the Cheesley's bottle of port to teleport there directly. However, Hermione was also a powerful enough spell caster to teleport without a portal key, or as the wizards call it – abberate. She was also very familiar with the destination, which is necessary for teleportation, and she could instantly bring Harry along with her.

Or the whole lot of them could have piled into Fabulous Butterpant's giant pickup truck. The little man had the magically extended cab edition, so everyone could have piled in comfortably and stayed together to protect Harry.

Or Harry could have disguised himself so whoever was watching would not have been able to recognize him. He could have accomplished this simply by shaving off his eyebrow. Or he could have disguised himself as a zombie and shuffled away unnoticed. No one would be able to distinguish him from normal late night foot traffic consisting of the undead and sleepwalking neighbors.

Or they could have distracted any onlookers and while they were glancing the other way, they could have high-tailed it out of there. For a distraction, they could have set off a few fireworks, waited for the ice cream van to come by in the afternoon, or had a few members of the group walk about outside in hazmat suits while looking concernedly at hand-held devices such as a cell phone or a meter of some kind.

Or they might have smuggled Harry out in something big, such as a piano, a coffin, a basket, a giant wooden horse, a rolled up carpet, or a mattress.

That Really Gets My Goat!

Instead, someone suggested a different plan. One of them had the brilliant idea to fix up seven decoy versions of Harry. Only a close observer would be able to distinguish the real Putter from the imposters. Then to further confuse their enemies, they would split into small groups, each escorting one of the seven dummies, eight if you count Harry. Finally, they would take a variety of routes to the Boil and a couple of other false locations. In the end, the Fungus Eaters would become as confused as they were. Their enemies wouldn't know where Harry was at all.

When the plan was first suggested, no one thought it was a very good idea. However, someone eventually spoke up and said it was a fine idea. One person even went so far as to call it a fabulous idea. A few people agreed, mostly because they thought it was Fabulous Butterpant's idea.

Fabulous Butterpants is a very short man who overcompensates by wearing cowboy boots and a cowboy hat, by driving a giant pickup truck, and by starting fights. He gets his name from wearing pants that are so tight that he uses butter to get them on. He sells light-up merchandise for a living – light-up gloves, light-up belt buckles, light-up sneakers, light-up ice cubes, etc. However, most of his income comes from selling fireworks. He likes country music and sings and dances to it.

Fabulous Butterpants has the annoying habit of writing everything down, whether it's important or not. He's usually very quietly taking notes on what everyone else says. Once in a great while, it's a useful reference, but in general, no one knows what he does with all the notes he takes or all the notebooks he fills.

There was something scary about the little man and several of them were quite afraid of him. He seemed the type that might turn his rage upon them at any moment. He might berate them, or start a fight, or quite possibly grab a shotgun out of his pickup truck and start shooting up the place and everybody in it.

No one spoke up to tell him the plan was stupid and once someone said it was a fabulous plan, others kept their mouths shut and went along with it. Still others were bored and didn't really care or feel like arguing about it anymore. Flour Delacour silently thought the whole thing reeked of unwarranted paranoia. But she was from France, and did not know the ins and outs of British eccentricity. Furthermore, she wasn't quite used to

Chapter 2

Bill's weird family yet, so wasn't really up to diagnosing the family's friends.

They all began to prepare for the big move, by obtaining the mannequins to pull off the grand scheme two days later. Now was two days later.

Under the cover of darkness, the large group left the Dirtley home en masse.

Fabulous Butterpants, Neville Largebottom, and Looney Luvnoodle escorted a version of Harry to Fabulous's large red pickup truck. Wrestlemania Trunks and Rhomulus Loopin along with Jan and Cindy Cheesley unceremoniously crammed themselves and one of the imposters into the Dirtley's mini cooper. Meanwhile, Greg, Marsha, Fred and George Cheesley carried a mannequin to a waiting rickshaw, they propped it up, and began to pull it at a run down the street. Minerva McGooglesnot and Kingsley Shuckthecorn accompanied their facsimile to a group of three waiting centaurs. They strapped it on the back of one, and each mounted one of the other two. They took off at a gallop. Frommundigus Filcher and Mad Dog Hooty put their dummy on the back of a stolen golf cart and peeled out. Hermione and Ron balanced themselves and one of the decoys on Harry's John Deer 2000 lawnmower and sped away. Bill and Flour conducted their rendition of the teenager down the street to the nearest bus stop.

Cubious Hasbeen carried the one and only Harry Putter under one arm and Harry's suitcase under the other to his motorcycle. He placed the suitcase in the side car, where Harry's goat was already waiting and busily chewing the upholstery. In the meanwhile, Harry held himself as stiffly as he could in order to best resemble the seven decoys. Hasbeen placed Harry on the bike and mounted in front of him. He kick-started the engine and took off.

Cubious Hasbeen is the groundskeeper and manager of the Hogwashes Magical Creatures Petting Zoo in the back of the school. Being 1/32 part giant, Hasbeen is more than just a big man, he is humongously large and fat. Hasbeen always reminded Harry of a large grizzly bear that had escaped the circus wearing a small tent. It was probably because Hasbeen

That Really Gets My Goat!

got his clothing from Omar the Tent Man's Big and Tall Fashions, that, and all his hair.

In fact, Harry found it difficult to ride behind the giant oaf, as his long hair was constantly whipping in Harry's face. He could barely tell where they were, with the big man's body and wavy tresses blocking his view. It was only when the bike rolled to a stop at a red light that Harry could finally spit Hasbeen's locks out of his mouth and take a good look around him.

The roads were wet with puddles from the recent rain. The suburban traffic was light since it was so late at night. Harry watched a large black SUV roll to a stop next to them. The showy car had dark tinted windows, spinning wheel rims, and a flashing license plate that read, "Thug Life." Harry stared at it impressed.

Then the passenger side window rolled down and Harry could hear the strains of some rock n' roll classic coming from the car stereo inside. It seemed hauntingly familiar. Harry started to hum the tune, waiting for the chorus to come, just knowing once he heard it, he'd remember the song's title.

That's when the spells started coming fast and furious. His enemy Lord Moldyfart was singing out the lyrics:

> "In a gadda da vida, honey
> Don't you know that I'm lovin' you
> In a gadda da vida, baby
> Don't you know that I'll always be true."

With each "In a gadda da vida," the Fart Lord stabbed his wand toward Harry and a blast of energy accompanied the words to the worst of the unforgettable curses, the Iron Butterfly Curse, also known as the Death Curse.

If it wasn't for Hedbutt, Harry would have died. The goat leapt up from the side car and came between Harry and the Death Curse's malignant energy. Harry's poor goat was dead before he hit the asphalt.

Harry cried out, "Cripes, it's Moldyfart!" He pulled out his wand from his robe pocket and began defending himself. Meanwhile, Hasbeen with a quick turn of his wrist, hit the gas. The rear tire accelerated too fast and

Chapter 2

spun on the wet road surface without gripping. The bike slued a little bit forward and to the side.

Moldyfart continued to sing, barely heard over the screeching tire:

> "Oh, won't you come with me
> And take my hand
> Oh, won't you come with me
> And walk this land
> Please take my hand
>
> In a gadda da vida, honey
> Don't you know that I'm lovin' you
> In a gadda da vida, baby
> Don't you know that I'll always be true."

His driver, Vermintail, one of the Fungus Eaters, joined him on the chorus, shooting more Death curses out the SUV's window. Harry was hard pressed to block all their spells. His enchantments of protection shot forth with bright silver flashes of energy to meet and dissipate their unforgettable curses.

Harry yelled out again, "Cripes! CRIPES! CRIPES! It's Moldyfart!"

The Fart Lord bellowed in return, "I changed the secret word, you moron!"

Finally, the motorcycle tire began to grip the road and the bike surged forward through the red traffic light. Fortunately, Hasbeen was able to avoid a collision with a car crossing his path. The SUV blasted through the red light, following the motorcycle and side car.

There was a final exchange of spells between He-Who-Should-Not-Be-Smelled and Harry, and then Hasbeen pulled far enough away to prohibit more dueling. Soon, he was able to shake their pursuit. They were safe for the moment.

Chapter 3 – Everything Comes to a Boil

 Harry and Hasbeen were first to arrive at the Boil. Ron's parents heard the loud motorcycle and rushed out the door in order to meet them. However, they were a bit surprised to see Harry alone. Cubious Hasbeen had departed, his bike accelerating thunderously down the avenue considerably far away from them already.

 Molly Cheesley had always been a sort of a surrogate mother to Harry. She was the short, plump, and frumpily-dressed mother of so many Cheesley children that Harry always lost count. Being a mom was what Molly did best. She had assisted Harry numerous times since the first time they had met, when she helped him get to the elusive train station area Platform π (Pi) in preschool. She had hair so orange it always reminded Harry of the rind of Muenster cheese.

 Arthur Cheesley had curly nuclear-orange hair. It almost seemed to glow. Ron's father works in the Ministry of Magic. For a long time he was in the Department of Muddle Artifacts. However, recently he had been promoted to head of the Office for the Detection of Evil Objects that No One Can See or Touch. It was about as cushy a job one could possibly find.

 Every so often, the Minister of Magic, Dufus Dimeeyore, would walk into his office. All Arthur had to do was get up to greet his boss and then exclaim, "Watch out, you almost knocked over the Poisonous Cup of the Villain Iago!" or some other such nonsense. He'd pretend to catch the

Chapter 3

falling object before it hit the ground, dust if off a bit, and place it back on an invisible shelf.

Dufus always fell for it. He'd nervously excuse himself saying, "I'm so sorry! I see you're quite busy here, uh … detecting things. Keep up the good work. Sorry to have bothered you. Please, go back to what you were doing."

Later, Dimeeyore would wonder how he could have bumped into an object that no one could touch. However, he always got so flustered when it happened, that he felt like a bull in a china shop. He immediately excused himself and so remained baffled. He was always quite glad to have Cheesley around to take care of all the evil intangible objects. The man had profound skills, yet he was not one of those terrible mimes. Dimeeyore made sure Cheesley was well compensated for his extensive knowledge and extraordinary abilities.

One look at the parents, and it was easy to see why all the Cheesley children had orange hair. Between the two, there was probably no other color available in their genes. They also seemed to have a lock on the nerd gene. One had only to look at them to see what house at Hogwashes they had belonged to back in their day. There was a clumsy, goofy, good nature to the Cheesley parents and most of their household.

One other common trait the Cheesleys all shared was the deficiency of their magic powers. While they were full-blooded wizards, their abilities were pathetic. The household was elfless. That is, they attracted no elven servants because their magical abilities were so weak that elves weren't interested in serving them. And they suffered for it. In the wizarding community, they were the butt of many jokes and never taken seriously.

Ginny ran past her parents and latched onto Harry in a tremendous hug. She said, "Thank God, you're alright!" She showered his face with kisses until her disapproving father pulled her away.

Molly noticed how pale Harry looked and worriedly asked, "Where's all my babies! Why aren't they here yet? Are they alright?"

Harry was a little surprised that he and Hasbeen were first to arrive. However, then he realized the big man had driven rather fast to escape their pursuing enemy. Fearing for his life, the giant oaf had driven his motorcycle like a madman. Furthermore, he barely slowed down outside

Everything Comes to a Boil

the Cheesley home to toss Harry and his suitcase off the bike and onto the strip of lawn outside the front gate to the Boil as he drove past without fully stopping. The rolling suitcase had opened up and Harry's things were scattered in front of the fence. Harry thought he could still hear the loud engine's roar in the distance as Hasbeen continued to hasten away from them.

Harry brushed some bits of grass from his shirt as he replied, "I'm sure they'll all be here soon."

Molly snorted, "Hmmph, I need a drink!" She went back inside, presumably to get one.

Just then, Harry heard the distinct clip-clop of approaching hooves upon the street pavement. Harry and the remaining Cheesleys turned and saw three centaurs approaching with Harry's transmogrification teacher, Mrs. McGooglesnot, Kingsley Shuckthecorn, and "facsimile" Harry.

McGooglesnot from the back of her centaur, cried out, "What a disaster! How did I ever get involved in this mess?"

Shuckthecorn nodded silently in agreement to her assessment of the situation.

Arthur asked, "What happened?"

McGooglesnot dismounted and answered, "We were attacked! That's what happened!"

"By the Fungus Eaters. They ambushed us en route," Shuckthecorn added.

Harry exclaimed, "Me too! Hasbeen and I were attacked by Vermintail and Lord Moldyfart himself! They even killed Hedbutt, my goat!"

Tears welled in Harry's eyes now that he had a moment to finally take in the fact that his loyal friend, and the deliverer of his mail, was indeed dead. Not only that, but Harry would not even have the chance to give his friend a decent burial. His body was probably still lying in the street. Poor Hedbutt! The goat had lovingly and loyally sacrificed his life to save Harry. Either that or it was just a dumb coincidence.

McGooglesnot said with derision, "Sure, make it all about you, Putter! I need a drink!" She headed toward the front door.

"I could do with one myself," Kingsley said as he followed.

Harry watched the two centaurs undo the straps holding the disassembled pieces of the dummy on their friend's back. They tossed the

Chapter 3

parts unceremoniously to the strip of lawn outside the gate. Then they trotted off without a word of goodbye.

Harry called after them, "Thanks, guys, uh, ... for all your help!"

Then he got a good look at the misused mannequin. A leg and an arm were no longer attached to the torso. The robe it was wearing happened to have been one of Harry's best. Not any longer. It looked like it had taken a severe beating. It was frayed, muddy in spots, and dusty in others. It looked like it had been dragged for several miles. There were even two noticeable hoof prints on its back.

Just then, the mini cooper raced down the avenue and came to a screeching halt in front of the Boil. It was in much worse condition than it had been an hour ago. The rear end had been smashed in. The rear window was shattered. There were several scorched areas, where spells had hit the vehicle and seared the paint. Harry noticed someone's ankle and foot were crushed in the driver's side door and hanging outside the car.

The driver, Rhomulus Loopin, opened his door and clambered out. He staggered a few steps to the gate, opened it, and flopped himself down on the front lawn. He said, "Holy crap!"

Wrestlemania Trunks opened the passenger side and slid the seat forward to allow Jan and Cindy Cheesley to struggle their way out of the back seat. Jan yanked the Harry imposter from the rear bench and wrenched it angrily through the car door. Harry noticed when she did the pant leg hanging outside the driver's door disappeared suddenly, and the plastic foot fell and rattled upon the street curb.

Her movements continued to be quick and angry as she stepped around the car and tossed the imposter on the strip of lawn next to the other mannequin. She briskly went to the front door, yanked it open and yelled, "Mother!"

Harry took a closer look at the second dummy. One plastic leg was in an inhuman position up around the ear and it wasn't missing one foot, but both of them. The head had a rather large hole blasted through it and the plastic wig hair was burnt and melted in clumps.

Harry timidly asked, "Errr, is everyone alright?"

No one answered.

Everything Comes to a Boil

Wrestlemania Trunks was trying soothingly to coax Cindy Cheesley out of the back of the car. The young Cheesley woman was curled up in a fetal position.

Molly Cheesley abruptly ran through the front doorway. The screen door slammed against the side of the house. She sobbed and yelled, "My baby!"

The frumpy housewife was able to eventually coax her daughter from the back of the little car. The stout woman carried her large sobbing child across the lawn and into the Boil. Wrestlemania held the gate and the front door open for them, then followed inside.

Harry nervously asked Rhomulus, "Heh, maybe you could use a drink?"

Loopin sighed and said, "Good idea. I'll have a gin and tonic."

He made no effort to move, so Harry felt obligated to fetch his order. A few minutes later, he returned with the drink that Arthur Cheesley had mixed for him. He offered it to Loopin. The man had momentarily drifted off to sleep and startled awake when Harry spoke. Rhomulus sat up and accepted the gin and tonic. He downed it in an instant. He let out a dry sigh and said, "I'll have another. Make it a double."

As Harry was heading back inside to fetch a double, he was surprised when Ron and Hermione suddenly appeared in front of him on the doorstep with a popping noise of displaced air. Hermione's hand was on Ron's shoulder. Though their backs were turned to Harry, he recognized his good friends instantly.

He called out, "Hey, guys!"

Ron visibly startled and let out a small cry of despair. His wand was already in his hand. Without even looking and before he recognized it was Harry who had snuck up behind him, he quickly turned around and shot off a magical attack. Harry flinched, but the wild spell missed him. The little bolt of electricity hit the mini-cooper several yards behind him, searing a relatively small burn mark in the driver's side.

Harry laughed and said, "Oh my God! Ron, look what you did to the car!"

Ron's eyes went wide when he saw the damaged vehicle. He looked at his wand and said, "Did I do that? I guess I don't know my own strength."

Chapter 3

Like the rest of the Cheesley family, Ron's magic powers were a mockery to the word 'powers.' Ron had the standard Cheesley nuclear orange hair, which was always a mess. He was a big young man with freckles and had become quite handsome as an older teenager. Yet he was a big galumph. He tripped over his own big feet often and broke magic wands with startling frequency. He was obviously still at that awkward teenage phase. As his body had grown, Ron still hadn't managed to compensate for it. He had been in this clumsy stage for years, and it was beginning to seem like he might never get past it.

Hermione tittered nervously. In one hand, she held a molded foam rubber arm of "decoy" Harry. Her other arm was looped through the steering wheel of Harry's John Deere 2000 lawnmower. Harry noticed Ron was holding the dummy's other arm. The rest of the mannequin was nowhere to be seen.

Though Hermione had grown up to become a lovely young woman with a beautiful figure, she had a disproportionately large head. The expanse of naturally wavy strawberry-blonde hair, which she wore down to her shoulders, made her head seem even larger. She had bushy eyebrows and more hair upon her cheeks and chin. Her mustache was one that any teenage boy would sport proudly. However, she was not bigheaded about that. More so, she was embarrassed of it and bleached it to make it less noticeable. It really didn't help a whole lot, if any.

"Sorry about your tractor, Harry. It didn't make it," she said, handing him the steering wheel.

Harry swallowed as he accepted it and replied, "Don't worry about it. I'm just glad the two of you are alright."

Hermione answered, "We're fine, but it's a good thing you weren't actually with us. There wouldn't be much left of you."

To demonstrate the truth of her statement, she held forth the dummy's arm, which was singed and still smoldering. Ron held his up too, which was in similar condition.

Ron blurted out, "We were attacked! Fungus Eaters were all over the place, like flies on jam."

Hermione corrected, "More like flies on a dead squirrel!"

Rhomulus brushed past Harry and muttered, "Never mind, I'll get my own."

Everything Comes to a Boil

However, they all turned when a vehicle skidded to a low screeching halt, skewed right in the middle of the street in front of the Boil. It was an old white delivery van with the logo, "Armond Hammer Plumbing."

Fabulous Butterpants hopped out. He cheerfully said, "Hey guys!"

However, Harry, Ron, Hermione, and Loopin simply stared, each of them silently wondering, "What the heck?"

Fabulous pushed his kangaroo-skin cowboy hat up on his brow a bit and scratched his forehead. He said, "Say, umm, you guys didn't happen to see them two students, Looney and what's-his-face?"

Now everyone was really worried.

Loopin answered, "Perhaps you should explain what happened to them? After all, they were last seen with you, and you were in charge!"

Fabulous spluttered nervously for several minutes explaining what happened to him with so many unnecessary words and so much extraneous information.

"Well, it's like this. You know how I like to be prepared for whatever comes up? How I keep all sorts of things in my satchel that maybe someone else might not bother to carry with them. For example, look at this."

From his leather satchel, he pulled forth a tin of mints. He said, "Now mind you, it may look like mints, but inside, I keep a small supply of animal crackers. Why? Because you never know when you're going to come across a food emergency! Say someone was a diabetic and hadn't eaten. Their blood sugar might drop to the point where it was dangerous. Or say there was a sudden snow storm. You might get stuck in it. It'd be a terrible thing to be stuck somewhere without anything to eat for days on end. So I like to be prepared."

Harry interrupted and asked, "What does that have to do with …"

Butterpants interrupted back, "I'm getting there. Anyway, another thing I like to keep in my pocket is one of them little packs of tissues and some hand sanitizer. Let me tell you, those things come in handy. Just this morning, I had a sneezing fit that made me think I might be allergic to something."

"Oh c'mon already! What happened?" asked Ron.

Chapter 3

Butterpants continued, "Well, I, that is, I saw one of those 'Best-One' convenience stores and figured I should stop and get another package of them little tissues."

Hermione interrupted with disbelief in her voice, "You stopped on the way?"

"Well, yes, but it was only for a minute," answered the little man.

When the cowboy paused, Loopin asked, "And?"

Butterpants finally admitted, "When I come back out, my pickup was gone."

"And Neville and Looney?" Loopin asked.

Fabulous replied, "Last I saw 'em, they were in the truck."

"And the keys to the vehicle?"

Fabulous sheepishly answered, "I left 'em in the ignition when I went in the Best-One."

Rhomulus blurted out, "You are a complete ..."

Harry interrupted, "What's that?"

There was a ba-bam noise, followed by another, and another. The noise was getting louder, coming closer. They all gazed out at the street and saw Greg and Marsha Cheesley pulling a wobbly broken-down rickshaw. Each time one of the wheels reached a certain point the whole rickshaw lurched, with a noisy ba-bam. The Cheesleys couldn't manage to pull it in a straight even path, but back and forth down the street. There were wisps of smoke trailing them.

George Cheesley was slumped down in the back of what was left of the man-pulled carriage. Fred was in the back pushing. They stopped just outside the front gate.

The exhausted Cheesleys rubbed their aching arms and shoulders.

Fred said, "At last. I don't think I had another spell left in me. I feel like I could sleep for a week."

Greg and Marsha were too tired to argue. Greg said, "Let's just get George inside."

Marsha called out to the others, "Give us a hand, guys. He's hurt."

Only then did everyone realize that George's shoulder and shirt were soaked with blood. Harry, Ron, and Hermione along with Fabulous and Rhomulus all moved to help. Harry noticed the back of the rickshaw had

Everything Comes to a Boil

been almost entirely shot out by hundreds of spells. There were even flames still burning feebly in a few spots.

The group quickly carried George inside so the older adults could examine his wound. Harry, Ron, and Hermione went back outside to wait for the others to arrive. While they were waiting Harry went to the rickshaw and discovered what was left of the mannequin, only his imposter's head remained. It was no longer attached to a body, and it was charred in several spots. The glasses it once wore were gone, and it had been solidly struck three times by curses and had many other grazes. Harry tossed it on the small pile of parts on the lawn. He wondered what could have happened to the rest of the dummy's body and his clothes.

He also decided to pick up the rest of his belongings from the Cheesley's lawn. As he was doing this, a taxi pulled up. Neville got out and called to Ron, "I need twenty Euros!" Largebottom likely was only carrying galleys – the gold coins that wizard's use as currency. Ron went inside to get him the needed fare.

Arthur Cheesley came out and paid the driver. Neville helped Looney Luvnoodle drag the decapitated remains of their version of Harry from the back seat of the cab.

Arthur said, "Thank God you are both safe. We would have had to kill Butterpants, had anything happened to you. Err, …what did happen to you?"

Looney told their harrowing tale. As soon as Fabulous went into the convenience store, they were attacked by Fungus Eaters. Neville slid over to the driver's seat and backed the pickup out. He nearly ran their enemies over and sent them scattering and diving for safety.

Then he took off. The Fungus Eaters got back in their car and gave chase. They began shooting spells and Looney began returning them as best she could. Neville got nicked by a blast and lost control of the truck. He crashed it into a fire hydrant, through a hedge, over a garden statue, through some shrubbery, and into someone's living room. Neville explained that it wasn't his fault. The airbags went off, so he couldn't see anything.

Looney disagreed, "that was afterward."

Fortunately, no one was hurt in the crash. They pulled the dummy out of the pickup, as the Fungus Eaters knocked in the front door of the

Chapter 3

residence. There was a quick exchange of spells while the two students made a hasty retreat out the back door. Out in the yard, as they were scrambling over a fence, Harry's head got blown off. The Fungus Eaters laughed evilly and gave each other chest bumps and high fives. Then they left.

Afterwards, the teenagers made their way on foot back to the Best-One. When they arrived, Butterpants was already gone, so Neville used his cell phone to call for a taxi.

Shortly after Neville and Looney had arrived, speculation and finger pointing began. Many felt the group had been betrayed by Fabulous Butterpants. It was his stupid plan in the first place. But worse still, it seemed that the Fungus Eaters were two steps ahead of them the whole time. They all began to feel Fabulous was not so fabulous after all.

Butterpants overheard those arguing on the front lawn and came outside to confront them. He said, "I heard that! I'm not so fabulous, am I? It was my stupid plan in the first place, huh? I'll have you know that's a bold face lie! It was not my plan. I don't know why you people think I would suggest something so stupid. I'll have you know, I bit my tongue when this plan first came up. I bit my tongue for a lot of the dumb ideas that were being tossed around. But this one? It was idiocy from the get go."

Just then, Frommundigus Filcher rolled up in what was left of his golf cart. The top half was gone. He got out and yelled, "Quick! Give me a hand! Mad Dog's hurt bad!"

The confrontation was put on hold as everyone rushed to help get old Mad Dog Hooty inside to medical attention. They laid him out on the long dining room table. A moment later, Mr. Cheesley pronounced the old man dead on arrival.

Arthur said, "Someone get the school nurse, Ms. Pomfrite."

McGooglesnot was the logical choice. She immediately said she would do it. A moment later, she abberated and was gone.

Molly Cheesley sobbed, "And what's become of Bill, my baby!"

Fred rolled his eyes and said, "Mum, he's your oldest."

She cried out, "Hmmph, he'll always be one of my babies."

Everything Comes to a Boil

They all tried to console her and tell her that Bill and Flour would turn up all right.

And then the arguing really got heated. Everyone felt certain there was a spy among them and that spy was Butterpants. Fabulous was appalled and insulted. He had been on their side for years. He'd been fighting Fungus Eaters since back when he was a student at Hogwashes. And if he were a Fungus Eater, he would not have been able to even get past the closed gate to the Boil. The strongest protection spells were in place to keep the Boil safe from enemies.

Rhomulus Loopin would not listen to a word of it. First he called Butterpants out, then he called Butterpants names, and then he got really ugly. He said, "You're not so tough without your stupid pickup truck, and your stupid cowboy boots, and your stupid cowboy hat."

And with that, he snatched the hat from Butterpants' head. Rhomulus threw it on the ground and he stomped on it with his foot, crushing it. The flattened hat, however, sprang back to its original form. Rhomulus tried again and again, and each time he lifted his foot, the hat returned to its normal shape. Bam, it was crushed. Pop, it was back.

Butterpants said, "Isn't it great. It's made to do that. You can stomp on it, sit on it, whatever. It never loses its form. Sure, it's a little more expensive than a regular hat, but if you've ever accidentally sat on your hat, you know…"

Loopin yelled, "I don't care!" He gave the little man a shove.

Butterpants got real mad then. He tossed down his satchel on the dining room floor and brought up his fists, saying, "There ain't no call for that, Loopin! There ain't no need to get all violent. We can settle this like gentlemen. But if you can't be civil, I'll whoop you fierce."

Loopin yelled, "Get out! Can't you tell you're not wanted here?"

Butterpants looked around at the others, waiting for someone to contradict Rhomulus. The others avoided his scrutinizing gaze. He saw then, Loopin was right. He wasn't wanted.

His voice cracked as he said, "Well, if, …if I ain't wanted…" He was choked up and did not finish his sentence. He picked up his Kangaroo-skin hat and left.

Chapter 3

Just as he was heading out, Bill and Flour walked in. They were noticeably scrapped and bruised. They conducted their rendition of Harry to a living room chair. It was missing both arms and legs. The head and torso had been thoroughly flattened and marked by tire treads.

Molly Cheesley ran to her son. She hugged and kissed him.

He asked, "Hey, what's going on?"

After they had brought Bill and Flour up to date, Hermione said, "Everyone, listen to this!"

She was holding Fabulous Butterpants' notebook. She had picked it up off the dining room floor after it had spilled from the little man's leather satchel. She recited:

> "Rhomulus: 'Even if we could teach a bear to sky dive, how would we get the Millennium Falcon?'
> Arthur: "Obviously that plan won't work."
> Bobby the Elf: 'Well, what we could do is make up seven decoys of Putter and split up into groups to escort them all. Then no one would be able to tell which was the real Harry!'
> Arthur: "That sounds like a fine idea."
> Molly: "Yes, finally, an idea that will work."
> Rhomulus: "I like it. In fact, I think it's a fabulous idea! It's certainly something we could pull off quickly. All we'd have to do is get some dummies. No offense, Putter.'
> Harry: 'Ha, ha, very funny.'"

Hermione added, "Looks like we owe Fabulous an apology." The others all silently stared at their own feet.

Harry cried foul, "Wait! Bobby the Elf? He wasn't even there when we were discussing it. That can't be right."

Hermione replied, "That's what it says here, and I remember, Rhomulus did call it a 'fabulous plan.' Maybe that's why we all thought it was Fabulous's idea. Does anyone remember if Bobby was there?"

No one could remember having seen the elf that day. Or at least, no one admitted to it.

Chapter 4 – Where there's a will

Harry felt much better once Nurse Pomfrite resurrected Mad Dog Hooty. Prior to it, he felt terrible. Their plan had been such a disaster from inception to completion. And as unlikely as it seemed, there was a possibility that the plan was really another attempt by Bobby the Elf to get Harry killed. It was well-known that Bobby hated the teenage boy and had plotted and schemed to bring about Harry's death. But how could the elf have snuck into their meeting? And how could he have proposed a plan without anyone noticing? How could they all have been so oblivious? Or was there something more to it?

The next morning, Harry, Ron, and Hermione began discussing their preparations for Hoaxcrock-destroying season. Harry, of course, put on his bravado. He tried to convince Ron and Hermione not to come with him, saying, "It's far too dangerous."

Ron sighed, "Phew, What a relief!"

Hermione elbowed him and said, "I've already packed and you're coming."

Then she proceeded to tell Harry all the efforts she had already made to get ready. She had even gone so far as to blatantly alter her parents' memories with her magic. They no longer think they have a daughter. And to keep them safe from the approaching Final Battle, she sent them

Chapter 4

off to live in the United States, in Akron, Ohio. Furthermore, she had given her pet cat, Croakshanks, to Looney Luvnoodle to take care of while she was away.

Ron said, "I'm sorry guys, but I can't go. Mum's already forbidden me. She says, 'If I don't start using my brain, I'm going to end up dead.'"

Just then, Mrs. Cheesley came in and added, "Hmmph, given the lethal combination of the dangerous company you choose for friends, and the fact that you're a nimrod, I'm surprised it hasn't happened already!"

Everyone was quite embarrassed and wondered how long Mrs. Cheesley had been listening. She sent Ron on an errand.

The rest of the day, Ron's mother kept not only the three teenagers, but the entire household busy with chores. Bill and Flour's wedding was now less than a week away. Everyone was busily preparing. Ron was sent off to be fitted for his wedding robe. Harry didn't see him until just before dinner. After dinner, Ron dejectedly told his friends he had to wash the windows.

Hermione objected, "But it's dark outside."

"That's what I said," Ron mumbled.

Hermione rolled her eyes, "No problem, I'll use my magic and we'll be done in five minutes."

Mrs. Cheesley came in and said, "Afterward, Ron's going to Aunt Pearl's to help her wax her legs."

Ron started to gag. He cried out, "Ugggh, I just threw up in my mouth a little."

The following morning, Molly Cheesley scolded Harry in a private conversation. She took him aside and let him have it, saying, "I hope you're satisfied! Another person, this time our good friend, Mad Dog, has nearly died, all because of the unending conflict between He-Who-Must-Not-Be-Smelled and you, Harry. Well, let me tell you something, mister. It takes two to fight. You insist on hostility, young man, and one of these days, something terrible is going to happen because of it. If you make a war of it, it's your friends, Harry, that will suffer. Do you want to be responsible for that?"

Where There's a Will

The tubby teenager replied, "Why are you blaming me? I was just a baby when Moldyfart murdered my parents and first tried to kill me. He's been trying to destroy me ever since."

"Don't you sass me, boy. I'll take a wooden spoon to you! Just what have you done to end this feud, hmmm? Have you even once tried to see things from his point of view? I'll bet he's not such a bad guy once you get to know him."

Now Harry was really confused. Moldyfart, not such a bad guy? Get to know him? This was crazy talk!

He angrily replied, "Not such a bad guy? What's the matter with you? He's insane and totally evil!"

Molly answered, "Stop being a drama queen, Putter! No one is totally evil. I'm quite sure Tom has some very lovely qualities."

"Tom?"

"Yes, The Fart Lord is an actual person and he has a name. Tom has feelings, too."

Harry felt like he must be on a hidden-camera show. His brain was having trouble comprehending this discussion. He repeated her words in the form of a question. "Tom has feelings, too?"

Mrs. Cheesley sighed, "Have you ever tried to work out your differences? Have you ever had a conversation with him? Have you ever even spoken to him?"

The teen with the L-shaped scar on his forehead, still consternated, asked, "Spoken to him?"

"Don't play stupid, young man! Answer the question!"

Harry felt so befuddled that he couldn't recall. All he remembered was dueling with Moldyfart. Maybe they had traded insults, but they certainly never held a conversation. Harry swallowed and sheepishly replied, "Well, no, but …"

"Well, I have."

At this, Harry had a sharp intake of breath. In that instant, he jumped to a quick conclusion. Moldyfart had gotten to her and put her under an evil spell! No wonder she was acting so strange lately. She was always around listening to his conversations with Ron and Hermione. She must be the spy!

Chapter 4

Molly said, "Yes, Tom and I went to Hogwashes together. And even though he was a Popular Rich Kid and I was in the Nerd House, he was always quite pleasant and sweet."

Harry deflated, thinking, "Oh well, scratch that theory."

He answered, "C'mon, Lord Moldyfart? Pleasant and sweet?"

"His name is Tom. And yes, not only was he pleasant and sweet, he was quite handsome, too."

Harry asked sarcastically, "Umm, you do realize he doesn't have a nose?"

The housewife scolded, "Don't you give me that! A person can't help it when something happens to disfigure them. You should feel sorry for him. He was handsome back when he was a teenager. And yes, he had a nose then, a cute one."

Harry thought, "Moldyfart was cute? This is too much."

Harry laughed and said, "You really had me going there for a minute. Good one, Mrs. C. But, you overdid it with the cute part."

"Harry, you need to think about what you're about to do before you do something you'll regret. A lot of people might end up dead. You just think about that, mister!"

And with that, she tromped off, leaving Harry with quite a lot to think about.

As he walked down the hallway in the Cheesley's house, he thought, "One thing's for sure, I can't mention this to Hermione in front of Ron. Ron would, first of all, never believe it. And secondly, he was such a mamma's boy! He'd likely get quite angry if someone talked badly about his mother. More likely, he'd go berserk."

As Harry mulled these thoughts over, he was suddenly abducted. A fiendish shadow grabbed him and placed a strong hand over his mouth to prevent him from screaming for help. A powerful and iron-like grasp irresistible pulled him from the hallway and into one of the bedrooms! And now, his kidnapper was kissing him! It was Ginny. He stopped struggling and kissed her back. It became a long ardent kiss. Like wind upon sleeping embers, it woke the passion within him.

Ginny pulled away and whispered, "Happy Birthday, Harry!"

Where There's a Will

Harry wanted more, a lot more. He kissed her again. Ginny eagerly kissed him back. But when his hand began to wander, she suddenly pushed him away from her. With a shocked expression on her face, she slapped his face and said, "What kind of girl do you think I am?"

Harry was the one who was shocked now. He stammered, "B-But, But..."

Ginny coolly pulled the door open and pushed Harry out of her bedroom. Then she closed the door in his face.

Harry held his cheek and whispered to himself, "Wow."

That evening the Cheesley family held a small birthday party for Harry. It was a simple and pleasant affair. Harry and Hermione were their only guests. There was a birthday cheese with lit candles on top. It was a large wheel of Brie. Mrs. Cheesley had baked it and brought it out with bread and sliced apples. They all sang 'Happy Birthday' and Harry blew out the candles.

Immediately afterward, the children especially the older ones all gave Harry the 'bumps.' They lifted him in the air by his hands and feet. Then they raised him up high and bumped him down hard on the floor. As they did, they all counted to seventeen – one for each year of his life. Then they added, "one for luck, two for luck, and three for the old man's coconut!"

While Mrs. Cheesley was cutting the cheese, there was a knock at the front door. Arthur got up and answered it. A moment later, he returned to the dining room, now holding a black briefcase, a shoebox, and another small parcel. By his side was a stranger wearing a dark gray suit. His hat was held in one hand and a large black portfolio case was in the other. Arthur said, "Allow me to introduce you to everyone. Everyone, this is Dufus Dimeeyore, the Minister of Magic, and my boss." He proceeded to introduce everyone by name to the unexpected guest.

Mrs. Cheesley said, "Please, do sit. We were just about to have birthday cheese. Won't you stay and have some with us? It's Brie, a mild cheese named after the French province where it originated."

Dufus replied, "Why yes, I'm quite familiar with brie. It's quite wonderful and I particularly like it on apple slices. But please forgive me for interrupting your gathering."

Chapter 4

Molly said, "Nonsense. We're happy to have you here and it would be an honor if you would take the first piece."

She held the tray piled with wedges of apple for the Minister. He set the portfolio down and took a slice, dipped it into the warm baked cheese, and took a bite. Then quite shockingly, he dipped the slice of apple right back in again, swirled it to coat it liberally with brie, and popped the rest in his mouth. Everyone's eyes went quite wide and they gave each other embarrassed looks.

Dimeeyore swallowed and said, "Simply fabulous. I wish I could take a seat and stay. However, I've got business to attend to."

Then Arthur said, "Harry, he's here to see you."

Harry was surprised. He asked, "Me?"

Dufus Dimeeyore added, "And Ronald and Hermione."

Arthur showed the Minister and the teenagers to his home office. He said, "Yes, this is the very place for you to discuss your business in private. I'll make sure no one disturbs you."

He placed the Minister's briefcase and boxes on the desk and left the room, closing the door behind him with a sudden loud snap.

Arthur opened the door again and asked, "What was that?"

He picked up a wand that had accidentally been snapped in two by the door.

"Oh, my!" He asked, "Whose wand is this?"

Everyone checked their pockets for theirs. Ron sighed and said, "It's mine. I must have a hole in my pocket."

His father replied, "Well, I hope we have a few spares left."

Ron assured him, "Yeah, Mum keeps them in bulk. I'll grab a new one in a bit."

Mr. Cheesley closed the door again. Once more, there was a sudden loud snap. Arthur opened the door again. Looking down at the floor, he said, "Whoopsie, looks like my wand dropped out of my pocket when I bent over. I hope Molly has stocked up. Oh, uh, sorry to interrupt. It won't happen again."

He closed the door quietly.

Where There's a Will

The three teenagers sat down in wooden chairs. Dufus set his portfolio against the side of the desk and put his hat down next to his briefcase. He said, "I have a bit of unusual business to transact with you. Let me commence by explaining that it is not of my origination. Had my advice been asked earlier, I should not be here now. However, it was not asked."

Dimeeyore had begun to pace for a moment, but he stopped and lifted his leg, setting it over the back of a wooden chair. There he stood with one foot on the seat of the chair and the other on the ground.

"Now, I have been named to execute the last will and testament of one, Elvis Grumblesnore, formerly known as Elvis Pressley. I am a busy man, and in hindsight, I wish I had not accepted this responsibility. At the time, I decided to honor his request because Elvis was always a good friend. However, since then, I have come to discover the unprofessional nature of the business contained therein. And I find the position of executor to my great dislike. He has left a most unusual last will and testament."

Hermione asked, "In what way?"

Dufus replied, "It is customary that one's will distribute the assets of the deceased. Elvis Grumblesnore has given clear instructions to his business in that regard. However, it is most unusual for the deceased to distribute assets for which they own no legal title and can make no legitimate claim of ownership."

The minister continued, "This applies to the property left to each of you."

Despite early misgivings, due to the introduction of the Minister, the three teens could not help but become excited by the words, "property left to each of you."

Dimeeyore looked at Ron and said, "Mr. Ronald Cheesley, it is the dearly departed Elvis Grumblesnore's wish to bequeath to you a rather large property in the United States."

Ron jumped up out of his chair, knocking it down, "Holy Crap, Graceland! I just knew it! Oh-ho-ho! I can't believe it!"

Dufus frowned. He wondered how the teenager could both 'just know it' and 'not believe it' in the same breath. He quickly chalked it up to idiocy. He said, "Sit down, young man, and stop jumping to conclusions."

Ron picked his chair up, sat back down in it, and was gripping the wooden arms tightly as he listened attentively.

Chapter 4

The Minister said, "The property in question is known as Ellis Island. However, there is no question about its ownership. Title of said property has already been established in a 1998 US Supreme Court case. Most of Ellis Island is part of the State of New Jersey and the remainder belongs to the State of New York. Whereas, no portion whatsoever is owned by Elvis Grumblesnore. Therefore, the deceased may have named you as beneficiary of said island, but never-the-less you have no legitimate claim to the property."

Ron said, "Whoo hoo! I own my own island! I own the Statue of Liberty!"

Hermione contradicted, "Sorry, Ron. The Statue of Liberty is actually on Liberty Island."

Ron asked, "How do you even know that?"

Hermione answered, "My parents took me there while on holiday, about five years ago."

Dufus said, "Do enjoy it, young man. Of course, you may visit Ellis Island as often as you like, but when you do, please, leave things the way they are. Any attempt to take possession of it is quite likely to land you in a psychiatric hospital."

He continued, "Additionally, Grumblesnore has left you one pair of soiled blue suede shoes." He handed Ron the shoebox. And here are your corresponding forms."

Dimeeyore pulled a manila folder from his briefcase and handed it to Ron. Then he pulled a pen from his breast pocket and offered it to the teenager.

He said, "I'll need you to sign that you received your property, specifically, the pair of blue suede shoes. Additionally, I am also giving you a signed and notarized statement from me in the capacity of executor. It states that despite Grumblesnore's wishes, possession of and title to Ellis Island cannot and will not be provided to you as part of the administration of the Grumblesnore Estate. It is your right to contest this in a court of law. However, should you choose to do so, you will have to first prove that Grumblesnore is the owner of said island, and not the states of New Jersey and New York. Good luck with that."

And as an afterthought, Dimeeyore added, "Oh, and Ron, it is Grumblesnore's last request that you make every effort possible to have the name 'Ellis Island' renamed to 'Elvis Island.' Good luck with that, too."

Ron replied, "I'll get right on it. It's the least I can do."

Then the Minister turned to Hermione, "And to you, Ms. Stranger, the deceased has left two famous paintings. First, to quote the deceased, 'the masterpiece titled, *Velvet Elvis.*' And second, the lesser known portrait, by the artist Leonardo Da Vinci, titled, *The Moaning Lisa.* The latter work of art, however, is completely and entirely the asset of the Nation of France and not Elvis's to give to anyone."

Hermione laughed, "It's mine and a sissified country like France isn't going to keep from me my rightful property!"

The minister replied, "For your own sake, I strongly suggest you not attempt to take possession of it."

Hermione laughed, "I was only joking! Anyone would be crazy to try."

Ron said, "Hey you know what's weird? The Statue of Liberty is French, and so's *The Moaning Lisa!*"

Hermione sighed, "Ron, The Statue of Liberty was a gift from the French to the United States, It's American, and in case you weren't listening before, it's not on Ellis Island. And Leonardo Da Vinci was Italian and so was the woman in the portrait. *The Moaning Lisa* isn't French, it's owned by France, and it's on display at the Louvre Museum in Paris."

Dimeeyore said, "Finally, Ms. Stranger, there is one more item Grumblesnore has left to you. It is a children's book titled, *The Drunken Tales of Beadie the Blowhard.* You will find the book and *Velvet Elvis* in this portfolio case. And, as you so aptly stated, you will find *The Moaning Lisa* in the Louvre. Please sign, here. And here is your corresponding legal notice."

Finally, the Minister turned to Harry. He said, "And if leaving property that the deceased has no legitimate claim of ownership to pass to his heirs isn't bad enough. Mr. Putter, it is further inconceivable for the deceased to distribute assets that do not materially exist, i.e., articles of a fictitious nature."

Harry asked, "Such as?"

Dufus replied, "Such as the sword, Excalibur, specifically named in the will and described as, 'the original and true sword named *Excalibur*, as

Chapter 4

described in *Le Morte d'Arthur* by Sir Thomas Malory and the known weapon of the legendary Briton, King Arthur of Camelot, and to the exclusion of any replica or substitute sword, which might falsely bear the name Excalibur or its likeness.'"

Hermione said, "Well, actually quite a lot of historians think that Arthur was in fact a real person and became king after the Romans left Britain. However, I'm sure a lot of the story is just a tall tale."

Dufus sniffed, "True person or not, the sword is not known to exist. There is no evidence that Grumblesnore possessed it or any other sword, for that matter. Though, even if he did, ownership of such a vitally historic artifact would likely be contested."

Harry said, "Cool, I'm the owner of a legendary sword!"

Ron congratulated Harry with a high five.

The minister added, "Elvis has also left you one other item." He handed Harry the small parcel. Harry proceeded to open the box. He pulled forth an item wrapped in layers of newspaper. He unwrapped the object, finally revealing it to be a glass snow globe. Inside was a small plastic figure of Elvis dressed in black leather and holding a guitar.

Harry read the caption on its small pedestal out loud, "I'm All Shook Up." Then he noticed there was something floating inside the globe, something brown, hairy and gross-looking. He said, "Ewwwww! What is that? It looks like a hairball!"

Dimeeyore answered, "That would be my guess, too." He added, "Sign here, please. And, ... your notice."

Once the Minister had received signed papers from all three, and had in turn provided signed statements regarding the property that would not be distributed, he was finished. He placed his documents in his briefcase and took it up. He grabbed his hat, and he said his goodbyes, first to the three teenagers, then to everyone in the dining room.

Meanwhile, Harry, Ron, and Hermione sat in Mr. Cheesley's home office. They discussed what had just happened. What was the meaning of the items left for them – the blue suede shoes, the portrait *Velvet Elvis,* the book of children's tales, and the glass snow globe? Did they have anything in common? What about the things that they received, but did not receive? Why did Grumblesnore leave Ellis Island, *The Moaning*

Lisa, and Excalibur to them in his will? The only conclusion they came to was Grumblesnore must somehow be leaving them a message from beyond the grave. What was the message? That was the mystery.

    Mrs. Cheesley came to the office and asked the three to rejoin the others in the dining room. Shortly afterward, it was birthday present time. Mr. and Mrs. Cheesley gave Harry a pager. Arthur said, "It's from the Department of Muddle Artifacts. When someone calls you on the telephone, the pager goes off alerting you that you have a call. That way, you don't have to wait by the phone all day when you are expecting a call. Isn't it ingenious?"
    The teen wizard said he was thrilled.
    Hermione gave Harry an invisible electric guitar. At first, he thought it was a gag gift, an 'air' guitar. However, it was an actual guitar, only invisible. So when he plays 'air' guitar, he can really rock out. Harry loved it.
    Harry was also touched and amused to be given a book from Ron, written by Ron, *How to Stop Dating my Sister*. He was supposed to have stopped seeing Ginny years ago. But if she kept trying to kiss him, how could he help it? Maybe Ron's book would somehow prove useful.

Chapter 4

Chapter 5 – The Wedding Crashers

Friday night, the evening before the wedding, at Bill and Flour's rehearsal dinner, Ron stood up and tapped his wand against his glass. He announced, "If I may have your attention for a moment, I'd like to …"

Percy abruptly stood and loudly interrupted, "Introduce, my brother, Percy, who will make the first toast!"

"Hey, it was my idea!" Ron asked, "Why do you get the first turn?"

Percy answered, "Because I'm older. We'll take turns in order, oldest to stupidest."

Greg, George, Fred, all nodded agreement at first. However, in order of stupidity, they realized their mistake and respectively scowled, frowned, and shook their head in disagreement."

Ron asked, "Why can't we go in order, stupidest to oldest? Uh, I mean, oldest to youngest. D'oh! I mean… darn, I never get the first turn." He plopped down in his chair and waited for his chance. Long before that, the show started.

The affair was at Molokai Munchies Hawaiian Restaurant and Luau, a traditional Hawaiian feast hall in downtown London. Years ago the restaurant had been a smash success and the long table rows were filled to capacity nightly. No more. The place was on the verge of bankruptcy and was cutting corners and employees regularly. The featured program, Huluali'i's Hula Hula Show, once featured true Hawaiian masters of their

Chapter 5

dance. The entertainment was now called Julio's Hula Hula Show and featured truly amateur Hispanic dancers pretending they were Hawaiian.

That evening, the Cheesleys had the place to themselves, though it was not planned so. It just happened to be an even slower night than usual. Only the Cheesley family and their many close friends were there.

The food in general was terrible. However, Harry particularly liked the Hawaiian sweet bread. It called to him, literally. Every time, just before he finished off a piece, the other slices on the platter began vying for his attention. They'd call out, "Ooh, Pick me, next! Me, Me, Me. Pick me!" It was enough to give him a headache.

Harry was a morsel-tongue. He could talk to his food. It was a rather dull and unrewarding superpower, conferred to him accidently when Lord Moldyfart attacked him for the first time as a baby.

Harry particularly did not like poi and he discovered that poi returned his disdain. When Harry announced, he didn't care for it, it quite frankly told Harry, "What do you know? You're a tasteless jerk!"

Meanwhile, the large fancy Mai Tai and Piña Colada cocktails were all depressed and raving drunk. They spoke foolishly and with heavy slurs. Harry felt obliged to put them out of their misery by drinking them. After a while, his headache disappeared. After a while longer, all feeling in his head disappeared.

When he woke early the following afternoon, he had a hangover. Someone was shaking him and his brain felt like it was rattling in his head. He opened blood-shot eyes and saw it was Mr. Cheesley, who was doing all the shaking, and he was saying something.

Harry scolded, "Shhh!"

Mr. Cheesley replied, "Drink it, Harry. It's for your own good. Nurse Pomfrite mixed it herself. She says it will cure your hangover instantly."

Harry leaned over the bed and barfed on Mr. Cheesley's perfectly polished shoes.

"Goodness, I don't know where it all comes from. I would think your stomach would be empty by now," said Mr. Cheesley.

Harry took the hangover remedy and drank it to get the bad taste out of his mouth. He was not overly pleased with the taste of it, but anything was an improvement.

The Wedding Crashers

He felt instantly well again. He said, "Wow! I feel so much better. Sorry about your shoes, Mr. C."

Arthur replied, "That's quite all right, I'll have them cleaned up in a wink. You, however, are going to need a bit more work."

Then he whispered, "And between you and me, you did a great job last night. You almost managed to do in one evening what I've been trying for months to accomplish. You had the bride-to-be in tears and she came this close to calling the whole wedding off! Had I known you didn't like her either, perhaps we could have pooled our efforts and accomplished together what neither of us managed to do separately."

Harry confusedly asked, "What?"

Arthur confided, "Girls like Flour are far too common. Bill is way too good for her. Really, he can do so much better. But don't worry, I still have a trick or two left. With a little luck, I'll still put an end to this before it's too late. Maybe, you can try somehow to keep Bill from reassuring her. That might just be the icing on the cake."

Harry dumbly asked, "Huh?"

Arthur whispered, "That is, if you can think of something to keep him busy. Oh, never mind. Just, whatever you do, don't apologize to the bride for what you did last night."

Then Mr. Cheesley spoke up and said, "And for heaven's sake, get yourself cleaned up already! The wedding's in an hour."

An hour and forty-five minutes later, Harry was clean, dressed, and sitting on a folding chair in the back yard at the Boil. He was hunched over to avoid the searing gazes of many of the other guests. Hermione was with him, however, she was busy talking with Rhomulus Loopin, Wrestlemania Trunks, and Looney Luvnoodle's father, Xylophonius.

Ron, however, was in the wedding party and so had spent the last two hours escorting guests to their seats and standing stiffly up front with his older brothers and the groom. They were waiting for the bride to come outside and be escorted down the aisle between the rows of guests. Everyone had been waiting and wondering what was taking so long.

Then, there was a sudden stir among those in attendance. The bride had finally come out of the house. Everyone was whispering to each

Chapter 5

other, saying how beautiful Flour looked in her wedding dress. Many stood to get a better look or to take a picture.

Mad Dog Hooty poked Harry from behind.

Old Mad Dog Hooty was a former auditor with the Ministry of Magic. In his time, he was the craftiest Certified Public Accountant around. He could beguile anyone with talk of tax laws, credits, loopholes, and other financial talk. He was as tenacious as a mad dog. They said he never failed to dumbfound his quarry, bring in their account, and prepare their financial statements and tax returns.

He had retired a long time ago and now spent much of his day filling out crossword puzzles, while using a large magnifying glass attached to a headband. He had become so used to it, he regularly forgot it was even there and went out with it still in front of his one eye. It was quite effective in making him look crazy. Yet despite appearances, he was one of the most sane members of the Order of the Harry Putter Fan Club.

He said, "Don't worry about it, Putter. At some point in their life, everyone vomits on the..."

That moment, the organist played the introductory notes to the wedding march. Mad Dog Hooty stopped mid-sentence and pulled out his wand. He had been in this situation many times. He was instantly more ready for a fight than those who where bringing it. He was ready seconds before they arrived. Just after the notes, "Here comes the bride," were struck, his first spell took out the organ with jolts of electricity that ruined the instrument. There was a final hideous chord lingering in the air that sounded not unlike the loll of a slowly dying cow.

Everyone was shocked, no one more than the poor organist, who was truly jolted by the nearby bolts of crackling electricity. Everyone's mouth was agape. The already too emotionally-fragile bride stopped after only two steps down the aisle. Her pouting lip was trembling and her eyes were filling with tears.

Harry could only wonder what made Hooty react so. It was the wedding march, for crying out loud, not "In-a-Godda-Da-Vida!"

However, in the sudden silence, Harry heard it. It was a distant and minute sound. He heard the base notes and percussion of a rock song.

The Wedding Crashers

The tempo matched the tempo of the legendary evil rock song. Though he could not hear the tune itself, the hairs on the back of Harry's neck bristled and shivers went down his spine.

He wondered how Hooty could have heard it with the organ playing. He realized, for experienced auditors, like Mad Dog, a single and distant note sends them into immediate action.

Suddenly, people began to shout. "You've ruined the wedding!"

"What's wrong with you, Hooty?"

"He's gone mad!"

Mad Dog yelled, "Get ready! They're coming!"

Harry knew. Mad Dog was right. He pulled out his wand, too. Harry was not the only one. Xylophonius Luvnoodle cast a spell, disarming Hooty. The man thought Hooty was crazy and too dangerous to keep his own wand.

Harry yelled, "No, the Fungus Eaters are coming!"

No one could hear anything in the chaos that ensued. There were cries of dismay, there were screams of fright. Some began to run, knocking down other guests and folding chairs.

And then the approaching nightmarish strains of the legendary evil rock song, "Inna Godda Da Vida" rose in volume until it was blaring over all the other noises.

Fungus Eaters were storming into the back yard. One of them, somewhere in the back of the group was holding a CD player up high, blasting the haunting melody and sending terror into the ranks of guests.

The first two Fungus Eaters to arrive were taken out by the spells of Harry and Rhomulus Loopin. However, there were many more behind them, and they pressed forward to attack.

There were too many. As Harry fought to defend himself and the others, he saw Nurse Pomfrite go down. She had been humbly sitting in the back row of chairs, and so was one of the closest people to their enemies' point of attack.

He also saw Rodolphius Le Deranged, one of the Fungus Eaters, sneer and attack the defenseless Mad Dog Hooty, who was standing close to Harry. The evil man had been captured by Hooty and jailed in Azcabanana, the prison for wizards. Rodolphius saw his chance and took

Chapter 5

it, exacting revenge on the wandless old man. Harry's defensive spell struck Le Deranged down a moment later.

Suddenly, the next thing Harry knew, he was no longer in the back yard. Instead, he was looking at the front door of the Boil. He could still hear the screams of terror and the horror-inspiring Iron Butterfly tune, only no longer so close and loud. Hermione was pulling open the front door and saying, "Quick, Harry, we have to find Ron!"

Only then did Harry feel his stomach lurch from the aftereffects of the teleportation. Hermione had grabbed his shoulder and abberated them to the front of the house. She continued to pull Harry's arm and tow him into the house and through the living room. Twice Harry rebounded off the hallway walls, knocking framed pictures askew. She opened a door. Inside was a closet. It was filled with winter coats, sports equipment, and suitcases. Hermione grabbed a large brown sack and handed it to Harry.

Harry could still hear the chaos going on outside, as she slammed the closet door and bounced Harry back down the hall again. She opened another door and tromped down a stairway into the basement. There she opened the laundry room door, turned on the lights, and dragged Harry inside. Past the washing machine and dryer, there was a utility sink with a large cabinet front.

She pulled open the cabinet under the sink and there was a high-pitched scream. At this, Harry felt Hermione jump and heard her sudden shriek. Ron was curled up in a ball, hiding in the space under the sink where all the pipes were. Hermione grabbed him, and an instant later, they were in a dusty and creepy looking old house.

They were in the entrance hall at Grim Old Place, the childhood home of Serious Smack the Clown and Regular Smack the Mime.

Chapter 6 – Grim Old Place

Ron stood, brushed himself off, and sighed, "Phew! We're safe."

He took a step forward, intending to go into the living room, flop down on the sofa, and rest a bit to give his nerves a chance to calm down. However, with that one step, he felt his shin press against a trip wire and he was struck suddenly in the shoulder by a crossbow bolt! He screamed in pain.

The clumsy teenager stumbled forward and spun around seeking Harry and Hermione's help for the agonizing wound. As he did, he heard an audible click and was almost impaled by a spear that shot out of the wall a mere two centimeters from his face. His eyes went wide at that. He backed away from the deadly weapon.

Hermione yelled, "Watch out!"

Ron turned and saw a suit of armor had dropped its pole axe. It was falling directly at him. He dove forward and fell to the floor, narrowly escaping the sharp blade. It was so close it put a slice in his rented wedding robe and chopped his magic wand in two. However, the young man didn't notice, as a shot gun blast had blown an array of holes into the wall a half meter above his head. If he hadn't fallen, he'd likely be dead.

Hermione yelled, "Ron, stop moving."

Chapter 6

Just then, a small duffle bag jumped out from behind a plant and started scratching and clawing at Ron as the teenager struggled to fend it off. Ron screamed again. He fought his way up to a standing position where he'd be better able to contend with his small attacker.

Harry recognized the assailant. The duffle bag was actually Kreeper the Smack residence House-Elf, which meant he served in a household. He was also a Free-elf, meaning he served the household of his own will. (As opposed to a Slave-elf, one that serves due to a life-saving debt.) Kreeper was slightly less than a meter tall. He had long pointy ears and nose, and beady eyes. He was wearing a small duffle bag with arm, leg, and neck holes cut out.

Harry called out, "Kreeper, stop! It's us!"

Even as he shouted, a trap door opened up. Ron nearly tumbled in. He was teetering on the brink, his arms flailing frantically to avoid the pit behind him. He yelled, "Help!" However, Kreeper the House Elf gave him a shove.

Though the elf was not very strong, the push was enough to send the off-balance young man tipping slowly and inexorably backwards. Realizing he was about to go in, Ron kicked off from the edge and managed to jump to the other side of the pit, landing on his butt. He said, "Phew! That was close!"

The next moment two things happened at once. Kreeper leapt over the pit to continue his attack and a grenade rolled next to Ron's side. The orange-haired teenager screamed his high-pitched shriek. He amazingly caught the elf by the throat with one hand, and picked up the grenade with the other. He handed Kreeper the grenade and dropped him into the pit.

Ron heard a splash and a low guttural growl. A moment later there was an explosion that shook the house. The next thing he knew, a gush of water and a large crocodile flew out of the pit. The monstrous reptile landed on him with a wet thud. He was slammed to the floor under its massive weight. Fortunately, the crocodile was either too stunned or too dead to attack him.

Suddenly, everything was quiet and still. Harry and Hermione turned and looked at each other in surprise. A moment later, they couldn't help but laugh at the bizarre turn of events. However, Hermione went from laughing to crying.

Grim Old Place

She hugged Harry and said, "It's so terrible, Harry. They killed Pomfrite. There's no one who can raise the dead like her. There's no one to resurrect Mad Dog this time."

Harry said without conviction, "We don't know that she's dead. Maybe she survived somehow."

Hermione asked, "Do you think?"

Harry frowned and shook his head.

After they rolled the dead crocodile off their unconscious friend, Hermione took care of Ron's injury. She saw the crossbow bolt had pierced both the front and back of his shoulder. She snapped the fletched end off and pulled the rest of the short shaft through the hole in his shoulder. Then she bandaged the piercing wound.

While she was working, Kreeper the Elf came nonchalantly down the hallway stairs.

Harry noticed him and called out, "Wow, I thought you were dead for sure!"

Kreeper said in a squeaky voice, "Once I realized who you actually were – oh, and sorry, I didn't recognize you at first. It's been a long time since I've seen you three. Anyway, I took the grenade from Ron and let him drop me. It was the only way to get rid of it in time. Then I quickly abberated out. I was gone long before I would have hit the water. Good thing for you, too! You wouldn't like me when I get wet. It makes me crabby."

Harry knew that it was a very bad thing to mix Elves and water. "Crabby" was an understatement. It would have been monstrous. He would have turned into a living holy terror.

Harry asked, "So what's with all the traps?"

Kreeper said, "Mad Dog Hooty set them up. He was worried about Fungus Eaters breaking in."

Harry replied, "I thought the place was protected by spells."

Kreeper shrugged and said, "Spells keep enemies from abberating in, but they don't keep 'em from bashing down the door. With only me around, he thought it would be a good idea to set up a little extra protection to keep the house safe."

Harry scoffed, "Well, he could have warned us!"

Chapter 6

"He said he was going to. I guess he forgot."

Harry asked, "If there are any traps left, would you please disarm them? Someone could get hurt."

Kreeper grinned, "Right away, Master."

Harry raised an eyebrow at that. He asked, "Master?"

"It's been a long time since there's been anyone around to call Master. Can't you just humor me?"

It had been a long time since Serious Smack had died. No one had been around after the Order of the Harry Putter Fan Club had helped Harry sort through the clown's belongings years ago. Meanwhile, Regular Smack the Mime's whereabouts were still unknown.

Harry replied, "Sure, go ahead and call me Master, if it makes you happy."

Kreeper's grin widened, and he said, "I'll go disarm the remaining traps. Let me know if you require anything else."

Harry said he would.

Hermione pouted and said, "You shouldn't encourage him Harry!"

Harry remembered Hermione's feelings about house-elves acting as servants to wizards and witches. She was adamantly against it. He said, "Sorry, I wasn't thinking."

Just then, Ron stirred in half-consciousness. He said, "Mommy!"

He opened his eyes and looked at Hermione for a short while. Then he said, "Hermione, I just had the weirdest dream, really it was a nightmare."

She replied, "Let me guess, you got shot by a crossbow, nearly killed by several other traps, were attacked by an elf, and had a half ton crocodile land on you?"

Ron said, "You dreamed it too?"

Hermione answered, "No, Ron, that really happened."

Ron exclaimed, "Holy crap! I'm lucky to be alive."

Hermione said, "Sometimes I think you have nine lives, Ron."

Harry asked, "Can I get you anything, pal? Would you like some water?"

Ron answered, "Why yes, that'd be nice."

Harry left to get his friend a glass.

Hermione suggested, "You should move over to the sofa, lie down, and rest a while."

Ron said, "That sounds good. I am tired."

Hermione helped him to stand up. As Ron slowly walked over to a dusty chair in the living room, he said, "First the Fungus Eaters and now this. I can't remember ever having a worse day."

Hermione said, "Well, then, cheer up, you have nowhere to go but up."

Ron flopped down into the chair with a poof of dust. Electricity promptly began coursing through his writhing body.

Hermione ran and grabbed the pole axe from the hallway. She ran back and swung the blade down on one of the electrical wires leading to the chair. There was a small spray of sparks. Once severed, the circuit was broken and the current stopped.

Hermione looked at Ron and noticed that his rented wedding robe was singed in many spots and wisps of smoke were rising from the scorched fabric. She quickly patted out a small flame that was sputtering and flickering to life on the front of his rented robe.

Ron said, "Ouch."

Harry walked in with a glass of water. He took one look at Ron and asked, "What just happened?"

Ron replied gloomily, "Nothing. Just me, being me."

At that moment, Harry's phone buzzed. He pulled it from his robe pocket and read a text message that had just arrived. It was from Kingsley Shuckthecorn.

Like old man Hooty, Shuckthecorn is one of the best auditors around, only Shuckthecorn is still currently employed by the Ministry of Magic. He is the Fan Club's official spy within the organization.

Shuckthecorn asks a lot of question and he never answers a question without asking a question in return. This is one of the reasons he's gone far in the ministry. He's so personable and seems to care enough to ask the employees at the ministry questions about their personal lives. The other is that he is a pathological liar who just hasn't been caught lying yet.

The people at the ministry all believe he is a nephew of the Prime Minister of England. That's why the ministry assigned him to the role of protecting his 'uncle.' Once Shuckthecorn was able to get in proximity to

Chapter 6

the head of Parliament, he altered the Prime Minister's memories to make him think he really is Shuckthecorn's uncle.

His text message arrived bearing horrifying news. Harry read it out loud:

OMG Ministry fallen. Dimeeyore's dead ☺. LOL, they are coming!!! Sux 2BU!!!

Ron jumped out of his chair, he had half of his sliced-in-two wand out. He nervously said, "I hear music! Quick we have to hide! Which way's the laundry room?"

Harry gruffly reassured him, "Ron, snap out of it. They're not coming here. No one knows where we are, especially not Shuckthecorn. He was trying to warn us that the Fungus Eaters were about to crash the wedding. Unfortunately, his message arrived too late."

Ron said, "Oh no. I forgot all about that. I hope everyone's all right. I better call and find out."

Harry said, "Yes, you certainly should. Just one thing though, Ron – don't mention where we are."

Cheesley asked, "Why?"

Harry was worried about Ron's mother. She had been acting so strangely. However, he didn't want to upset his friend. He simply said, "The less people who know, the better. You should call."

Ron was on the phone a long while with his mother. While he was talking, Harry received another text. It was from Ron's father.

It read:

Accidently **left gate open, ;) I guess the wedding's off, LOL.**

Harry was shocked. Good friends were seriously injured and most likely dead. Why would Mr. C. do something like that just to stop the wedding? Was he a spy and a traitor too? Both Mr. and Mrs. Cheesley were acting so strange lately. Harry was glad he had asked Ron not to tell

Grim Old Place

anyone they were at Grim Old Place. He reminded himself to talk with Hermione alone, when he got a chance.

A moment later the L-shaped scar on his forehead gave Harry shooting pains in his head. He knew Moldyfart was mad. His scar always hurt terribly whenever the Fart Lord became irate, which was quite often. Moldyfart was generally an angry person. Harry had a sudden vision of He-Who-Must-Not-Be-Smelled. He was yelling at a small group of the Fungus Eaters.

Vermintail was saying, "Cheer up, Master. We brought you a piece of the wedding cake."

The Fart Lord raged, "I don't want cake! The idea wasn't to ruin the wedding. It was to get Putter!"

Vermintail answered, "Look. It's got strawberry jelly inside."

Moldyfart begrudgingly looked at it. Another stabbing pain knifed into Harry's brain.

Lord Pull-My-Finger stormed, "What? It's got coconut on top! Who puts coconut on a wedding cake? I hate coconut!"

Harry mercifully passed out.

When Harry regained consciousness, Ron had gotten off the phone. He told Harry the terrible news. Nurse Pomfrite and Mad Dog Hooty were indeed dead.

Harry said, "I've got to put an end to this. I've got to find out more about these hoaxcrocks, so I can destroy them, and then kill Moldyfart."

Ron said, "No. We have to."

"I thought you weren't…"

"We're a team, Harry. We're like a shiny new…"

"Tricycle," said Harry, jumping in and finishing Ron's sentence for him.

Hermione sighed and muttered, "Can't we skip the tricycle analogy and just call ourselves the three musketeers?"

"I don't get it," Ron asked, "What's a candy bar got to do with the three of us?"

Hermione said, "I was referring to the Dumas book, Ron."

"Oh yeah?" Ron blurted out, "Well, your hair is so bad, it looks stupid."

Chapter 6

Hermione slapped her forehead and explained, "No, Ron. I was referring to the book, *The Three Musketeers*, by Alexandre Dumas."

Harry chimed in, "I think you're pronouncing it wrong. It's doo-ma. It's a French name and the s is silent."

Hermione answered, "I really don't care how those hoity-toity, namby-pamby poofs pronounce it. I wasn't talking about a candy bar."

"Ouch, Hermione," Harry asked, "What do you have against the French anyway?"

Hermione replied, "Oh, come on. They're all a bunch of baguette-munching, wine-sniffing women. And their women are all stuck-up, pouting, snooty snots. They think the rest of the world is beneath them."

"Yeah, but they make some awesome pastries - Napoleons, éclairs, crème brulée, tarts."

Hermione sniffed, "They're all a bunch of tarts, if you ask me. I'd rather have tiramisu. But can we just skip dessert?"

She continued, "Why don't we get back on subject. We need to make a plan to destroy Moldyfart's hoaxcrocks. Once we take care of them, the Fart Lord becomes vulner…."

Ron interrupted, "Wait? You guys don't even have a plan yet?"

Hermione and Harry answered, "No."

Ron became exasperated. He cried out, "I thought you said you were ready!"

Hermione replied, "I said I had already packed. And, I have. Everything we could possibly need is in my bag."

Harry asked, "Oh, is that what this sack is? I was wondering about that."

Hermione answered, "Yes, it's all in there."

Ron said, "Wait, everything we need is in just that one bag? I thought this was likely to take a couple of months."

Harry corrected, "Probably longer than that. We're gonna need a lot of supplies."

Hermione answered, "It's all taken care of."

Harry scoffed, "Oh, come on, Hermione. You must mean your stuff is in that bag. You can't have everything we're going to need in there."

Hermione stiffened, "That's what I said, and I mean what I say."

Ron scoffed too, asking, "What about all my personal stuff? My clothes? My toothbrush? My teddy bear?"

"I've got it covered."

"What do you mean, you got it covered? You couldn't have packed all my toiletries. I just used them this morning."

Hermione sighed, "All right, you two. You obviously don't believe me. So just what do you think I forgot to pack?"

"My underwear," answered Ron.

"Wrong." She reached into her sack, pulling out a package. It was covered in gift wrap with blue and white snowflakes. She handed it to Ron.

Cheesley asked, "What's with the wrapping paper? It's not my birthday."

"Just open it."

He tore the paper away and revealed pink underwear with white fluffy bunnies.

Ron blinked. He laughed nervously and said, "I don't wear fuzzy bunnies anymore, you know!"

Hermione replied, "I thought you might say that. Here." She reached into her bag again and pulled forth another package. This one was covered with green and red Christmas trees.

She handed it to Ron and added, "These ones are plain white."

Ron opened the present. He had a confused look on his face when he saw the new package of men's white underwear in size 38. He wondered how it was possible for her to pull out the right present so quickly.

She challenged him again, "C'mon. What else you got?"

Harry chimed in, "How about my toothbrush?"

A moment later Putter was staring confusedly at his very own toothbrush, which he had just unwrapped.

Ron asked, "What about spare magic wands?"

Hermione handed him a beautifully wrapped box. Inside was five of Ron's kind of wand. He took one out and put it in his robe pocket. Then he returned the remaining ones for Hermione to store. Hermione placed them back in her bag.

He continued, "Hmmm, how about a can opener?"

Chapter 6

Hermione looked miffed at Ron and said, "Please. Like I'd forget that! Now you're not even trying to challenge me."

Harry got excited. He asked slyly, "How about my Elvis Snow Globe?"

Hermione yawned and said, "I packed it."

A moment later, Harry had unwrapped his Elvis Snow Globe.

"All right, how about an accordion?" asked Ron.

"You don't own an accordion."

"Well, I'm thinking of taking it up."

She sighed and pulled out a present for Ron. It was an accordion.

Harry asked furtively, "How about an extension ladder?"

Hermione cocked her head to the side and asked, "Think not?"

Harry was feeling a bit smug. He thought he had her now.

Hermione scoffed, "Wrong!"

She pulled a very long present out of her bag. The boys' eyes became wide. This package was longer than the whole sack. Together they unwrapped a brand new extension ladder.

Next Ron asked for the latest video game system. When he got it, he exclaimed, "This is the best Christmas ever!"

When Harry had opened up a new laptop computer, he concurred.

Ron asked, "How about the Statue of Liberty?"

"That's a place. It doesn't count. If you want the Statue of Liberty, go visit Ellis Island!"

Ron questioned, "I thought you said it was on Liberty Island?"

Hermione smiled and replied, "Well, what do you know? You do listen sometimes."

Harry jumped in, "All right. How about some French pastries?"

Hermione stuck her tongue out at Harry. She reached into her bag and rummaged around for several seconds, then she pulled forth a gift-wrapped box. It was covered in Wise Men heading for the Star of Bethlehem. She handed it to Harry. Harry tore the wrapping paper away. He opened the box and inside was a large tiramisu.

Harry called out, "Ah-HA! This is Italian pasty, not French."

"Close enough."

"I'm going to need a fork and a napkin."

Hermione handed him two more presents.

Grim Old Place

Yes, it turned out Hermione really had packed. Everything they could ever need was in just one sack. Of course, it really was the wizard Santa's magic sack. She had stolen it a couple years ago from Cubious Hasbeen. The big man was substituting for Father Christmas while he was on vacation recovering from a severe head trauma. Hermione was one of Santa's helpers. She had traveled the world with Hasbeen that magical night delivering presents to everyone. And after the last present was delivered, she stole the empty bag.

Ron and Harry were simply amazed at her ingenuity. They spent the rest of the night playing video games on a brand new gigantic television.

Chapter 6

Chapter 7 – The Most Exciting Monday Ever

The boys did not wake until Sunday afternoon, and when they did, they eagerly began to play video games again. Hermione was ready to take the pole ax to their games, however, instead she simply pulled the plug on them.

She scolded, "We need to make a plan. We need to find out about these hoaxcrocks. We don't know how many there are. We don't know what they are. We don't even know how they're made."

Ron complained, "Aw, I don't even know where to begin."

"We begin by going over what we do know about them," said Hermione. "Basically, we know that hoaxcrocks are totally evil. Only the worst sort of wizard or witch would resort to rending their soul in two and placing a piece of it into an object in order to obtain a wicked immortality of sorts. They can still die, but their soul continues to live in its repository. And their friends or family or followers can restore the soul, by extracting it from the hoaxcrock and placing it into a living person's body. Basically, it's a form of possession. The person's soul is forced to vacate the body and the witch or wizard takes over.

Ron said, "Eww, that would be so weird, especially if you took over a girl's body."

Hermione sniffed, "And what's so weird about being a girl?"

Ron spluttered, "Oh, I didn't mean it that way. I just meant it would be weird for a guy to become a girl. That's all."

Chapter 7

Hermione ignored this and continued, "There isn't much history regarding hoaxcrocks. I've researched it on the Internet. There are no ancient ones. There are no medieval ones. There aren't any records or occurrences of them until modern times and even then, they are extremely rare. The first known person to have made one was Sigourney Weaver."

"Oh! She's totally evil!"

"Then of course, it became a celebrity rage. You had other malevolent actresses following in her footsteps; Morgan Fairchild, Joan Rivers, Jaclyn Smith, Christie Brinkley, and Goldie Hawn to name a few."

"Evil, Evil, Hot, Hot, and Evil."

Hermione gave Ron a look of contempt.

He said, "What? Go on."

She turned to Harry and said, "That's it for me. Harry?"

Harry began, "Well, my good friend Grumblesnore was the one who seemed to know all about them. Unfortunately, he's dead, and I don't really know all that much. First of all, Moldyfart hated Grumblesnore and wanted to kill the Headmaster. Ever since Grumblesnore and I fooled the Fart Lord at the diving board two years ago, Grumblesnore's been near the top of Moldyfart's list.

And so, Grumblesnore was researching the hoaxcrocks, so that together we could destroy them and afterward, kill the Fart Lord. Grumblesnore told me everything I know, but again, that's not much. He told me that I had already inadvertently destroyed one hoaxcrock, the Frozen Dairy Dessert Cookbook. He told me he destroyed another, a Hong Kong Phooey metal lunchbox. It was Moldyfart's from when he was a boy. Grumblesnore bought it on Ebay. He said it was listed under hoaxcrocks.

He also learned about two others; Moldyfart's pet anaconda, Snakey, and a pair of light up sneakers.

A few months ago, the Headmaster and I tried to obtain the pair of light-up sneakers. Unfortunately, after risking our lives to get them, they turned out to be knock-offs and not genuine L.A. Gear light-up sneakers. They weren't the real hoaxcrock."

Hermione asked, "L.A. Gear? Didn't we throw a pair of L.A. Gear sneakers out when we were cleaning this place up like two or three years ago? If I remember correctly, no one wanted them."

Harry answered, "I doubt it."

The Most Exciting Monday Ever

Ron chimed in, "No, I remember. We definitely threw an old pair of L.A Gear sneakers away. But, don't worry, they weren't the light up kind."

Harry asked, "Are you sure?"

Ron answered, "Positive, I wouldn't throw out light-up sneakers. Who would?"

Hermione agreed, "Only an idiot! Oh, uh…I mean, what if you didn't realize they were the kind that light up?"

Harry reasoned, "Why would they be here anyway? They're probably in Moldyfart's closet or under his bed or something."

Ron blurted out, "Are you kidding? Did you ever see Moldyfart wearing light-up sneakers?"

Harry answered, "No."

"Well, that proves it then."

Harry laughed, "Proves what? I don't quite follow your logic."

"If you had light-up sneakers, wouldn't you wear them? I know I would! Say, you didn't happen to pack any did you, Hermione?"

Hermione made a wry face, "Sorry, Ron, I forgot to put them on my list when packing."

Harry found the whole idea silly. He said, "Ron, it doesn't matter. If you threw them out three years ago, it's too late now."

Hermione disagreed, "Maybe not. Let's check to make sure they aren't in Serious's bedroom."

They searched not only Serious's old bedroom, but the rest of the house as well, but they did not find a pair of sneakers.

Finally, Hermione called loudly for Kreeper. When the House-Elf arrived, she asked him, "Kreeper, by any chance, do you remember when we were sorting through and cleaning up the place three years ago? There was a pair of Serious's sneakers that got thrown away."

Kreeper answered, "Well, yes and no. There was a pair of sneakers you guys tossed, but they didn't belong to Serious. Those were Regular's sneakers."

"Wow, I'm surprised you remember them," said Hermione.

Kreeper shrugged and replied, "I've good reason to remember them. First of all, they were stolen from Regular and I helped my master steal

Chapter 7

them back. Secondly, they're only the best pair of sneakers in the whole world!"

"Who stole them from Regular?"

"He-Who-Must-Not-Be-Smelled."

She was shocked. That meant the sneakers were The Sneakers! To confirm it, she asked, "Then they were L.A. Gear sneakers?"

Kreeper affirmed, "Yes."

Hermione excitedly asked, "You didn't happen to take them out of the trash, did you?"

Kreeper rolled his eyes and said, "Well, duh! Yeah, they're light up footwear! Of course, I took them."

Harry and Ron waited breathlessly, their hearts were in their throats. The sneakers weren't plain ordinary sneakers. They were light-up sneakers! They were L.A. Gear light-up sneakers! They were The Sneakers. And Kreeper had them!

Hermione asked, "Do you still have them?"

"No."

With just one word, all their enthusiasm deflated like an untied balloon.

Kreeper added, "That stinkin' Frommundigus Filcher stole them from me."

And suddenly, there was hope once more.

Hermione immediately suggested, "Harry, send Frommundigus a text, ask him to come here."

While they were waiting for Frommundigus to arrive, Hermione looked out the front window. She noticed there was a suspicious-looking man standing in an empty lot across the street. She looked closer, shrieked, and hid behind the curtain.

Ron asked dumbly, "What?"

Harry called out, "What's wrong?"

Hermione answered, "I think there's a Fungus Eater outside. Isn't that the notorious criminal, Yahtzee? One of the ones they broke out of Azcabanana Prison a few years ago?"

Harry peeked out and then said, "Crap! How did they find out where we are? We haven't come here in years."

The Most Exciting Monday Ever

Ron said, "Maybe they scout the place every so often to make sure. If they came by last night, wouldn't they have seen the lights and the television on?"

Hermione said, "Oh, I feel so stupid! This would have been such a great place to hide while we figure out what to do."

Harry said, "Well, it's not like they can just come in. Remember? There's spells protecting the place."

Hermione said, "What's going to keep them from busting in?"

Harry said, "Hmmm. I guess we better reset all the traps just in case."

Harry felt his phone buzz. He looked at the message, hoping it was Filcher replying to his earlier text.

It wasn't. It was from a fellow Nerd House student, Rusty Pipes. It read:

So is Elvis *really* dead?

Harry got that question a lot. He wasn't sure why. He thought, "It must be because it was so shocking for everyone. Other people are having as much trouble believing it as I did."

Harry quickly texted back:

Yes, definitely. Was @ his viewing and funeral.

Just then, Frommundigus Filcher arrived. He abberated into the living room.

Filcher was a filthy homeless man who never did an honest day's work in his life. He was a petty thief always looking for a way to make a galley or save one. It was said that he was not born, but had crawled out from under a rock. Others said, 'Frommundigus' referred to his cheese. However, from under what part of the body the cheese came, was disputed by the other members of the Order of the Harry Putter Fan Club. Despite all of his hardships and lack of resources, the homeless man seemed to exude an unmistakable air of superiority. They had often commented on how Filcher for some stuck-up reason thought he was better than everyone else.

Chapter 7

Ron raised his voice, "Filcher, you ought to be ashamed of yourself! You…"

Hermione clamped her hand over Ron's mouth and put her finger to her lip to shush him.

Kreeper scowled at the sneaky thief.

Harry said, "Thanks for coming, Frommundigus. We were just wondering something. Do you remember a pair of sneakers from when we were cleaning this place up a few years ago."

Filcher nervously said, "Hmm. Not sure. Could you describe 'em?"

Harry said, "L.A. Gear. Light up ones."

Kreeper accused, "The ones you stole, Filcher! Remember? You stunned me and ran away with them!"

Frommundigus stuck a finger in the collar of his robe to loosen it from his throat. He seemed to shrink a little as he said, "Oh, uh, those sneakers."

Hermione asked, "Where are they?"

Filcher bit his lip, thought for a moment, and replied, "If I remember correctly, I sold them about a year ago. Yes, that's right. I was having a yard sale, and I remember a funny-looking fellow bought them. He had a big nose and…"

Harry said, "C'mon, Filcher! You don't have a yard to have a yard sale."

Hermione asked, "Where are they?"

Filcher answered, "I don't know. Someone stole them from me."

Hermione asked, "Who?"

Frommundigus said, "Her name's … Trollores Underbridge."

Trollores Underbridge was Harry, Ron, and Hermione's preschool teacher. She was a troll and loved children – that is, she loved to eat children. The class had gotten considerably smaller as the year went by. Of course, she was no longer at Hogwashes, she was now working at the Ministry of Magic.

Harry asked, "Trollores Underbridge! Why would she steal them? They wouldn't even fit her! You're lying again, aren't you?"

The thief answered, "Oh, come on, would I lie to you, Harry?"

Putter snorted, "Pffft! Of course, you just did a second ago."

The homeless man indignantly said, "Well, I'm not lying now."

The Most Exciting Monday Ever

Hermione asked, "Do you mean the woman who is Head of the Department of Transportation and Tolls?"

Filcher answered, "See! Your friend's heard of her. That proves I wasn't making it up."

Harry reasoned, "It doesn't prove she stole your sneakers. How do you even know her?"

Frommundigus answered, "We're both members at the same gym. She was admiring my light-ups one day. And, after I had taken a shower, they were gone."

Harry asked, "Wait. You took a shower and when you got back they were gone? And you think that means she stole them?"

"Absolutely. I knew she was bad the moment I first saw her. You should have seen the gleam in her wicked beady eyes. She wanted them for herself. I know it was her that took 'em."

Ron reasoned, "But that means she would have had to have gone in the men's locker room to steal them while you were showering? Right?"

"Well, actually, I was showering at the water fountain. They won't let me in the men's shower anymore."

Ron asked, "Why not?"

Hermione cried out, "Ugggh, Ron. Do you really want to know the answer to that?"

"Oh, uh, I guess not," Ron answered.

With a note of worry evident in her voice, Hermione pled, "Frommundigus, please, just tell me you don't go to 'The Palatial Pilates Palace' in Hogsbreath."

"Yes, that's the very one!"

She groaned.

Harry threatened, "If you're lying to me, Filcher, I'm going to … why, I'll get the rest of the Harry Putter Fan Club on you! And let's face it, neither of us knows just what *that* means!"

Hermione shuddered and embellished, "Oh, I don't even want to think about it! Rhomulus Loopin, Wrestlemania Trunks, Kingsley Shuckthecorn! It's enough to give me the willies! And if that's not bad enough, there's Butterpants! Who knows what he'll do to you?"

Chapter 7

Frommundigus visibly and audibly shook away the shivers those thoughts gave him. Then he swallowed and said, "I swear. It was Trollores Underbridge. Find her, and you'll find your sneakers."

Harry said, "For your sake, we'd better."

That evening, Harry, Ron, and Hermione made daring plans. Hermione would ransack Trollores Underbridge's house looking for the sneakers. Meanwhile, Ron and Harry would disguise themselves, dressing as interns, and infiltrate the Ministry of Magic. Once inside, they'd locate the troll's office and search it. And they'd even go so far as to find Underbridge and see whether she was wearing the light-up sneakers or not.

Everything they went through the following day was completely unnecessary. The light-up L.A Gear sneakers weren't in Trollores Underbridge's home, they weren't in her office, and they weren't on her feet. Filcher lied. He was wearing the light-up sneakers the whole time he was talking to the three teenagers. If it weren't for the long robe he was wearing, they would have spotted the footwear easily.

However, that Monday was not uneventful. Within the Ministry of Magic the day became known as, "The Most Exciting Monday Ever."

Meanwhile, in Hogwashes on the Most Exciting Monday Ever, two Popular Rich Kids stepped out of the PRK Common room and into the dungeon hallway. They were heading to the Great Eatery, when one of them spotted a large mean-looking cat in the corridor ahead. He noticed several frays in the feline's ragged outer ears, scars from countless cat fights. The tawny animal turned and padded away.

However, one of the two large boys was in a mischievous mood. He pulled his wand out and said the magic word, "Stupidify!" His spell struck the poor cat. The animal was balanced in motion before the spell struck. Afterward, it fell over senseless.

Shabby complained, "Aw, why'd you go and do that for?"

Foil replied, "Stupid cat doesn't belong down here. Must be someone's pet wandering around looking for trouble. I thought I'd oblige."

"You're mean!"

The Most Exciting Monday Ever

Foil exemplified this comment, when he replied, "Hey, I just got an idea. It'd be really funny if we tie-dyed its fur!"

"Where are you going to get the dye from?"

"I've already got some. It's leftover from when I tie-dyed Faco's white polo shirt. That's what gave me the idea."

Shabby smirked and said, "That *was* funny!"

Foil replied, "Yeah, but this will be even better. Wait until everyone sees a cat walking around with green and pink swirly stripes! People will think their hallucinating!"

Shabby's smirk widened. He said, "Let's do it!"

Faco Maldoy, the son of Luscious Maldoy and a PRK student at Hogwashes, was the first person to come upon the consequences of Shabby and Foil's attempt to tie-dye their first feline. They had unknowingly chosen the worst cat ever to mess around with. Faco entered the men's bathroom on the second dungeon level and came upon a scene of frightening death in vivid colors. The two large students were lying on the floor. There were two overturned buckets. One had poured forth a florescent pink liquid, the other bright green. These two colors had splashed the two young men, dousing areas of their clothing and skin. These hues had swirled around their fallen bodies and left trails of color on the floor all the way to the drain.

Faco was shaking as he called out, "S-S-Shabby? F-F-Foil?"

His friends did not move.

He stepped closer, avoiding the remnants of colorful liquid. He noticed the small prints of an animal's feet in pink and green.

He saw two red claw marks, deeply scratched into Foil's arms. He saw a pink florescent ball of fur on Foil's brightly dyed neck.

He surveyed Shabby and found a similar raking set of scratches on the back of his wrist and hand and a tawny hairball resting in the corner of his eye, alongside his nose.

He called out loudly, "Shabby! Foil!"

Neither boy moved.

He looked closely at their chests, neither was breathing. Faco couldn't believe it. They were dead!

He screamed and ran to find the Headmaster, Carnivorous Ape.

Chapter 7

The tawny cat leapt silently from its hiding place and dashed through the bathroom door before it swung closed.

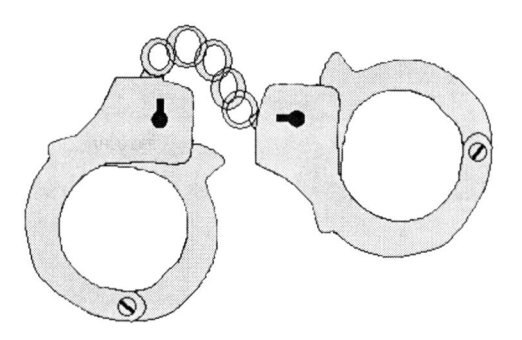

Chapter 8 – Aftermath

When Harry came to, he was surprised to find himself in a forest, lying on top of a pile of gold coins – galleys. The scar on his forehead hurt terribly, until he realized it wasn't only the scar, but his whole head that hurt.

Next to him was an expanse of wavy strawberry-blonde hair. Harry knew immediately it was Hermione.

When he sat up, he felt a twinge in his upper arm and wondered if he had bumped into something. From a sitting position, he could see Hermione was asleep. However, it was odd that she was wearing an orange jumpsuit and had a pair of handcuffs attached to one wrist. He moved her hair aside to make sure it really was Hermione after all. Despite a noticeable swollen black eye, Harry recognized his good friend.

However, other observations now vied for his attention. The foremost was Frommundigus Filcher. His dead body was fifteen meters away and had been run through. A heavy jousting lance was sticking upward at an angle from his chest. On Frommundigus Filcher's head a half-gallon of chocolate chip ice cream was melting and oozing into his hair.

Putter knew without a doubt, the thief was dead. Harry's sudden and rapid intake of breath made Hermione stir. She let out a tiny sweet little mew of dismay.

He also noticed Ron was lying nearby, next to Santa's sack. His best friend was still wearing his rented wedding robes, which were in horrendous condition. They were noticeably singed, cut, ripped and stained. His hair was also messier than usual. Harry's eyebrow knit when

Chapter 8

he noticed there was a sock on one of Ron's hands. He looked carefully and saw the rise and fall of Ron's chest. Thank goodness his friend was alive and breathing.

Harry stood up and again felt the momentary pain of his upper arm. Gold coins slid and clinked as he moved. Hermione opened her good eye, winced, and made a noise that wasn't nearly as cute as her previous one.

Harry whispered, "Hermione, where the heck are we?"

She hoarsely said, "Where we camped during the World Tea Cup a few years ago."

She sat up, stretched, and added, "I abberated us here last night."

Ron snorted, "Mommy." Then he stirred awake with a groan, "Oh, my aching back! Oh, my neck!"

Harry asked, "What happened to Frommundigus?" He stepped over to the thief's dead body.

Ron answered, "Oh, he died."

Harry scoffed, "Obviously, but how?"

Cheesley returned the sarcasm, "Obviously, he lost a joust."

Harry ignored this comment. He had just noticed that Frommundigus was wearing sneakers. Harry looked closer. They were L.A Gear sneakers. Harry kicked the bottom of Frommundigus' foot.

Hermione called out, "Don't tell me you're still mad at him?"

Harry kicked again, harder. The heel of the sneaker lit up with flashing red lights.

Filcher was wearing the light-up sneakers.

Harry whooped with delight. "We've got The Sneakers!"

Ron said, "Oh, wow! This is so great. I thought this whole hoaxcrock thing was going to be difficult, but this is going to be a snap! We're practically done. All we got to do now is kill Snakey the Anaconda."

Hermione corrected him, "Actually, Ron, we don't know how many hoaxcrocks there are. For all we know there could be two or three more out there."

Harry said, "I'm going to try them on."

Ron asked, "Why do you get the first turn!"

Harry replied, "Because I'm older."

Ron said, "Darn, I never get the first turn."

Aftermath

Harry removed the light-up sneakers from the dead man's feet. It felt immensely great just to be holding them. He took off his own sneakers and put the L.A. Gear on. As he did, he was annoyed at the twinge he felt in his upper right arm. However, once he was wearing the light-ups, he felt so wonderful, he promptly forgot all about it. Harry already thought he was so much better than everyone else, without the light-up sneakers. With them, he felt incredible, just incredible.

He exclaimed, "Whoa! These really are the best sneakers in the world!"

"That's what Kreeper said." Hermione asked, "What's that supposed to mean anyway?"

Harry cried out, "I feel like I could conquer the world!"

Hermione scowled. She didn't like the sound of that. She suggested, "Maybe you should take them off. It might not be a good idea to wear them. After all, there's a portion of the most evil wizard known to man's soul inside them. Who knows what that might do?"

Harry ignored her and said, "Hermione, you've got to try these on!"

Harry took the sneakers off and begrudgingly handed them to Hermione to put on. He suddenly was annoyed that he couldn't both wear them and share them at the same time. Not only that, but his arm was now bothering him again.

As Hermione changed into the light-up sneakers, Harry pulled the right sleeve of his robe up and found a bandage on his arm. He said, "Hey, do either of you remember what happened to my arm?"

"Beat's me," answered Ron.

Hermione exclaimed, "Holy Crap! These sneakers are…" She jumped up and began a happy dance.

Ron wanted a try. He called out, "My turn!"

"I just got them on. You have to wait!"

"Then, I call next turn!"

Harry was annoyed. He wished he hadn't said anything out loud about the sneakers, then he wouldn't have to share them. He peeled back the bandage. Beneath it, he had a Fungus Eater Mark, a mushroom, newly tattooed on his upper arm.

Chapter 8

Now, he was really annoyed. He cried out, "Oh, come on! A Fungus Eater Mark? You've got to me kidding me!"

Hermione sang, "Oh, well."

Then she took a more serious tone and said, "Wait, I just remembered something. Last night, I think we were all drunk."

Ron scoffed, "No duh!"

Hermione stuck her tongue out at him and said, "Anyway, a bunch of friends you guys made at the ministry came back with us to Grim Old Place. They wanted to help beat up Frommundigus for lying to us."

Ron asked, "So what?"

Hermione replied, "Some of them could have been Fungus Eaters. After all, a lot of Fungus Eaters work there. There's likely more than ever, now that they've taken over the Ministry. And since some of our 'friends' last night were probably our enemies, our enemies have now been inside Grim Old Place. The protection spells won't keep them out any more."

Harry exclaimed, "Crap! So we can't go back there then? Oh, man. That place was so great. It was the perfect headquarters for our hoaxcrock destroying mission. Can't you update the protection spells?"

Hermione scoffed, "As if! We'd have to get the whole Order over to help us do that. Plus the Fart Lord would know exactly where we were. He'd come after us for sure. But don't worry, we can camp out here. We still have everything I packed including a tent and sleeping bags. We're totally set, and no one will know where we are this time."

Ron exclaimed, "My turn!"

Hermione knew he was referring to the sneakers. She ran and called out after her, "First you have to catch me!"

Much later, after they had pitched a tent and set up camp, Ron finally got his turn to wear the L.A. Gear. When he put them on, he said, "I don't know what we did to Frommundigus, but it was worth it."

Hermione and Harry agreed.

Ron asked, "Are we really going to destroy these sneakers? I mean, do we have to?"

Hermione chimed in, "Well, we don't have to destroy them now. We can wait and destroy them after we find all the other hoaxcrocks first."

Aftermath

Suddenly, they all found themselves thinking the same thought, however, none spoke of it. They each realized how horrible it would be if they were to find and destroy the remaining hoaxcrocks. If they managed to accomplish this, they'd have to destroy the light-up sneakers. And that would be a travesty! They could barely stomach the idea of sharing the L.A Gear by taking turns with their two friends. However, if they destroyed the footwear, they would never have another turn again. It was a revolting thought.

And so, that afternoon, the Quest to Destroy Lord Moldyfart hit a giant speed bump. The three teenagers did absolutely nothing to find out anything more about the remaining hoaxcrocks. And they were all quite relieved that there was a ready excuse, for they simply didn't know what to do next. They often told each other they were busy "thinking about the problem" or "contemplating a solution." However, none of them ever did.

When they were wearing the sneakers, they felt so magnificent, they couldn't waste the opportunity with such negative thoughts. It seemed the problem was all blown out of proportion anyway. It was really too insignificant to consider. Instead, they often made the fascinating observation that it was really cool how the sneakers fit each of them, despite the fact that they all had different-sized feet.

And when it wasn't their turn, they became irritable and grumpy. It was easy to convince themselves that they were in too bad of a mood to do their best thinking anyway. Their thoughts were always focused on getting another opportunity to wear the sneakers. They brainstormed ways to prolong their turn at the expense of their friends.

And so, the three teenagers camped in the nameless woods. Their camp site became larger and larger as the days passed. They were constantly improving it. When they needed something, a moment later, they had pulled it out of Saint Nick's sack. They had electrical generators running on gasoline. They had television and video games. They had furniture and home appliances. They became lazier and lazier as the hot days of August turned to warm days of early September. And they marveled at the size of the pile of discarded balled-up gift wrap as it grew larger and larger as the arrival of autumn came and went.

They ate the food that Hermione had packed in abundance. Harry's belly was growing noticeably. Ron was becoming bigger too. However,

Chapter 8

his larger frame could carry more weight, and so it was less noticeable as he packed on the kilograms. Only Hermione managed to maintain her figure.

The nights became colder as October slipped away. And then one November night, Harry heard a disturbance outside the tent. He heard the sound of voices. Quickly, the three teenagers went out to investigate. Outside they discovered some goblins, including their leader, Gripbutt, country singers Tim McGraw and Faith Hill, actor Harrison Ford, weatherman Al Roker, half a dozen alpacas, their fellow Nerd and Harry and Ron's former roommate at Hogwashes, Spleen Thomas, and Sir Robin and his minstrels.

When asked, they explained that they were all fugitives on the run from the Ministry of Magic, as were all who opposed the Fart Lord. While Harry was growing fatter, Lord Pull-My-Finger had begun his reign of terror. He was persecuting his many enemies.

Harry, Ron, and Hermione all felt quite guilty and embarrassed. They fed the large group dinner and assured them that the three teenagers were working hard to defeat He-Who-Must-Not-Be-Smelled. They lied and said they felt confident a breakthrough was imminent.

Spleen Thomas asked them, "Dudes, did you hear that Gringo's Bank got robbed? Totally outrageous. A terrible run on the bank happened right after. No one thinks their money is safe anymore. The Ministry had to guarantee everyone's funds, otherwise the bank would have folded without any customers."

Harry, Ron, and Hermione all felt quite guilty and embarrassed again. They pretended to be surprised.

When the eclectic group left, they went away with a large tiramisu. The three teenagers fell right back into their recent habits. November slipped away, and when the first snowfall arrived in mid-December, the three admired the tracks the sneakers left behind in the snow.

And then, one December night, Hermione went to bed wearing The Sneakers, and the next morning, Harry had them on.

Ron cried foul, "Hey! You skipped my turn!"

Hermione raised her voice to accuse Harry, "You took them in the middle of the night!"

Aftermath

Harry replied, "I did not. I was asleep. Someone must have put them on my feet and framed me."

Harry was looking at Ron as he said this.

Ron blew up, "Someone? You mean me! Why don't you come right out and say it?"

Harry shrugged his shoulders and said, "Fine, Ron, you framed me."

Ron was livid. He yelled, "Did not, LIAR! That's so dumb! Why would I even do that? I'm the one who was sleeping."

Hermione said, "Calm down, Ron. I think it's more likely that Harry stole them in his sleep."

Harry cried out, "Stole them? They're mine, you know! I'm the one who found them."

Hermione was outraged, "Wow, what a jerk! You really do think you're better than everyone else. We were all here Harry. Just because you woke up first, doesn't make them yours. They're ours."

Harry snottily said, "I'm not the one with the big head."

Ron reasoned, "Look, you two, I haven't had a turn for, like, sixteen hours. I'm the one who got skipped. It's my turn and you both know it! You're always pulling stunts like this and I'm sick of it. Did I get the first turn? No. I went last, remember! And now, you're trying to take advantage of me like this? Gimme them!"

Hermione argued, "Like hell, it's your turn! It was my turn to wear them last night and you know it. I'm the one whose turn got stolen in the middle of the night. If it's anyone's turn, it's mine."

Ron yelled, "That doesn't mean I should be skipped. Take it out of Harry's next turn."

Hermione explained, "Ron, it doesn't work that way. And I'm not taking half a turn. I get to finish my turn, then it's your turn. We have to go in order."

Ron yelled, "What's going on with you two? You're always against me. Plotting to steal my time every chance you get. Don't you think for a minute I don't notice how you're always working together to shave minutes off my turn. I have to constantly fight the two of you, just to get my fair chance. I'm sick of it. This time, I'm putting my foot down! It's my turn!"

Chapter 8

Harry was not in the least afraid of Ron's stance. He knew Ron didn't have the magic power or the guts to reinforce it. He scoffed, "Ooh, Hermione, Ron's put his foot down! He's so scary! What will we do?"

Ron scowled and said, "Why don't you shut up? Moron."

Harry continued to jeer, "Or what, Ron? What will you do?"

Ron shouted, "You know what? I don't need a pair of sneakers to know I'm better than you two losers! You're pathetic. You've just been pissing in the woods for the past three months. Everyone's waiting for you to kill the Fart Lord, Harry, and you're letting all your friends down. I thought you guys knew what you were doing, but you don't know anything. I keep waiting for you to come up with a plan, but all you two do is spend your time thinking up ways of screwing me out of my turn. Well, I'm done. I'm going home."

Cheesley stormed off.

Hermione called after him, "Ron?"

He didn't bother turning around.

Hermione tried again, louder, "Ron!"

Again, he ignored her.

She called out, "You're going the wrong way."

Chapter 9 – Goldbrick Shallows

What Ron said when he left, cut like a sword – not Harry – Hermione. She was ashamed of herself for having let everyone down. She knew Harry and Ron were both morons, and they couldn't come up with a plan if their lives depended on it. Just look how dumb the move to the Boil went. That's what happens when a committee of idiots is in charge.

At that moment, she took it upon herself to finally come up with a plan. Even then, it was difficult for her to puzzle through the problem because she had too many clues and not enough information. It didn't take her too long to figure out that she needed something more solid. However, it took her two weeks to finally realize where she might be able to find some answers.

She announced one evening, "Come on, Harry. We're going to Goldbrick Shallows."

Harry asked dumbly, "Goldbrick Shallows? What for?"

Hermione answered, "We're going to search Grumblesnore's house for clues about hoaxcrocks."

"Grumblesnore lives in Goldbrick Shallows? I didn't know that. You know my parents used to live there?"

"Yes, I know."

Then Harry remembered out loud, "But, wait. Grumblesnore's house? Isn't that empty by now? I mean, they settled the estate, right? That means they would have cleaned it out and sold it by now, doesn't it?"

Chapter 9

"It's possible, but we just don't know. The house could have been cleaned up by now or not at all. It might have been left to a relative, or it could be up for sale. Anyway, let's go find out."

Harry said thoughtfully, "If we're going to break into Grumblesnore's house, we'd better bring some flashlights."

"We'll bring the whole sack. That way, if we need anything else, we'll have it."

"How are we going to get there?"

"I'll abberate us there."

"You know Grumblesnore's place well enough to?"

"Not exactly, my parent's church is just two streets away. I'll abberate us and we'll walk from there. As a matter of fact, while we're there, you might want to visit your family's graves. Your parents and your uncle are buried there."

Harry swallowed, "I don't know if this is such a good idea. I mean, do you think we should take any precautions? What if there's Fungus Eaters staking the place out?"

Hermione answered, "I don't know. When was the last time you visited their graves, Harry?"

He spluttered, "Well, that is, I've been meaning to … I just haven't gotten around to it."

"I think it's safe to say, no one will be expecting you. The Fungus Eaters probably have a better chance of finding us here in the woods, than there."

Harry admitted, "Yeah, but, the whole idea kinda gives me the creeps."

"Visiting your parent's graves?"

"No, visiting a cemetery after dark."

Hermione rolled her eyes and said, "Don't worry, big guy. I'll protect you!"

A moment later, they were outside the small church in Goldbrick Shallows. They made their way to the cemetery. They searched around, using their flashlights to locate the gravestones of James and Lillyput Putter, and Serious Smack.

Goldbrick Shallows

James Putter
1966 – 1988

The first enemy to surrender is France.

Lillyput Putter
1034 – 1988

Serious Smack
1976 – 2004

What's the worst that could happen?

When Hermione saw the grave of James and Lillyput Putter she said, "That's so true! The French are such blatant cowards. If we're not kicking their butts in a war, then it's the Germans."

Harry said, "Uh, I thought France and England were allies."

Hermione replied, "Don't swallow everything you hear, Harry. I don't think there are two countries on the planet that have fought more wars than the English against those filthy Frenchies."

Harry asked, "So, is there, like, a personal reason you don't like them? Did they kill a relative or something?"

Just then, a red sleigh pulled by eight reindeer, nine if you count Rudolph, flew overhead. They could hear Father Christmas's laugh, "Ho, Ho, Ho! Merry Christmas!"

Hermione dove for the cover of a large tombstone. She exclaimed, "Holy Crap! The old fart is after us! He's trying to get his bag back!"

Harry said, "More likely, it's Christmas Eve."

Hermione asked, "You sure you want to take that chance? You more than anyone should know he's partial to using a shotgun."

Harry stood watching the sleigh come to a rest on a nearby roof top.

Hermione whispered, "Come on, Harry, get down before he spots us."

Harry replied, "It's dark out, and we're in a cemetery. Why would he spot us?"

Hermione pulled out her wand. She said the magic word, "Stupidify!"

Harry became more stupid than usual, actually, rather senseless. Hermione pulled him down and sat him against a tombstone.

Just as Harry was starting to regain his senses, Hermione was pulling him and saying, "C'mon, now's our chance!"

She ran, leading Harry by the hand. They made their way down the lane taking cover behind hedges, garbage cans, and automobiles. She

Chapter 9

turned the corner and made a dash for it. She ducked behind a pickup truck and stopped to rest. Harry was so out of breath, he was wheezing.

As he huffed and puffed, Hermione was looking over the bed of the pickup for signs of Santa. She said, "If I'm not mistaken, he was heading down the street the other direction, so we should be safe for now."

Harry, meanwhile, was noticing the large Victorian house behind them. There was a sign that said, "Crabby Cots Bed and Breakfast." However, he found the smaller sign even more interesting. It was hard to read in the dark, but he eventually made the words out. It read, "A historic landmark: The only B&B where infant Harry Putter defeated the evil Fart Lord."

He pointed the sign out to Hermione. He sadly said, "Wow, look at how big that house is. If it weren't for Lord Fartypants, I would have grown up there, instead of in the Dirtley's dog house. I might have had brothers and sisters and a pet dog and cat. I'll bet we would have had a swing set in the back yard."

Hermione consoled, "But then, you wouldn't be you. You'd be just like every other nerdy teenager. Harry, you're special. You're an exception. If you were just like every other twit, you wouldn't have a fan club and books written about you. And let's face it, it's only a matter of time before they turn your adventures into a colossal summer movie blockbuster."

Harry's eyes glazed over at that. He whispered, *"The Quest to Destroy Lord Moldyfart."*

Just then Saint Nick's sleigh flew over the rooftops. Santa called out, "C'mon, Comet, get the lead out!" There was a crack of a whip and a reindeer's bray.

Hermione gasped, "Run!"

Harry ran.

Minutes later, Harry was retching in the gutter on a different residential street. Hermione said, "I don't know where we are now. I think we ran the wrong direction. I think Grumblesnore's place is back that way, somewhere. Maybe, if I walk down to the corner, I might recognize the name of this street."

Goldbrick Shallows

A strange woman's voice kindly offered assistance, "Maybe, I can help? What street are you looking for?"

A middle-aged woman walking her dog, a Jack Russell Terrier, had happened upon them in the dark.

Harry retched again noisily.

The woman said, "Oh, my goodness. Are you all right? Why don't you come in and have a glass of water. My place is right over here."

Harry croaked, "That would be awesome. I'm parched." He used his robe's sleeve to wipe the sweat from his brow.

The woman suggested, "Maybe you should try breathing through your nose."

But then the woman suddenly recognized Harry. She gasped and said, "You're Harry Putter!"

Harry lied, "My name's … Shameonus, Shameonus Finnigan."

The woman was not fooled. She replied, "Don't be silly. I recognize the scar on your forehead, Harry. Allow me to introduce myself. I'm Butthilda Bigshot."

Harry gasped, "Bigshot! As in Benny Bigshot? The movie producer?"

"Why, yes, that's my husband. I see you've heard of him."

"Everyone's heard of him. And, today's your lucky day! You just became my next best friend."

Butthilda mused, "Hmmm, well, I may be more of a friend than you realize. Let's get some water and we'll discuss a little plan I have. I think you will find it to our mutual satisfaction."

Butthilda led the way to her house. When she opened the front door, she was greeted by one of her many, many cats. There were more cats than Harry could count. Some of them dashed for cover when strangers arrived. Others were more outgoing and curious.

The movie producer and his wife had a lovely home, and Harry said so. He wisely kept his opinion about the odor of the place to himself. Butthilda led them into the kitchen, she was nearly tripping over two cats, which were vying for her attention.

In the kitchen their host quickly got Harry a glass of water. Then she offered them both tea and cookies. The two teenagers sat at a large butcher-block kitchen table, while Bigshot put a kettle on the stovetop,

Chapter 9

heating it up in the old-fashioned manner. She said, "I hope you don't mind waiting a moment for it. I prefer tea the English way, though it takes a bit longer than zapping it hot with a wand. Tea needs a good five minutes to thoroughly brew. That's what I always say."

Meanwhile, Harry and Hermione watched as cats came and went about the kitchen. Several congregated around Mrs. Bigshot's legs, rubbing against them. One tabby-striped cat was particularly friendly and took especial liking to Hermione. When she sat at the kitchen table, the tabby jumped up into her lap. Hermione ran her hand over its head, neck, and back and soon had the cat purring.

Suddenly, Harry heard a strange hacking noise coming from under the table. He looked and saw there was a tawny cat beside him. Harry wondered if it was choking on a fish bone or something. He asked, "Is this one alright?"

Butthilda answered, "Oh, it's just coughing up a hairball. It'll be fine."

Harry was disgusted and yet morbidly fascinated by the process. He had never seen it before. Hermione was not looking, but she had a cat and knew all about hairballs. Harry noticed the cat was hovering over her foot. It was her turn, so she was wearing the light-up sneakers. Harry did not want them to become sullied by contact with the hairball once the cat eventually cacked it up. Hermione didn't notice as she was petting the tabby in her lap. Harry tried to call her attention to it. However, she ignored both him and the tawny cat under the table. Three seconds later, Harry kicked her in the shin. She pulled back her leg just in the nick of time. The wet hairball of tawny fur landed on the kitchen floor. The cat ran away like it was shot from a gun.

Hermione cried out, "Ow!" She gave Harry a scowl. "What was that for?"

Harry smiled mischievously and answered, "Sorry, I slipped."

Butthilda sighed as she grabbed a paper towel from the kitchen dispenser. She said, "They're always leaving hairballs all over the house. They get in the darnedest places, too. Why, I even once found one inside one of my shoes! Found that one the hard way."

As she used the paper towel to clean up the cat's mess, she continued, "The worst is in the middle of the night. Imagine trying to sleep with that hideous noise going on. I can't remember the last time I slept through the night without interruption."

Hermione said, "But you must love them. After all, you have so many."

Bigshot replied, "Oh, without a doubt. I truly do. They bring me such joy. Each one has its own personality and they're all my babies. That one you're holding is Mr. Buzzywuggles."

Hermione shook the cat's paw and said, "Nice to meet you, Mr. Buzzywuggles."

Butthilda continued, "Buzzy is very instinctive. He can always recognize a cat lover. You do own a cat don't you, Ms. Stranger?"

Ms. Stranger replied, "You can call me Hermione. And, I do, her name is Croakshanks. How many cats do you have, Mrs. Bigshot?"

"Call me Butthilda. And, seventeen in all. The dog is really Benny's. The cats are mine. Yes, I'm what you might call a crazy cat-lady."

Hermione exclaimed "Well, seventeen is a lot of cats."

Harry brown-nosed, "Nonsense, you can never have too many cats. That's what I always say."

Butthilda asked, "Oh, and how many do you own, Mr. Putter?"

Harry replied, "Call me Harry. And, uh, none. That is, unless you count dust bunnies."

They all laughed at Harry's joke.

Mrs. Bigshot put out a tray of assorted Christmas cookies, scones, and fruitcake. She poured the tea and there was sugar, milk, honey, and sliced lemon to prepare it to personal taste. Finally, Butthilda sat down and joined them at the table.

She began, "My next door neighbor is someone I believe you are familiar with."

Hermione said, "Oh, is he your next door neighbor? And here I thought we had gone the wrong direction. I guess I got turned around so much, I didn't know which way I was going."

Harry felt suddenly excited. Perhaps, Grumblesnore had entrusted Bigshot with some big information. Perhaps he had left her some important artifact for her to give to him – something that would help him on *The Quest to Destroy Lord Moldyfart*. His eyes glazed over for an

Chapter 9

instant. However, he quickly realized that Butthilda was talking and he should be listening.

She was saying, "...not the sort of neighbor I had hoped for when he first moved in. I can tell you! He was rather unfriendly from the start. Though Benny and I always smiled and waved, he deliberately ignored us. And then, there are the garbage cans. He always puts them out next to my fence. We've asked him not to. However, for some reason, he thinks he's putting them in front of his property. We've tried to show him, but he just doesn't seem to get it. Really, I think he's doing it on purpose, just to annoy us. And, I can tell you, his garbage stinks, and I mean, really stinks. Some days, especially in the summer, I can smell it from inside the house."

Hermione sympathized, "It sounds horrendous."

Bigshot agreed, "It is. And you should see his lawn. He hardly does anything to take care of it. And we get so much lovely rain, you'd think it would at least be green, but it's mostly dead and brown. It's such an eyesore. I just know it brings down the property values in the neighborhood."

Harry nodded knowingly, though he knew virtually nothing about being a home-owner and trying to get along with next-door neighbors.

She added, "Not to mention his taste in lawn decorations."

Hermione could only imagine. American's were notorious for their lack of refinement and inexplicable partiality to the plastic pink flamingo. Besides, she had heard of tacky displays on the lawns of Graceland, Elvis' former home in the states, back when he was a much younger man and a rock legend.

Butthilda continued, "Then there was the swimming pool incident. The pool liner has been stained ever since. And believe me, we've tried everything. We've had experts in, and try as they may, they simply cannot do a thing about it."

Hermione asked, "And you're sure it's his fault?"

Bigshot admitted, "Well, I don't have any proof. But, Benny and I feel certain, it was him."

Harry nodded and said knowingly, "I see."

She added, "Oh, and don't get me started about that loud music he plays, and always so late at night. It's a good thing we don't have any babies, or they'd never get their sleep. I don't know how the Cromwell's put up with it. They've two toddlers. I can barely tolerate it, but if I were them, I'd have called the police and had them put an end to it."

Now Harry was confused. He wondered, "Why was she still complaining about his music when Grumblesnore has been dead for over six months? I guess some people are just whiners."

Hermione said, "Yes, but given his past in show business, I'm sure you must have expected rock music when he moved in?"

Butthilda laughed and said, "Rock 'n roll? I wouldn't mind it so much, if it were rock 'n roll music! Personally, I like to rock out once in a while. I was referring to his late night organ playing."

Harry asked with surprise in his voice, "Organ playing?"

Bigshot confirmed, "Yes, it's eerie and well, bizarrely eccentric of him!"

Harry agreed, "That certainly sounds bizarre. But considering the circumstances, things must be pretty quiet now that he's gone."

Butthilda snorted and said, "Yes, but for how long? And if that weren't enough, ever since he moved in, every night, thunder and lightning storms! Why, with the organ playing, the thunder, and the cats coughing up hairballs, is it any wonder I need a nap each afternoon?"

Hermione said, "Well, you can hardly blame him for the weather!"

Bigshot disagreed, "Why not? We never used to have thunder and lightning but once in a rare while, like everyone else. Somehow, it's got to be his fault."

Harry nodded reassuringly and knowingly said, "I see."

She complained, "And to top it all off, he wants me to water his plants while he's gone!"

Harry and Hermione were shocked. Hermione's mouth was agape and the mouthful she had been chewing was showing in a most rude and unattractive manner.

Harry swallowed and asked, "While… he's gone?"

Bigshot confirmed, "Yes, I've been taking care of his plants for the past two weeks while he's been away recruiting allies for the Final Battle."

Hermione asked, "Who? Grumblesnore?"

Chapter 9

Butthilda laughed, "Mr. Grumblesnore? Certainly not! Oh my, no wonder you thought I was talking about rock 'n roll music. No, no, no. My next door neighbor is Mr. Moldyfart."

A Surprise Christmas Visit

Chapter 10 – A Surprise Christmas Visit

Butthilda Bigshot and Harry Putter had something in common, their mortal nemesis was Lord Moldyfart. Since she believed the tenet, the enemy of your enemy is your friend, Bigshot was only too glad to help Harry. In doing so, she was hoping that Putter would finally rid her of the neighbor from hell, who had been a thorn in her side and bringing down property values in her neighborhood ever since the day he moved next door. She was counting on Harry to restore peace to her local community as well as to the larger wizardly community as a whole.

And so, she handed Harry the key to the Fart Lord's castle crib. As she did, she said, "Merry Christmas, Harry, and many happy returns!"

Harry laughed and said, "I only hope that I can return the favor."

Bigshot said, "Just bring the Kitten Killer down, Harry, and no one will be happier than I!"

Harry was eager to search Moldyfart's place for clues while the Fart Lord was away, as Butthilda said, "recruiting allies for the Final Battle." It was a golden opportunity, and he was ready to make the most of it.

In the early hours of Christmas Day, most children were nestled in bed with visions of sugar plums, dolls, toys, and excessively violent video

Chapter 10

games dancing in their heads. Harry and Hermione, however, were anticipating a successful breaking and entering operation. Their visions were filled with mischief-making and getting a quick jump to the top of Santa's naughty list for the following year.

They made their way past the offensive garbage cans lined up against Butthilda's fence. They ignored caution signs that read, "No Trespassing, Violators will be Persecuted!" and "Warning! Solicitors will be tortured to death and have their souls eaten," and "Dead People's Things for Sale, Inquire Within." They opened the spiked black-iron gate decorated with skulls and other human bones. They admired how the lightning crashed perfectly on cue with their first good glimpse of the eerie old castle.

They took a short-cut and walked across the lawn consisting of mud and brown patches of dead grass. They walked past a small cemetery to the excessively large iron-studded front door. Harry inserted the key in the lock, turned it, and pushed the door open with a noisy creak. He turned on the lights.

Inside the old castle they discovered a stunning modern mansion. They were standing in a giant entrance foyer with a beautiful staircase and chandelier. They admired the large expanses of marble and crystal before them. There were many beautiful plants and even two small trees. To his left, Harry noticed a movie poster on the wall. It advertised *The Lady in the Water*. Harry hadn't seen that one, but he seemed to remember that it was not favorably reviewed. He noticed someone had scribbled something on it. When he looked closer, he saw it was someone's signature.

To his right, he spotted another signed movie poster. This one was for, *The Happening*.

Harry let out a gasp and said, "This is truly an evil place."

Hermione suggested, "Let's split up and look for clues."

Harry laughed and replied, "All right, Velma."

"Velma? Ha ha," Hermione laughed sarcastically. "I'm serious. This is a big place, we should split up, and that way, we'll cover more ground. That is, unless you're too afraid?"

Harry scoffed, "Afraid of what? Aside from his choice in movies, I don't see anything too scary."

A Surprise Christmas Visit

"Fine, I'll take the left, you cover the right, and we'll meet back here in fifteen minutes. Holler if you find anything interesting."

"Will do."

Hermione explored the rooms in the left wing of the castle. She discovered a room filled with the skulls of kittens and bunnies, the room of Lost Souls, the room of Evil Ambiance, the Hall of Masks, the Chamber of Unearthly Horrors, a bizarre alternate universe, the secret séance room, The Dining Room of Death, the crazed scientist's laboratory, the Unholy Chapel, the mortuary, the mausoleum, the catacombs, and a torture chamber. As she explored there were several deadly traps to be eluded and many unfathomably fiendish monsters to be battled and destroyed.

Harry searched the right wing of the castle where he found the game room, a yoga room, an exquisite tea room, a fabulous ballroom, a candy making kitchen, a room filled with Moldyfart's gigantic Barbie doll collection, a luxurious spa room, and the Fart Lord's home entertainment room with a huge television.

When he entered that last room, Harry became terrified. There were more movie posters! They were to some of the most awful movies known to man. And there was a voice, even though the television wasn't on! The hairs on the back of his neck stood on end, when he heard the disembodied voice whisper, "The horror. The horror."

Harry couldn't stand it another minute, he dashed from the hideous room. He ran down the hall and back to the entrance foyer, where he met Hermione again. She knew immediately something was amiss. She could tell by Harry's more pallid than usual complexion.

She asked, "What's wrong?"

He answered, "Oh, it was horrible. Just ghastly! This place is worse than I ever could have imagined."

She agreed, "I know what you mean."

Harry disagreed, "No, I don't think you do."

"Why? What did you find?"

"Words elude me. I don't even know how to express it."

"Oh, my goodness! That bad?"

"It was the worst decorated room, I've ever seen in my life!"

Chapter 10

Hermione laughed and hit Harry playfully on the arm. She said, "Oh, Harry, you really had me going there for a second."

"I'm serious, Hermione! The room was so badly decorated, it was audible! I heard it saying, 'The horror! The horror!'"

"You lost me. Just what are you talking about?"

Harry shrugged and said, "I guess you'll just have to take a look for yourself. Follow me."

He led her to the entertainment room.

Hermione went in, but did not experience the same thing as Harry. Though the movies posters were indeed terrible, it wasn't like she had to endure the movies themselves. That would have been much worse. And there was no whispering voice. It wasn't such a bad room. It was rather cozy and lived-in compared to many of the rooms she had been in earlier.

She said, "I don't hear anything."

Harry peeked in. He heard it again. The whispering voice said, "The horror, the horror."

He swallowed and said, "Yikes! Didn't you hear it just now?"

Hermione said, "I didn't hear anything."

The disembodied voice said, "Who's there?"

Harry suddenly realized, it was not English he was hearing. It was Morsel-Tongue."

He replied, "Just me. Harry Putter."

The voice said, "Eat me, Harry Putter! Please, for the love of God, put an end to this eternal nightmare. Eat me!"

Hermione couldn't hear any of the lengthy conversation that followed. It took place in frequencies beyond the normal human capacity to discern. However, Harry told her to be quiet while he conversed with a stale, half-eaten tub of popcorn on a shelf. Even so, she was bewildered as to how long her friend could spend wasting his time supposedly talking to food. In exasperation, she interrupted several times, asking Harry to hurry up. She didn't realize it was the single most important conversation in Harry's life. The half-eaten tub of popcorn was the first Hoaxcrock made by the Fart Lord long ago, and what it knew was simply astounding.

A Surprise Christmas Visit

At first, the popcorn begged for Harry to destroy it outright. However, Harry was in no hurry to comply. He had a hunch the popcorn knew some vital information and could tell Harry something helpful. He persisted in asking it questions.

The popcorn was a reluctant informant. First, it made Harry promise that he would destroy it and put an end to its unending misery.

Next, it fully explained hoaxcrocks to Harry. Hoaxcrocks occur by watching any M. Night Shyamalan movie in its entirety. When subjected to such hideous plot flaws, highly melodramatic themes, wildly outlandish exaggerations, cool visual cinematography, and if you are unfortunate enough to make it to the end of the movie for the gratuitous plot twist, it always fractures the soul. Soul fragments will then take refuge in nearby objects, usually ones being held at the critical moment. (Please be warned, if you have ever watched any of his movies from beginning to end, your soul may have trouble finding eternal peace, but likely, you already knew that.)

Anyone's first Hoaxcrock is likely to be a tragic accident. The half-eaten tub of popcorn was no exception. And it almost didn't happen. In the middle of the movie, *Signs,* the Fart Lord made himself more comfortable. He lied down on the sofa and in doing so, the remote control became out of easy reach. Had he moved the remote control with him as he shifted and kept it within arm's length, he would have eventually turned the movie off.

Instead, he continued to watch. Moldyfart was, of course, holding his tub of popcorn at the critical moment of the movie. When it was over, the Fart Lord recognized immediately the impact on his soul. He realized at once the powerful consequences of splitting his soul. He already knew a lot about possession of another human being. And he knew that a portion of his soul could be used to restore him to life after death. He understood that a form of immortality was in his grasp, literally. He decided at once to make more hoaxcrocks. The only drawback was that he would have to watch other movies by the same director.

Of course, he also realized the leftover popcorn could not be discarded, but must be saved forever. And so, his first hoaxcrock remained on a shelf in the entertainment room, where it was subjected to all of M. Night Shyamalan's movies, some of them on multiple occasions. Is it any

Chapter 10

wonder that it was reduced to pathetically calling out over and over, "The horror. The horror!"

And because it was always in the entertainment room, it knew about many evil acts perpetrated by Moldyfart. The most insidious of which was when he wickedly declared Tuesday night to be movie night. His movie buddy laughed evilly and agreed. Each Tuesday, for the following several months, Shameonus Finnigan abberated over to watch horrible motion pictures with Moldyfart. Tuesday nights became dreaded and despised by the tub of old popcorn.

Harry asked, "Wait? Shameonus Finnigan? He's the Fart Lord's movie buddy?"

The stale popcorn confirmed it.

Harry's old roommate at Hogwashes was not only Lord Moldyfart's movie-watching pal, he was one his many hoaxcrocks – a living hoaxcrock. Then Harry vaguely remembered, his roommate used to go out on Tuesday nights. He used to always happily say the same thing, "I'm going out to visit my chum. I'll be back in a couple."

Harry seethed, "Shameonus Finnigan must die!"

Hermione perked up and asked, "What? Why?"

Harry said, "Never mind, I'll tell you later."

The stale popcorn knew a lot about the other hoaxcrocks and there were more than anyone would have ever imagined. In that very room there were several. The barcalounger in the corner was a hoaxcrock. There was a curio cabinet in another corner and inside a moldy half eaten tub of Ben and Jerry's ice cream – Everything but the Kitchen Sink. It was a hoaxcrock. The leftover box of Raisinettes? A hoaxcrock. And the pair of 3-D glasses from going to see *Avatar: the last Airbender*? Duh! Of course, it was a hoaxcrock. The popcorn was even aware of the presence of the stolen pair of light-up sneakers. Hermione was still wearing them at that moment. The popcorn confirmed, the pair was also a pair of hoaxcrocks.

Yet, there were so many hoaxcrocks, even the tub of popcorn couldn't remember of all of them. In fact, the Fart Lord himself would not be able to keep track of them all, if it weren't for "The Master List."

Harry asked, "And just where is The Master List?"

A Surprise Christmas Visit

The popcorn told him, "Moldyfart keeps it in one of the most secret hiding places known to mankind – under his mattress upstairs."

When Harry told Hermione all that he had found out, she was shocked. She quickly tried to remember if she had accidentally made any hoaxcrocks herself. She felt a surge of relief as she realized, she hadn't ever watched more than a few scenes of any of Shyamalan's movies before becoming disgusted and turning it off.

When he got to the part about the mattress, she laughingly said, "Under the mattress! How stupid can you get?"

When they were finished asking the tub of popcorn all their questions, Harry made good on his promise. He turned the gas fireplace on, and tossed the tub in to burn. A moment later, the popcorn released its portion of Moldyfart's soul and finally found peace.

Next, Harry tossed the moldy tub of ice cream in the fire. Hermione tossed in the 3-D glasses. However, when the box of Raisinettes realized it was next, it spoke up. It said, "You can't destroy me that way!"

Harry stopped and asked, "What do you mean?"

The Raisinettes smugly replied, "I can only be destroyed in the volcanic fires of Mt. Doom!"

Harry skeptically answered, "All right, in you go."

The Raisinettes cried out, "Wait! Would you believe, in the fire of the candy-making kitchen where I was first crafted?"

Harry responded, "Not for a second."

He was on the verge of tossing the box into the flames. Once more it called out, "Wait!"

The teenager sighed and asked, "What, now?"

The Raisinettes replied, "Take a closer look and you'll see."

Harry peered into the dark box. All he saw was Raisinettes. He asked, "What?"

But, there was no reply.

He removed his glasses and bent the cardboard box to let more light in and peered closer still.

"Get 'em, boys!" yelled a Raisinette as it shot forth and hit Harry in the eyeball. Another said, "Run for your life!" It plinked Harry's nose.

Chapter 10

He tossed the box in the fireplace and stepped on the two rolling Raisinettes.

One of the squished morsels of candy said, "Drat."

The other said, "Darn."

For good measure, Harry scrapped them off the bottom of his sneaker and flicked them into the flames.

The barcalounger was not going to be so easy.

Harry said, "Too bad we don't have that pole axe from Grim Old Place. That would have been perfect for smashing this thing up so we can fit it in the fireplace."

Hermione asked, "We don't?"

She reached into Saint Nick's sack and pulled out a pole-axe-shaped present. She offered it to Harry and said, "Merry Christmas, Harry! I know it's something you can use."

Harry replied, "You shouldn't have! Well, actually, I was hoping you might do the honors. I'd like to go explore upstairs and see if I can find The Master List."

Hermione sighed, "Sure, I'll just be the man of the house and chop this thing up for you, you big woofter."

Harry laughed and said, "I knew I could count on you."

He stopped for a moment on the staircase and watched Hermione whale with the pole axe on the barcalounger as it yelled, "No!" and tried to run away. Harry shook his head, and thought, "Now the furniture is talking."

He turned. As he departed, he heard Hermione ruthlessly say, "Take that!"

There was loud whack and a feeble cry of dismay.

There were many bedrooms on the second floor of the mansion. Harry thought he was looking for the master bedroom. However, when he finally found it, it wasn't the right bedroom at all. It did not have a lived-in look to it. More importantly, it did not have a slip of paper under the mattress.

The bedroom Harry was looking for was the one with the NASCAR racing car bed in it. Harry reached under the mattress and pulled out a slip of paper. He said, "Bingo!"

A Surprise Christmas Visit

However, Harry was not paying attention to a monstrous reptile in the room. Just then Snakey, Moldyfart's pet, a giant anaconda, latched onto Harry's leg with its strong jaws. Fortunately for Harry, the anaconda is not a poisonous snake. Unfortunately for Harry, the anaconda prefers to crush it's victims in the strong muscular coils of its body. Harry tried to get his wand out from his robe pocket, however, he fumbled in his efforts. His body was tossed about as the giant snake began to loop itself around Harry's legs and torso. He fell. His wand slipped from his grasp and rolled on the floor.

He tried to call out for help, but it was already too late. His lungs weren't able to draw in enough air to carry his voice all the way downstairs. He stretched for his wand, but it had rolled just out of his reach. He tried again in vain to call for help. It was useless. He could barely gasp for air. His lungs labored taking short rapid breaths. He was in a panic. The snake squeezed harder still. Now he was suffocating.

He heard Hermione call out, "Did you find it yet?"

He couldn't reply. He tried banging his fist on the floor to alert her to his predicament.

He heard her shout, "Hurry up already!"

He was starting to feel numbness in his feet and hands. He thrashed as hard as he could, trying to make enough noise to bring her running up the stairs to his rescue.

He heard her call out, "What's taking you? It's under the mattress!"

His body was running out of oxygen. He couldn't move. He felt his muscles relax despite his terror. He felt dizzy and the room began to spin.

He heard Hermione yell something, but he couldn't decipher the words. A moment later, he blacked out.

Hermione muttered to herself, "If you want anything done right, you have to do it yourself." She tromped up the stairs and thought she heard a noise coming from one of the nearby rooms. When she entered, she saw Snakey wrapped around Harry. Her friend's lips were already blue and he wasn't moving.

She quickly reached into Santa's sack and pulled out a present. She tore the paper off and excitedly said, "It's just what I wanted!"

It was a blowgun and snake-tranquilizing darts.

Chapter 10

Harry felt something tickling his lips and an undeniable urge to cough. He coughed and spluttered back to life. He heard Hermione say, "Thank God!" He felt her weight upon him as she hugged him tight. His chest ached.

He coughed again and hoarsely croaked, "Ow, get off!"

She let go and kissed him on the mouth. He felt it again, the tickle of her mustache on his upper lip. He felt the wetness of a teardrop on his cheek. It was hers. She slowly drew her lips away from his and he tasted the salt of her tears.

She whispered, "Thank God, you're alive."

He suddenly remembered and realized what had just happened. He had died. There had been a floating sensation and a dark tunnel. He had seen a small crowd of shining people made of golden light beckoning to him. Though he didn't recognize their faces, he instinctively knew who they were – his mother, his father, and his uncle. He also saw and recognized the faces of people he did know: Elvis Grumblesnore, Cedric Biggleby, Dufus Dimeeyore, Nurse Pomfrite, Mad Dog Hooty, Frommundigus Filcher, Gandulf-the-Off-White, and his goat, Hedbutt. They were all standing on a small boat, except for Mad Dog Hooty. He was on the shore and was being beaten with a long oar by a skinny old man.

Harry heard Mad Dog yelp and get on the boat as the man with the oar wanted him to do. When Harry approached, the skinny old man held out his hand expectantly.

Harry, like a gentleman, shook it.

The oarsman bonked Harry on the forehead with his long wooden paddle. He said, "One galley, Dipstick!"

Harry checked his robes, but couldn't find any money.

The skinny old man bonked him on the head again and said, "Then kisses off, Landlubber!"

That's when Harry woke from his dream.

He whispered, "I see dead people."

Hermione asked, "What?"

"Oh, nothing," Harry asked, "Did you find The Master List?"

"It's in your hand."

A Surprise Christmas Visit

    Harry looked. Slightly worse for the wear of having been squeezed tight in Harry's fist, there was a crumpled up piece of paper – The Master List.

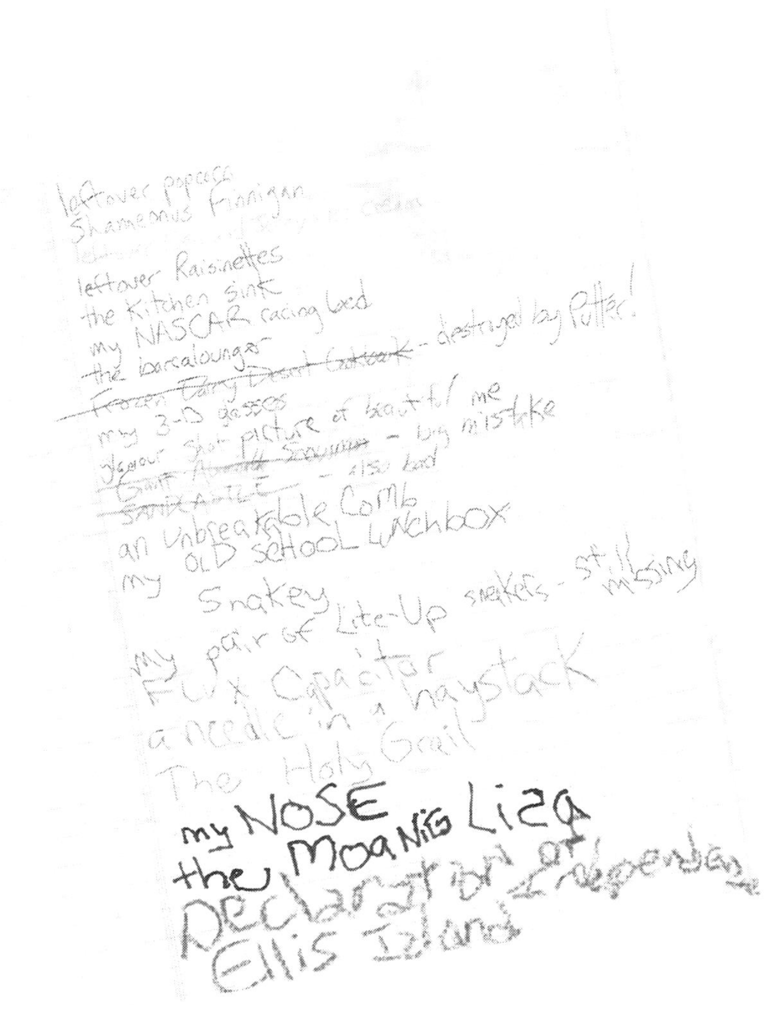

The handwritten list reads:

- leftover popcorn
- Shameanus Finnigan
- leftover Raisinettes
- the kitchen sink
- my NASCAR racing bed
- the barcalounger ~~destroyed by Potter!~~
- ~~frozen fairy~~
- my 3-D glasses
- ~~your shot picture of beautiful me~~ – by mistake
- ~~Snape~~ ~~Statue~~ – also bad
- an unbreakable comb
- my OLD SCHOOL lunchbox
- Snakey Lite-Up sneakers – still missing
- my pair of
- Flux Capacitor
- a needle in a haystack
- The Holy Grail
- my NOSE
- the Moaning Liza
- the Declaration of Independence
- Ellis Island

Chapter 10

Chapter 11 – Christmas List

They were still in Moldyfart's mansion because there was more work to be done. However, Harry had rested a bit from his deadly ordeal and had a snack – a bowl full of Cereal Killers. With the way that the breakfast cereal carried on as he mercilessly ate it, Harry felt a little like a Cereal Killer.

Afterward, Harry read The Master List aloud to Hermione:

leftover popcorn
Shameonus Finnigan
leftover Ben and Jerry's ice cream
leftover Raisinettes
The kitchen sink
my NASCAR racing bed
the barcalounger
~~Frozen Dairy Desert Cookbook~~ – destroyed by Putter!
my 3-D glasses
glamour shot picture of beautiful me
~~Giant Abominable Snowman~~ - big mistake
~~Sandcastle~~ – also bad
An unbreakable comb
my old school lunchbox
Snakey
My pair of light-up sneakers – still missing

Chapter 11

flux capacitor
a needle in a haystack
The Holy Grail
my nose
The Moaning Lisa
The Declaration of Independence
Ellis Island

Harry asked, "So how do we destroy the kitchen sink? Clog it up?"

Hermione asked in return, "Really, out of all these, that's the one you're worried about?"

"Well, yeah, I know the others are bad too. I mean, really bad. What I meant was we have to destroy the kitchen sink before we leave. Now's our big chance."

"Hmmm. Just how destroyed does it have to be? I suppose for good measure, we'd better completely melt it down to slag. That should be at about 1500 or 1600 degrees Celsius. That's not going to happen here, unless we burn the place down."

Harry laughed and jokingly asked, "Got any matches?"

"Sorry, Harry, we'd likely set the whole neighborhood on fire. We're just going to have to remove it and take it with us to destroy later."

"Well, that leaves only one question."

Hermione rose to the bait, "What?"

Harry answered, "Do we turn the water off first, or leave it running?"

Hermione shrugged and said, "Actually, I've got a lot of questions. First of all, is this list for real?"

Harry replied, "Didn't you hear the barcalounger? Didn't you see it try and run away from you? That barcalounger had a piece of someone's soul in it."

Hermione sighed, "Yeah. I know. I just don't want this list to be true. Some of these are going to be impossible to destroy. I mean, c'mon, Ellis Island? How do we destroy an island? We don't have a nuclear arsenal and we couldn't really nuke it even if we did."

Harry shrugged.

Hermione added, "And just how did he make *The Moaning Lisa* and the Declaration of Independence into hoaxcrocks?"

Harry shrugged.

"And what the heck is a flux capacitor?"

Harry shrugged.

"Does The Fart Lord really think that an unbreakable comb can't be destroyed?"

Harry shrugged.

"And isn't it odd? Grumblesnore left us two of these items in his will – *The Moaning Lisa* and Ellis Island. That can't be coincidental. How could he have known about them? And why did he leave the sword to you Harry? It's not on the list. If he were being consistent, he probably should have left you the Holy Grail."

Harry winked and said, "I've got my best person on it. She's a genius. She'll figure it all out."

Hermione sighed, "Thanks, I hope so."

"In the meanwhile, we need to kill Snakey, chop up and burn the Fart Lord's bed, and find the "glamour shot," his comb, his nose, and anything else on the list we can locate."

"Don't forget, we need to pull out the kitchen sink."

Harry added, "And find his television remote."

"What are you talking about? That's not on the list."

Harry laughed and said, "I know. I just think it would really mess with his head if I were to steal it. He'll probably have a cow!"

"You know, I think you might really be the evil one."

They returned upstairs and eventually located the glamour shot of Moldyfart. When Harry saw it, he said, "Eww, if any hoaxcrock deserves to be destroyed, this is it!" They chopped up the Fart Lord's NASCAR racing bed and destroyed the pieces, burning them up in the fireplace.

However, they had failed to find the unbreakable comb and many other hoaxcrocks on the list. Even though they used our new sponsor's magic words to the summoning spell, "Hess Premium Gasoline, Unbreakable Comb," the summoned item did not appear and apparently was not within the spell's range.

Furthermore, Snakey was nowhere to be found. The snake had escaped while they were downstairs. They had missed a golden opportunity to kill the giant anaconda.

Chapter 11

Yet, all in all, it had been a very successful mission. They had destroyed seven hoaxcrocks: the half-eaten tub of popcorn, the leftover Ben and Jerry's Everything but the Kitchen Sink ice cream, the leftover Raisinettes, Moldyfart's NASCAR racing bed, his barcalounger, his 3-D glasses, and the glamour shot picture of the Fart Lord. Additionally, they had an eighth, the kitchen sink, packed away in Santa's sack. Hermione used a powerful summoning spell to wrench out the Fart Lord's kitchen sink, leaving broken water pipes shooting water throughout the room. She packed it in her magic bag.

Furthermore, they had obtained a lot of useful information about hoaxcrocks in general. And perhaps most importantly, they now had The Master List.

Before they left, they spent two hours rearranging all the furniture. And for the finishing touch, Harry stole the television remote.

An hour after dawn, they locked the front door to Moldyfart's castle. They stopped back at the Bigshot's, to return the key to Butthilda. She marveled at their devilish tales of mayhem and destruction. When they were finished, she hugged herself and said, "This is the best Christmas ever! And she wrote down her cell phone number and handed it to Hermione while telling the two, "If you ever need anything, don't hesitate to call."

Harry assured her that he would, saying, "When this story's finished, your husband Benny's going to have his next big blockbuster on his hands." Then he slyly asked her, "So, who do you think he'll get to play your role in the movie? Sandra Bullock? Jennifer Aniston?"

Her eyes glazed over. She cooed, "Ooh, Scarlett Johansson."

They said goodbye and Hermione abberated them back to their camp. They spent much of Christmas Day catching up on their sleep.

Three days later, Harry felt the scar on his forehead erupt with agonizing pain. He had a vision. Moldyfart had returned home. He placed his suitcase on the floor beside him. He was already livid. Someone had tracked mud on the carpet!

Harry panicked. If his head hurt this much just for mud on the carpet, his head was going to simply explode when his archenemy saw his home flooded with three days worth of water.

Christmas List

Holding his head, he whispered to Hermione, "He's finally back. He just walked in the door."

Harry's vision continued. The Fart Lord was taking a closer look at the muddy footprints. He found something peculiar about them.

There was a moment of recognition and another burst of outrage and anger. Harry winced and gritted his teeth as pain stabbed into his brain like a knife. He almost wished it were a knife, so that the agony he felt would go away.

Moldyfart yelled, "Those are from my light-up sneakers! Who's got my light-ups! Who dares to steal MY light-ups!"

Harry was really worried now. He knew the worst suffering in his life was moments away.

And then it arrived. Every nerve-ending in his body screamed out with suffering. His body writhed and he wanted to scream in agony. However, he could not even draw his breath in to yell. Once more, he mercifully fell unconscious.

Chapter 11

Chapter 12 – Silver and Goat

It was the middle of January, in the brunt of winter. However, the temperature was barely freezing and so the snow was coming down in fat wet clumps. Everything was covered in white and the unnamed woods looked beautiful with every tree adorned with bright snow. The evergreens were especially gorgeous with thick piles of it clasped in their branches.

Though it was cold out, Harry was dressed in layers and felt pretty comfortable. There had been a few really cold nights – ones where Hermione and he cuddled together to keep warm. Harry had asked her for more blankets, but she said she had already brought out all the ones she had packed.

However, there was something in the way she had kissed him after saving his life, that made him suspect that she might not be telling him the truth. In many ways, it seemed like they were almost an old married couple. They had fallen into such a daily routine.

Though they had not made any progress over the past three weeks, Harry knew that Hermione was thinking hard about The Master List. She had done some research on the Internet, finding out as much as she could about *The Moaning Lisa*, the Louvre Museum, and the Holy Grail. Every so often she'd tell him something new she had learned.

Chapter 12

However, having had such a recent breakthrough in *The Quest to Destroy Lord Moldyfart*, Harry was eager for more progress. Earlier in the day, he felt apprehensive and crabby because things had slowed down once more. But now that it was finally his turn to wear the light-up sneakers again, he felt much better, even though his boots had been a lot warmer.

What he really wanted to do was go for a walk and admire the beauty of the freshly covered landscape, the falling snow, and the cool tracks the sneakers left behind in it. However, he knew his feet would freeze if he did, and if he took the light-ups off, he wouldn't feel like going for a walk any more. He decided he'd simply have to put on a pair of dry socks and warm his feet up near the wood burning stove when he got back.

When he returned an hour later, Hermione was in a bad mood. After he changed his socks, she complained, "Ugggh, your feet stink! Do you have to put those atrocities inside the sneakers? Can't you just wear them on your hands or something?"

Harry sprinkled some more of the foot powder she had given him inside the light-ups. He said, "There, now you can relax."

However, she complained about his wet socks, "They smell like two dead skunks. Go hang them outside to dry!"

Harry was pinning the socks up on their clothesline outside, when he noticed a silver light in the gloom of the overcast afternoon. He watched curiously as the light approached, weaving between the trees. It was a being made of light, not the warm golden light of the spirits in his near death experience. It was a creature formed of a cold silver radiance with highlights of white and shadows of blue and gray. It was a goat. It was a beautiful goat. It seemed oddly familiar. When it got closer still, Harry recognized it. It looked like Hedbutt, only more lovely than Hedbutt had ever been while living. It was the spirit of Hedbutt.

Harry and the goat stood watching each other for a long moment. Then the silver goat turned around and began picking his way through the trees, wandering back the way he had come. Harry called out, "Wait!"

But the goat only turned its head back toward Harry for a second before it began walking away again. It appeared as though Hedbutt wanted Harry to follow, so Harry obliged. At first, it seemed he was falling behind and

Silver and Goat

so moved quickly to try and catch up. However, the Spirit of Hedbutt always remained within sight, but well ahead of Putter. And so, he decided not to rush.

He followed the silver goat for nearly an hour. And even though he was still wearing the light-up sneakers, after a while, Harry was starting to feel tired and cranky. His feet were cold again. His fresh dry pair of socks was wet from trudging through the deep snow. Though he couldn't smell them, he figured they probably weren't so fresh anymore. He was weary of hiking and consequently was moving at an even slower pace now. Plus, it was getting to be late afternoon and with the sky still overcast, it was likely to become dark quickly.

He had half a mind to turn around and go back, when the Spirit of Hedbutt arrived at a small unfrozen pond. Then the creature of light abruptly disappeared.

Harry groaned and said, "Oh great, lead me to the middle of nowhere and then disappear. You always were a stupid goat!"

However, Harry surveyed his surroundings. The pond was of fair water and broad. In the midst of it, Harry noticed what he first thought to be a snow-covered tree branch sticking up out of the water, was actually an arm clothed in white samite, that held a fair sword in that hand aloft.

Just then a damsel appeared. Harry hid behind a thick tree. He peeked out, watching to see what would happen.

"What lady is that?" Harry whispered to himself.

Then he heard something behind him. He turned and there was Ron. His best friend was holding a half gallon of chocolate chip ice cream, his weapon of choice, which he immediately hid behind his back. Harry was shocked to see him. He cried out, "Ron!"

His friend answered, "Hey, Harry, ol' pal."

"What are you doing here?"

Ron replied, "Well, that is, I got to thinking about those light-up sneakers and I felt bad that I left you guys in such a huff. I figured, what the heck, I can just take two turns next time mine comes up. Say, it's got to be my turn by now, right?"

Harry had gotten used to only sharing the sneakers with Hermione. He did not want to go back to a three-way share. Plus, Ron was acting very suspiciously, sneaking up on him like that.

Chapter 12

Harry sounded a bit irked as he said, "First things first, Ron. Do you know who that lady is?"

"Why, that's the Lady of the Pond," said Ron; "See how grand this place is? It's as fair a place as any on earth. Look, she's headed this way. Hey, maybe if you're nice to her, she'll give you that cool sword!"

The lady was so beautiful that Harry swallowed, then chickened out, "I-I-I don't want to talk to her! You talk to her! Maybe she'll give you the sword." He pushed Ron forward.

Anon withal came the damsel unto Ron and saluted him, and he her.

Ron spoke with fluster in his voice, "Err, Ma'am, that is, uh, what sword is that held above the water yonder? I've never seen such a sweet, uh, that is, righteous, sword!"

"Sir Ronald Cheesley, King," said the damsel, "Behold Excalibur! That is as much to say as Cut-steel. The sword is mine and if ye will give me a gift when I ask it you, ye shall have it."

"Shucks, Lady, but I'm no king."

The Lady of the Pond replied, "Well, then, never mind."

And she bid Sir Ronald Cheesley farewell and was turning to depart, when Harry spoke up. He cleared his throat and said, "I'll give you what gift you, I mean, ye, what gift you, err, thee, ask!"

The damsel said, "You speak graciously, but art thou a king?"

Harry was feeling quite regal, perhaps it was the sneakers. He replied, "But, of course, you may call me, Harry, King Putter of the Britons."

"And when I see my time and come to you anon to ask my gift, you will give what I ask ye?"

King Harry replied, "Ask what ye will and ye shall have it, and it lie in my power to give it."

"Well said," answered the damsel, "go ye into yonder pond to the sword, and take it and the scabbard with you, and I will ask my gift when I see my time."

Harry stepped to the snowy edge of the pond's fair water. He realized the pool must be nearly freezing. He did not care very much for the idea of wading in such cold water. He looked for another way. He pulled out his wand. He didn't think it would work, but he tried anyway. He said our proud sponsor's magic words, "Hess Premium Gasoline, Sword!"

However, the white-sleeved arm did not move and the hand continued to grasp the sword.

The only way to get it, Harry knew, was to go in and retrieve it. He gritted his teeth and stepped into the ice cold water. The pond was not too deep. The water was only to his knees when he stood beside the arm and sword. However, his lower legs ached and were so cold it felt like they were burning. He could never be one of those human "polar bears," plunging themselves into the January ocean. His teeth were already chattering.

As his hands closed around the hilt, the light-up shoes suddenly sent a burst of electricity into Harry's feet. Electricity crackled as it coursed through Harry's body and shot from his hand to the sword. Harry felt sure he was about to die of electrocution.

The Lady of the Pond called out, "Liar! Thou art no king! The sword Excalibur knows it well! Ware it smites thee for thy sin! The hand that clasps it will not let go for any but a true king."

Ron saw immediately his best friend's predicament. He was either very brave or very foolish when he clenched his teeth and ran into the pond to help. The water burned it was so cold. It conducted electricity very efficiently and so Ron immediately subjected himself to the same jolts Harry suffered. Yet, he would not let that deter him from coming to the rescue of his best friend. He pushed forward, ignoring the pain and the spasms of his muscles as electrical energy coursed through his body. He struggled to maintain his balance on legs that were not completely under his control and responding unnaturally to his brain's guidance.

He attained Harry's side and immediately grabbed the sword. Ron took the sword and scabbard from the hand that held it. He wrenched the bright silver blade from its sheath. He could not help but notice the sword glowed with white light and white fire. And he felt a sense of purpose in that weapon. It was a powerful magic sword that exemplified all that was good and just.

Ron knew immediately what he had to do. He could see the sneakers now for what they were. The light-ups were evil. They emanated an aura of evil. It was radiating from then in a manner that was not visible, yet he could somehow sense the presence of their malevolence as never before. They had to be destroyed immediately and he had no misgivings about their destruction. Something that evil deserved to die.

Chapter 12

However, he hesitated with a sudden realization. The sneakers were still on Harry's feet. To use the sword upon them would also harm and maybe even cripple his friend. Yet the evil sneakers were killing them both with crackling jolts of electrical energy. The sneakers must die! Ron had to kill them even if it meant harming his best friend to do it. Surely, it is better to live without feet, than to die with them.

Suddenly, the jolts of electricity stopped and Harry's foot kicked out at Ron, catching him in the groin. There was a distinct snapping noise.

Ron hunched over clutching at himself and crossing his eyes. He said, "Ow, I think that broke my wand."

Harry gasped, stunned for moment. When he recovered, he called out, "Oh my God! I'm so sorry, Ron! It was the sneakers, not me!"

A deep malicious voice resonated in the air nearby. It was the voice from inside Ron's head, only now it was outside his head. It said, "Lies! He's lying to you, Ron. He hates you. He's jealous of you. It was Harry that kicked you in the family jewels! They're the best sneakers in the world, they'd never do that to you! They love you, and you love them."

Ron was bewildered and still hunched over in pain. He answered the voice outside his head, "I might have believed you, if you hadn't said that out loud."

The deep malignant voice audibly winced, "D'oh!"

Harry took a wild kick at Ron. He lifted his leg so high, he fell over, splashing in the frigid water.

Harry's head rose from below the surface. He spluttered and called, "Ron, pull me out, I think the sneakers are trying to drown me!" His feet jerked upward again and his head went back underwater.

The voice spoke to Ron's deepest fears. It said, "I've walked a mile in your shoes, Ron Cheesley! I know you! From the tip of your toes, to the bottom of your ankles! And your soles are mine!"

There was an evil laugh.

Ron could not help it, he listened horrified.

The light-ups continued, "I can make all your dreams come true, Cheesley! The sneakers can be all yours – you won't have to share with anyone! I will make you a hero and a king! I can make Hermione love you again. Use the sword! Kill Harry! If you don't, I'll make your every worst nightmare a reality!"

Silver and Goat

Again, there was evil laughter.

Ron didn't know what to do. He listened with an expression of deep anguish on his face. Harry put his hands behind him and pushed his head and shoulders back out of the water. He gasped for air. His feet were still held up high above him.

Meanwhile, the sneaker's voice said, "Already, Hermione loves Harry and not you. You are history to her. She is glad you left. Like a spider, she's got him all wrapped-up in her little web. She's even kissed him on the mouth."

Ron looked to Harry to either confirm or deny it.

Harry spluttered and said, "It's not like that. She saved my life. She kissed me because she was so glad I lived."

Ron yelped. He had not expected Harry to confirm what the sneakers said. Ron still liked Hermione and wanted her to be his girlfriend again. Harry knew that. How could he kiss her? Ron felt so betrayed.

Harry suddenly flipped over, his feet were sticking out of the water again and his face went back under.

The sneakers said, "Don't listen to him. He's not your friend, Ron. He's a backstabber. Now stab him back! Otherwise, on the next plane ride you take, I'll make the movie be *Maximum Overdrive*! And you'll be so bored that you'll watch the whole thing without sound."

Yet again, there was evil laughter.

Ron's eyes went wide when the voice continued, "And next Christmas, I'll make you sit on Santa's lap again!"

Harry forced his feet back down into the water. The L.A. Gear, which was laughing evilly, wheezed, and then had a coughing fit. Putter lifted his head and called out, "Help me, Ron!"

However, his feet quickly shot back up out of the water, and his head went under again.

Ron hesitated as the sneakers recovered from their coughing episode. They yelled, "Gah! Too much water under my tongue! Quickly Ron, use the sword! Kill Harry while his back is turned to you. Do it now, while you don't have to look at his face. If you don't, you'll never be the true hero of this story but only a subordinate character – a mere side kick, who's only good for a laugh. Speaking of which…"

The voice of the shoes laughed with malignant delight.

Chapter 12

They continued, "And, I will have your mother make the 'Great Zucchini Experiment' for dinner again."

Ron's tongue stuck out of his mouth. He cringed with a look of disgust.

The light-ups laughed until they wheezed again.

"And there will be more very long words in your life, such as, 'Hippopotomonstrosesquipedaliophobia,' otherwise known as, 'fear of big words.'"

Ron shuddered and said, "Yikes, I'll never remember all that!"

Harry pushed his head up and his feet back under the water. The light-ups coughed loudly instead of laughing.

Harry gasped for air and cried out weakly to his friend, "Help... Ron... I'm... drowning!"

Ron was terrified. However, before he could do anything, the L.A. Gear spun Harry around again. The teenager was now on his back again with his feet high in the air. Harry's head was underwater and he was thrashing.

The footwear spluttered angrily, "Now Cheesley! Kill him or I'll make the squirrels come and get you!"

Ron shuddered and said, "Ahh! Not the squirrels!"

Harry drove his feet back down to the bottom of the pond and his head popped back up. He greedily gulped at air and coughed up water.

The disembodied voice was coughing and wheezing too. Harry struggled while holding his feet down on the bottom of the pond. There was a choking and gagging noise, almost like someone dying.

Meanwhile, Ron was paralyzed by fear. All his secret thoughts were being voiced aloud by the light-up shoes. While Ron just stood there terrified, there was a tiny surge of electricity and two small popping noises in rapid succession, followed immediately by two plumes of smoke rising from the water just over Harry's feet.

And then there was silence. No more thrashing. No deep evil voice, no laughter, no coughing or wheezing. The shoes had shorted-out from the pond water. They were ruined. They released the fragments of the evil soul that resided within them.

In frustration, Ron called out, "NO!" He plunged the sword, Excalibur, into the water, into the light-up sneaker, and into Harry's foot.

Silver and Goat

Harry screamed in pain!

Hermione was already in a sour mood. She had not had a chance to wear the light-up sneakers since noon. Harry had been gone for hours in a snow storm and now it was dark out. She was worried about the sneakers and wondered where he was. She wondered if he was out there somewhere inconsiderately lying in the snow, perhaps he was even dying. He left without a word to say where he was going, without even a word of goodbye, telling her that he was leaving. He just vanished. Her stomach was upset from worrying so much.

When she heard his weak voice coming from outside the tent, she rushed to open up the entrance flap.

She gasped, "Ron! Oh my God! Please tell me you weren't followed back here!" She looked behind him, but it was too dark to see anything.

He replied, "Uh, I don't think I was."

Hermione scolded, "For your sake, I hope not."

She held the flap as the two boys limped into the tent. Ron was supporting Harry's side. Cheesley had the sword Excalibur sheathed in its scabbard, attached to his waist. Hermione was glad Harry was finally back. However, she was upset to see Ron again. She was angry at him for abandoning them in the first place. Some friend he was!

She was annoyed he was back too, because that meant he'd want his turns in the rotation of sharing the light-up sneakers. She had gotten quite used to sharing less, and did not relish the idea of having shorter turns and more time waiting for her next chance to wear them.

She finally noticed Harry's foot and exclaimed, "Oh, NO! Are the sneakers alright?"

When she found out the light-ups were destroyed, she went ballistic. She cursed enough to make a sailor blush, and even used a few select terms Harry didn't quite understand but wasn't about to ask her to explain.

She was especially mad at Ron for letting the sneakers get destroyed.

Ron retorted, "But I wasn't even wearing them! It's all Harry's fault!"

Meanwhile Harry plunked his wet shivering body down in front of the wood stove. He opened the iron door in front and tossed in two pieces of wood.

Chapter 12

Hermione spent several minutes making a special poultice of Knotweed and salt for Harry's foot. She applied it liberally and then wrapped it up in a bandage.

Harry complained that the concoction stung his injury terribly.

Hermione answered, "Good, that means it's working. Get out of those wet clothes or you'll never warm up."

Meanwhile, Ron discovered Harry's or the sneaker's kick had indeed snapped his wand. He asked, "Hermione, do you still have my backup wands?"

She crabbily replied, "What do you think? Of course, they're in the bag, simpleton."

Ron pulled out a present and unwrapped it. The box had originally held five wands. There were two left. He took one out and placed it in his robe pocket. Then he put the box back in the sack.

Later, as they were all eating dinner, Ron and Harry told her about their adventure – meeting the Lady of the Pond and battling the evilly possessed sneakers.

Hermione gasped suddenly when she realized something from their rendition of the events. She exclaimed, "Ron, you were able to take the sword, Excalibur! Do you know what that means?"

"Yeah, it means I've got to give the Lady of the Pond her gift whenever she decides what it is she wants."

Hermione sighed.

Ron tried again, "It means Harry can use the sword to destroy the hoaxcrocks?"

Hermione answered, "Harry doesn't need the sword to destroy the hoaxcrocks! That would be dumb if he did. Items don't become virtually indestructible just because they contain a fragment of someone's soul, just like we aren't indestructible, even when we have our entire soul. Besides, while you were gone, Harry and I destroyed a bunch of them.

Furthermore, it would be way too convenient and contrived if something like that happened to be in a nearby pond and showed up just when we needed it. It'd almost be like pulling it out of a magic hat. Heck, I don't even know why we need the sword. What it means, Ron, is you're a king! Only a king could have gotten the sword! So, at what age do you inherit your kingdom? When you're 18? 21?" What country is it?"

"Hermione, don't be silly. I ain't a king."

She whispered furtively, "Don't worry, I can keep it a secret."

Ron turned to Harry, "Tell her, Harry, I ain't a king."

Harry laughed and said, "I don't know, Ron, maybe you are and just don't know it."

Hermione suddenly began to scold Harry. She blamed him for ruining the light-up sneakers. She cried out, "It was so stupid of you to wear them in the water. Why didn't you take them off first?"

Harry shrugged and said, "It was cold out, I just couldn't go in barefoot."

Hermione said, "You're a butt-headed idiot. You could have returned from the cold water to warm dry sneakers. You should have known better."

Ron changed the subject. He said, "Hey, guess what I found out while I was home? Oldyfart May has a hex placed on his name. Whoever says it out loud, their location becomes instantly known to him. He can send his Fungus Eaters to teach them their lesson. And I suppose, that's probably how they found us at Grim Old Place so fast."

Harry asked, "You can't be serious?"

Ron replied, "I swear it's true. My mum told me so."

"That's so dumb! Hermione, did you happen to pack my new laptop?"

She reached into Santa's sack and pulled out a present, while saying, "Of course, dimwit. You know I did."

Harry unwrapped his laptop and said, "It's just what I wanted!"

He logged in and went online to the Facebook site. He said, "This ought to give him a headache."

He left a message for all his fans, asking them to start chanting Moldyfart's name. Then he logged out and shutdown.

Not long afterward, he began to feel the pain of his scar slowly building up with Moldyfart's rage. Within two hours, the taboo was lifted and Harry felt the pain begin to fade.

Two weeks later, Hermione announced that she has finally figured out why Grumblesnore left her the book, *The Drunken Tales of Beadie the*

Chapter 12

Blowhard. She read them one of the stories within, "The Three Bad Kittens."

Chapter 13 – The Three Bad Kittens

Three bad kittens, one stormy night,
began to quarrel, and then to fight.
One had a mouse, the others had none,
and shortly after the fighting begun.

"I'll have that mouse," said the biggest cat.
"You? Steal my mouse? We'll just see about that!"
"I will have that mouse," said the eldest son.
"Over our dead bodies," said the two smaller ones.

Chapter 13

Enough was enough, they began to fight,
to hiss and spit, to scratch and bite.
The old woman had enough. She seized her broom,
and swept the bad kittens right out of the room.

As she swept kittens, the old woman gruffly said:
"Hairballs on the floor, hairballs on the bedspread,
hairballs on the sofa, hairballs on the chair.
Even in the lasagna, there's hairballs everywhere!"

The Three Bad Kittens

Hairballs on the carpet! Even one on that dead mouse!
You live and eat and breathe hairballs, when cats live in your house.
Hairballs on my dresses, hairballs on my best coat,
I hope the next hairball you cack up, gets stuck in your throat!

Get out, you stupid kittens! Get out, you disgusting cats!
Take your hairballs with you, and that's the end of that!
She swept the kittens from the room, she swept the three out the door.
Then she spent the next half hour sweeping hairballs off the floor.

Chapter 13

Outside the ground was all frost and snow,
and the three little kittens had nowhere to go.
But go they must, to stay was to freeze,
or catch pneumonia and die from disease.

So they crept away as quiet as mice,
all wet with snow and cold as ice.
The wind was blowing, the snow, how it whirled,
as they made their way out into the cruel world.

The Three Bad Kittens

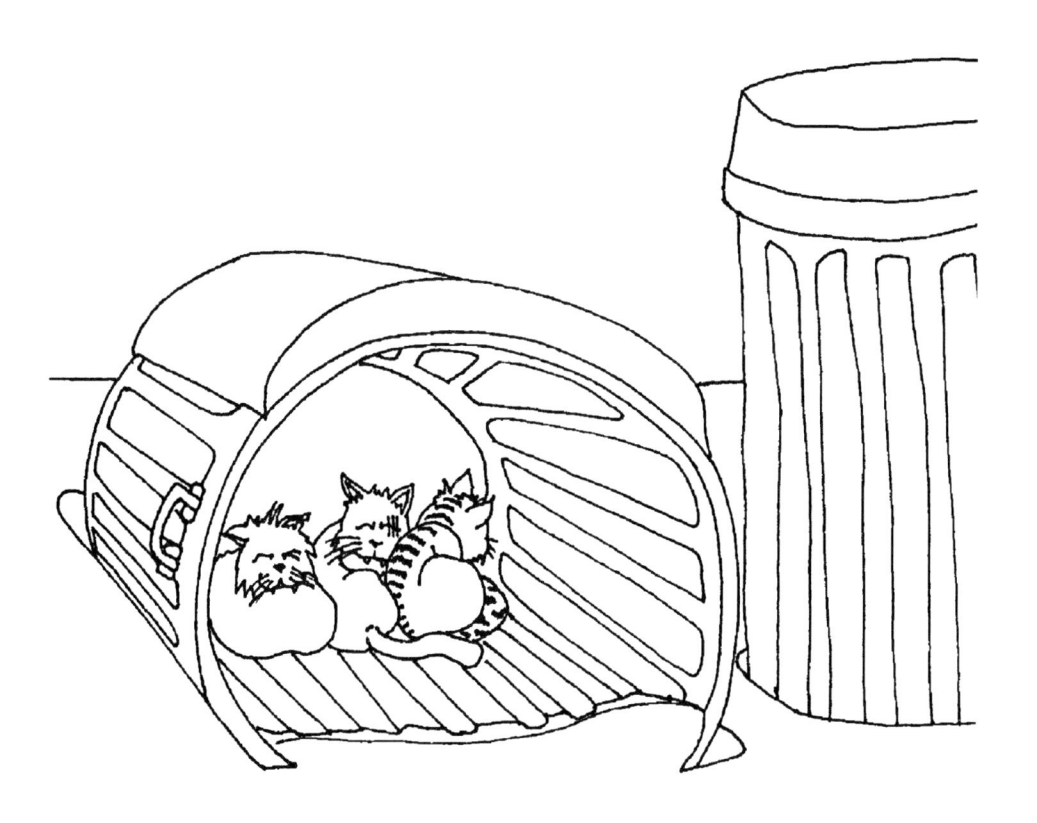

Yet the three bad kittens survived that harsh night.
The first thing they did was put an end to their fight.
They found a dry place and huddled together to stay warm,
and they slept that way, waiting out the night's storm.

Chapter 13

The next morning they fell in with a group of strays,
riotous cats, who weren't even neutered or spayed.
They lived on the streets, in back alleys, and tool shacks.
They cacked up hairballs and committed worse acts.

The Three Bad Kittens

How they fought to excess and lived wanton in their ways,
the three bad kittens learned bad things from these strays.
They learned to caterwaul, to revel and frolic,
and how to steal booze from sleeping drunk alcoholics.

And they learned blasphemous curses and oaths most profane.
They learned to raise their hackles in back alleys and lanes.
And how they fought and scratched with sharp claws,
biting their enemies with fanged teeth in fanged jaws.

Chapter 13

And sometimes the back alley strays fought 'til they died,
when faced with another cat they simply could not abide.
And it happened there were two toms, so shrewd and canny.
Each thought the other was one cat too many.

So they yowled at each other, they hissed and had fits.
How mean they fought, how they scratched and they bit!
And in the end of the battle of one cat too many,
instead of two cats, there were no longer any.

The Three Bad Kittens

Then all the dead toms' friends gathered to mourn,
and among them the three kittens felt quite forlorn.
'Twas said among them, a thief stole their nine lives,
against the assassin "Death," no cat ever survives.

Chapter 13

NO PITY!

But the three bad kittens, they were not afraid.
They were tougher than all the other cats who had strayed.
They would not wait for "Death" – for the bitter end.
They decided to find him and exact their revenge.

And so the three brave kittens boldly set out,
to find the thief "Death" and thrash him about!
They wandered the dark alleys around the whole city,
And said when they found him, they'd show him "no pity."

The Three Bad Kittens

Until in one dark alley, they found an old cat,
and the biggest one said, "Well, just look at that!
Hey, Old Tom, why do you cling so to life?
Wouldn't it be better to end all your strife?"

The aged old tomcat looked at him and he said,
"If I was as stupid as you, I'd be better off dead."
"Stupid as I? We'll just see about that!"
said the eldest kitten as he hissed and he spat.

Chapter 13

"Calm down, kitten, I've rubbed your fur the wrong way,
but I'm just an old tomcat, like you, I'm a stray.
And you asked me why to life I so cleave?
Let me answer now, I'm still here by God's leave.

And in return I ask you, why you find it so strange,
that wherever I've wandered, no one will exchange
their youth for my years, their peace for my strife.
Alas, not even Death wants my poor life."

The Three Bad Kittens

The kitten exclaimed, "Hear that! He speaks of Death,
the one who has stolen our friend's very last breath.
One of his loyal servants? Perhaps you are his spy?
Here to slay us young kittens? Is Death lurking nearby?"

Then the wily old tom laughed and he said,
"Death is waiting for you just down that alley ahead!
And if you are smart, kitten, take my advice,
don't walk down that alley or you'll pay the price!"

Chapter 13

Then the oldest bad kitten among the three cats
laughed and he said, "We'll just see about that!"
Down the narrow alley he led his sister and brother.
They slipped into the darkness one after the other.

And in the dark alley there arose such a fight;
three kittens against Death, robed black as night.
And each of the three little kittens almost died,
but they stuck together and so they survived.

The Three Bad Kittens

They fought meanly and scratched with sharp claws,
biting their enemy with fanged teeth in fanged jaws.
In the end they forced Death to cry out for mercy,
even so, they accepted his surrender quite adversely.

They had said when they found him, they'd show him "no pity."
Quite determined to do so, were the three little kitties.
It was not until Death offered something more,
And even then, they didn't stop 'til he swore

Chapter 13

that he'd grant each little kitten one wish come true.
Then finally from battle, the kittens withdrew.
And Death did not lie, he made good on his word.
He waited to find out what each kitten preferred.

And when he was ready, the oldest made the first wish,
He stepped forward excitedly, his tail all a swish.
With thoughts of his favorite cat story, Puss 'n Boots,
quite proudly he wished for a spiffy pair as his loot.

The Three Bad Kittens

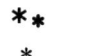

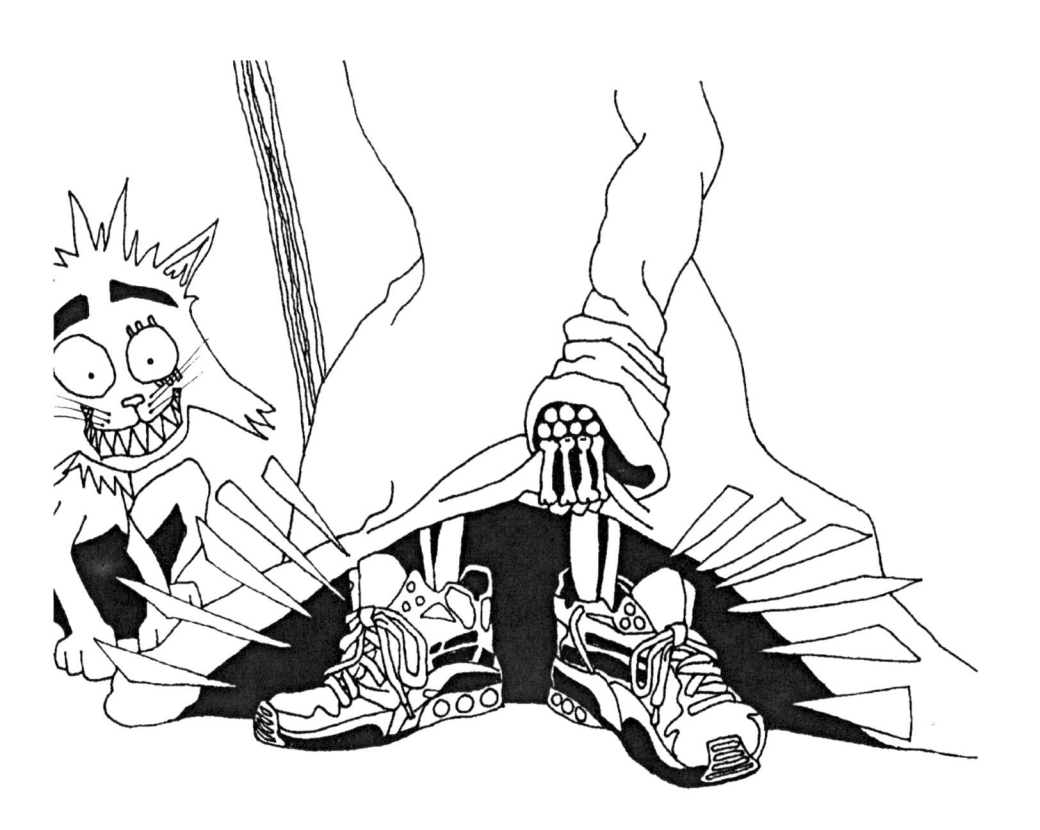

And just as quick as a stray can catch rabies,
Death said, "I'll do even better, take a look at these babies!"
Lifting his robe, to the kitten's delight,
he revealed a pair of sneakers with flashing lights!

And Death said, "But wait! There's even more!"
There was something quite magic about the sneakers he wore.
"They're not only great, these sneaker make you the best.
Better than everyone else! Better than all the rest!"

Chapter 13

Oh, how their eyes nearly popped out in awe.
and they called out, "Cool!"; "Whoo hoo!"; and "Hurrah!"
And the oldest cat took his light-up shoes with great pride,
"Hmmph, I'm already the best tom around, far and wide!"

Now, his brother knew what he wanted and could no longer wait,
but he simply could not ignore him and rose to the bait.
He said, "Best tom around? We'll just see about that!"
and with a swish of the tail, stepped forward, the second cat.

The Three Bad Kittens

And thinking of his own favorite tale, "The Cat in the Hat."
"I wish for a snazzy magic cap," said the second-most cat.
Now Death is a fast one, and just as quick as he could,
he upped with his hand, and he snapped back his hood.

On his head a hat with goat-hair tassels was revealed,
when they saw it, how the delighted kitties all squealed!
"But there's more to it," said Death. "It's got magic, too.
It casts an illusion no one can see through."

Chapter 13

"The person who wears this hat on his head,
can appear to everyone else that he's dead!
Your chest will seem not to fall and to rise,
so whenever you want, you can fake your demise.

Even a vet could not discern you're alive.
And when you're ready you can simple revive.
It's useful to get out of scraps quite varied,
just make sure you are careful not to get yourself buried."

The Three Bad Kittens

Then Death with a flourish, placed it on the cat's head.
A moment later, the second cat dropped down quite dead.
For a minute the two other cats thought he had been tricked,
The liar had betrayed them, the hat his death did inflict.

Chapter 13

But up popped the cat, ending his morbid disguise
and he laughed, "You should have seen the look in your eyes!"
"Hmmph," replied the two kittens. They didn't like that one bit,
but they knew that they'd somehow have to get used to it.

The Three Bad Kittens

And when she was ready, the third kitten made the last wish,
she stepped forward excitedly, her tail all a swish.
She said, "Death, grant my wish now! If you will permit,
when I cack up hairballs, let them instantly kill who they hit!"

"I'll do even better!" said Death, adding a small change,
"I'll also magically increase your cacked-hairball range.
And in addition to causing death to whomever you strike,
you'll now expertly cack hairballs whenever you like."

Chapter 13

Death granted her wish and oh, how he laughed,
as the bad little kitten gave each of her two brothers the shaft!
She cacked up a hairball on each kitten's head,
and an instant later they fell down quite dead.

She gathered up her dead brother's great magic loot,
the hat on her head, a light-up sneaker on each back foot.
And she knew in her heart she was the best cat in the city,
Yes, she felt rather proud when Death called her, "Good kitty!"

Chapter 13

Chapter 14 – Home is Where the Fart is

After she had finished reading the story, Ron said, "Thanks, Hermione. That brings back fond memories. My mum used to read me that one when I was little."

Harry said, "I never heard it before. The Dirtley's never read any stories to me."

Ron asked, "So, the light-up sneakers were really from the story?"

Harry scoffed, "No."

Hermione answered, "Yes."

The two looked at each other like they were crazy.

Harry said, "Don't be dumb, Hermione. It's a children's tale with talking cats and Death granting wishes. It's laughable."

Hermione asked, "Then why do the light-up sneakers exist?"

"The sneakers were just a hoaxcrock. They had a piece of the Fart Lord's soul in them. And that evil presence was working hard to break up our friendship. Making us think the sneakers were so great was just part of …Oldyfart May's scheme to divide us, not because they're Death's magic footwear."

"Good idea not to use Moldyfart's name anymore. He could set up his taboo again at any time."

"Thanks, maybe you should stop too."

"Oops! I guess I said Moldyfart by mistake. Whoops, I did it again. Hee hee. Anyway, why can't the sneakers be both a hoaxcrock and Death's sneakers?"

Chapter 14

Harry scoffed, "Because there is no such thing as Death or the Grim Reaper or whatever. That's all folk tales and malarkey. Death is a fact of life, not some supernatural being carrying a scythe. People are dying every second and that has nothing to do with Death personified. And even if Death did exist, I mean, c'mon, he goes around wearing light-up sneakers as his choice in footwear? Get serious. What did he wear before they were invented? I mean, he's been around a lot longer than L.A. Gear."

Ron replied, "A black robe and a hat with goat-hair tassels."

Harry gave Ron a wry look.

Hermione asked, "So, then, why did Grumblesnore leave the book to me and the hairball to you, Harry?"

He replied, "I don't know. He probably left the book to you, because you'd eventually read it. Why would you believe the hairball is real?"

Hermione sniffed and said, "Because that's what Grumblesnore is trying to tell you."

Harry said, "Oh. I see your point. It's not that a Death Cat actually cacked-up a deathly hairball. It's Grumblesnore. He's trying to give me an advantage, a chance to kill Moldy, …err, Oldyfart May in a wizard's duel. Grumblesnore must have used Advanced Poisons Magic to make it a super poisonous hairball. All I have to do is get close enough to hit the Fart Lord with the snow globe. The glass will shatter and the Deathly Hairball will kill him on contact."

Hermione said, "Something like that."

Ron said, "Cool! And then you steal his heart. And then you take a bite out of it! Bloody brilliant!"

Harry said, "Ron, I'm not going to take a bite out of his heart. Especially, after it's been poisoned."

With the light-up sneakers destroyed, Hermione felt so much more mentally competent. The shoes had really inhibited her ability to concentrate on what was essential – finding and destroying the hoaxcrocks. And perhaps more importantly, now that the sneakers were ruined, she could finally stomach the idea of conducting magical research experiments upon them.

Home is Where the Fart is

She wanted to find out if the sneakers retained any residual effects from the evil soul that had inhabited them. She hoped to discover a method of finding the remaining hoaxcrocks by detecting their evil emanations.

In her research she discovered there was a legendary group of holy knights, called "Paladins." The Paladins were from the medieval ages and the servants of the Knight Roland, who in turn served King Charlemagne. The Paladins were said to be able to detect the presence of evil.

And so, Hermione felt certain if a bunch of poofy French knights were able to detect evil, certainly she should be able to figure out a way to do it.

However, she was unable to discover the means and she became quite frustrated. It wasn't helping that Harry and Ron were always around lazily eating and playing noisy video games.

One day, she said in exasperation, "Can't you two do anything to help? What am I expected to do this all on my own? While you just sit around eating all the food I packed, leaving your mess behind, and playing stupid video games?"

Harry replied, "Well, you are the computer expert."

"You can research stuff on the Internet too, you know!"

"Fine." Harry asked, "What do you want me to look up?"

Hermione answered, "The Holy Grail."

Harry saluted her and said, "Aye, Aye, Captain."

She turned to Cheesley and said, "Ron, why don't you make yourself useful and … err, … start a letter writing campaign to US congressmen urging them to rename Ellis Island to Elvis Island."

Ron asked, "Really, I have to do that? I thought …"

Hermione interrupted, "If you have any respect at all for your dearly departed Headmaster's wishes, you'll do it. Or would you rather his ghost start haunting you?"

Ron eyes widened a bit. He grumbled, "All right, I'll get on it."

The boys turned off the video games.

Hermione went back to her research and was glad things were quieter now that the others were working too. However, she still made no headway. She soon found herself sighing, "It's like trying to find a needle in a haystack." That's when, she decided to take a break from her research and spend some time looking for the hoaxcrock needle in a haystack.

Chapter 14

Finding a needle in a haystack sounds impossibly difficult, however, for wizards and witches, it is trivial. The summoning spell makes it quick and easy. However, finding the right needle in the right haystack made the problem much more difficult. Worse still, it turned out that very few haystacks actually have needles.

The three teenagers spent a month roaming the English countryside trying to summon needles from haystacks. They had found just three and snapped them. Hermione thought for sure they'd somehow be able to tell when they located the right one. Yet, there had been no sign they had found and destroyed a hoaxcrock. In their hearts, they knew they had not succeeded.

One day Harry complained, "I think we've already been to this haystack before."

Ron asked, "How can you tell? They all look the same to me."

Harry said, "That's the point. We've been looking in all the haystacks in England. But what says it's in England? What if it's in the States or China or Africa? It would actually be smart for him to hide it in a different country."

Hermione asked, "So, if you were Moldyfart...er, Oldyfart May, where would you hide it?"

Harry answered, "How should I know?"

"Ron?"

Cheesley shrugged and said, "Beat's me."

Hermione sighed and said, "It's no use. We need a way to detect hoaxcrocks. Let's go back to camp, and I'll see if I can figure out what to do next."

A week later, Hermione decided she needed to talk to Arthur Cheesley. She abberated to the Boil that evening. She wanted to know more about Arthur's work in the Office for the Detection of Evil Objects that No One Can See or Touch.

She was astounded when, after being sworn to secrecy, Arthur finally admitted to her that he really had no means by which to detect intangible objects, regardless of their state of good or evil. He also told her he was not able to detect evil in objects that did exist, or at least not any better than anyone else.

Home is Where the Fart is

And so, Hermione hit another dead end. She felt like she had been banging her head against a wall for the past two months.

She decided to take another break from researching a means of detecting the evil hoaxcrocks. Instead, she researched the Fart Lord's "Flux capacitor." She found out a flux capacitor is the rare invention that makes time travel possible. And she shuddered at the implications. If Moldyfart has a flux capacitor, he could travel backwards and forwards in time and space. Who knows how his evil and insane mind might put such power to use?

Furthermore, once she knew what it looked like, she remembered having seen it in Lord Fartypant's mad scientist laboratory. And so, they raided Moldyfart's castle once more in the middle of the night. Only this time she abberated herself, Ron, and Harry inside the entrance foyer.

Hermione whispered, "Moldyfart didn't get his protection spells updated yet. I guess he didn't think we'd dare to come back while he's around. I thought we'd be blocked and have to borrow the key from Butthilda again."

Harry whispered back, "You did it again. Remember? Call him, Oldyfart May."

Hermione tittered in her embarrassment.

When Harry saw the signed movie posters hanging in the entrance foyer again, he shivered inadvertently and muttered, "M. Knight Shyamalan."

Lately, Ron had taken up the habit of wearing Excalibur strapped to his side. And so, he brought the sword along, as he put it, "just in case we happen upon Snakey."

Hermione led the way, leading them into the left wing of the castle.

However, even with the sword on his hip, Ron was a mess. The left wing of the castle was a frightful place, filled with peril. The dangerous traps had all been reset. However, Hermione remembered where they were located. The monstrous denizens had all been replaced. The three teenagers defeated several horrors.

Ron was constantly whining and complaining about the evil place. Several times, he asked, "Is it much further?"

Each time, Hermione replied, "We're almost there."

Chapter 14

Suddenly Harry felt his scar send a burning pain into his skull.
He cried out, "Oh no! The Fart Lord's angry!"
Hermione asked, "Does he know we're here?"
Harry had a vision. Moldyfart was at his home computer. He was on The Villain's Message Board. He was angry because Darth Vader had corrected his grammar in a post. He seethed, "That cursed know it all! I'll show him!"
Harry said, "Nope, false alarm."
A moment later, they entered the Hall of Masks. While there, Hermione got confused and began leading the boys toward the Room of Evil Ambiance instead of the mad scientist laboratory.
Ron, however, balked. He said, "You're going the wrong way!"
Hermione sniffed and did not like his blatant accusation that she was making a mistake. She said, "Oh, stop being a baby, Ron, just follow me."
Ron pointed the opposite direction and said, "I'm serious, Hermione. The flux capacitor is this way. I don't know what room you're heading for, and I don't like it a bit. But, regardless, it ain't the right direction."
Hermione was really miffed now. She just knew she was right. She said, "Look, Ron, I'm the one who's been here before. Don't you think I know better than you, which way to go?"
Harry said, "C'mon, Ron, we don't have time to argue. We need to quickly find the flux capacitor before Moldyfart figures out we're here."
Ron mumbled, "Fine, let's just get this over with. This place gives me the creeps."
Hermione replied, "We know. You've only said it like four times."
She led the way to the Room of Evil Ambiance. Meanwhile, Ron's knees were shaking in fear, yet he bore the burden of his terror silently.
When Hermione came to the Unholy Chapel, Ron's whole body was shaking with fright and his teeth were chattering. Hermione felt abashed. She knew what rooms were beyond the Unholy Chapel – only the mortuary, the mausoleum, and the catacombs. She reluctantly had to admit her mistake, turn around, and go back to the Hall of Masks.
When they returned, Hermione became curious. She asked, "Which way did you say to go, Ron?"
Ron, who was feeling slightly better now, pointed. Hermione said, "Lead the way."

Home is Where the Fart is

Ron took them to the mad scientist's lab. And though Hermione did not see the flux capacitor at first among all the experimental equipment and strange objects, Ron took them right to it. It was attached to a lawn mower.

If Moldyfart's nose was on his face, they would have destroyed the flux capacitor right under his nose. However, his nose was hidden elsewhere so they simple destroyed it while he was still on the computer upstairs.

Harry felt another stab of pain from his scar. He saw Moldyfart pound his keyboard and shout at his computer screen, "That stupid moderator deleted my post!"

Finished destroying the hoaxcrock, Hermione asked, "Ron, by any chance, can you tell if there are any more hoaxcrocks around?"

Ron shrugged and said, "How should I know?"

Hermione said, "Just think about it. Do you know which way Moldyfart's comb is?"

"It's probably upstairs in his bedroom."

"No, I mean, do you get a feeling where it is? What direction?"

Ron laughed, "No."

Hermione sighed, "What about the Holy Grail? Can you tell where it is?"

Ron replied, "I've no idea."

Hermione sighed again and said, "Alright, then, let's go."

She abberated them back to their camp. Harry crossed the flux capacitor off the list, glad they had finally made some more progress.

Chapter 14

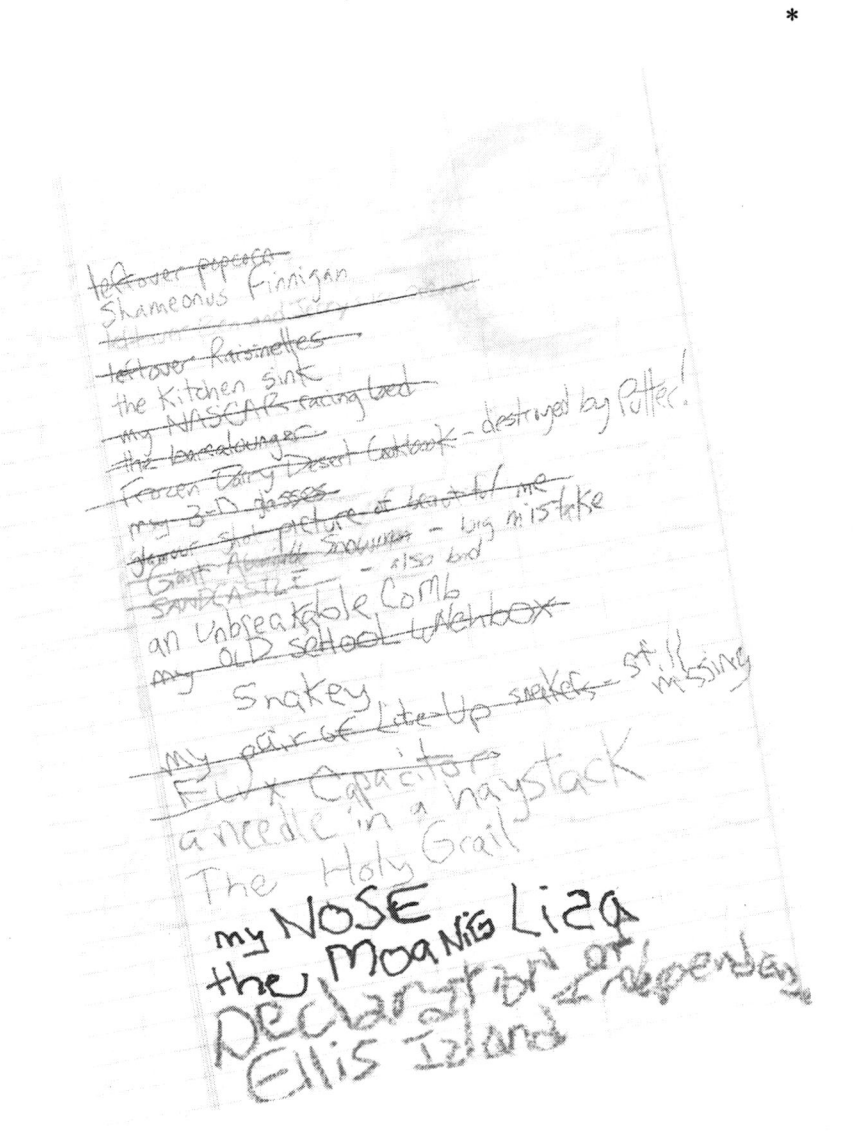

[handwritten list on notebook paper, with many items crossed out:]

- ~~leftover popcorn~~
- ~~Shameonus Finnigan~~
- ~~leftover karomettes~~
- the kitchen sink
- ~~my NASCAR racing bed~~
- ~~the barcalounger~~
- ~~Frozen Dairy Dessert Cookbook~~ — destroyed by Potter!
- ~~my 3-D glasses~~
- ~~Jamie's picture of herself~~ me — big mistake
- ~~Giant Armadillo Snowman~~ — also bad
- ~~SANDCASTLE~~
- an unbreakable comb
- ~~my OLD school lunchbox~~
- ~~Snakey~~
- ~~my pair of Lite-Up sneakers~~ — still missing
- ~~Flux Capacitor~~
- a needle in a haystack
- The Holy Grail
- my NOSE
- Moaning Liza
- the Declaration of Independence
- Ellis Island

Hermione sat down and said, "Oh, Ron, would you bring me the pair of light-up sneakers."

Ron brought them over.

Hermione asked, "All right, Ron. What gives? In this huge mess, how did you know where the light-up sneakers were just now?"

Ron shrugged, "I dunno. I guess I just remembered where they were."

Home is Where the Fart is

"Then how did you know where the flux capacitor was, when you'd never been there before?"

"I don't know, I just sort of knew."

"When did you first know?"

"When we were in the hall with all those creepy masks."

"Ron, I don't know how you're doing it, but I think you can tell what direction the hoaxcrocks are. You're like a modern day Paladin."

Ron blurted out, "Oh yeah? Well, you have a mustache!"

Hermione said, "It's alright, Ron. A paladin is a holy knight. All I meant by it is, it seems you can detect evil. Tell me something. Do you know which way the needle in the haystack is?"

"I have no idea."

"What about the unbreakable comb?"

"I haven't a clue."

"Moldyfart's nose?"

"Sorry, but I don't think I'm a pal of any of those things or a holy knight or whatever."

Hermione thought for a moment and said, "Hmmm. Ron, how did you find your way back here?"

"What do mean?"

"You left us and went home for over a month. When you came back, how did you find your way here?"

"I remembered which way to go."

"You remembered how to get to the camp from home?"

"Uh-huh."

"Then why did you end up at the pond?"

"Oh, I just happened upon Harry in the woods and thought I'd follow him and murder him for the sneakers. Heh, heh. Uh, I mean, to see where he was going."

"By any chance, were you thinking about the light-up sneakers while you were on your way?"

"Uh, not at all. I was thinking how much I missed seeing your beautiful face."

"Hmmm. And, if you were to go home right now, Ron, which direction would you go?"

Chapter 14

Ron faltered, "Uh, let's see, let me get my bearings…all right, that way." He pointed.

Hermione said, "Wrong. Which direction is the holy land?"

Ron asked, "The holy land?"

"Yes, Jerusalem."

"How should I know?"

"Just guess."

Ron pointed.

Hermione considered the direction he was pointing. It was mostly south but also a little to the east. It was a pretty good guess.

She said, "Ron, I think you're the descendent of a holy knight."

Ron said, "Oh yeah? Well, you're the descendent of someone with a big head."

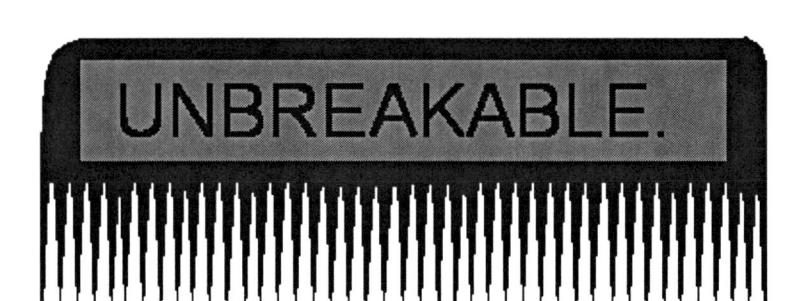

Chapter 15 – Hoaxcrock Destroying Rampage

Hermione knew just how to test Ron's ability to detect evil. She had a hoaxcrock in her bag – the kitchen sink. With Ron blindfolded, she pulled items out of the sack. Sometimes she pulled out Moldyfart's kitchen sink, sometimes she pulled out her toaster oven. He could instantly tell when she pulled out the hoaxcrock. Somehow he sensed its presence and accurately told her when it was in the tent and when it remained in the extra-dimensional space of Santa's sack.

She began training Ron. She would take the bag out into the woods, hide, pull out the kitchen sink, then text Ron to come find her. He never failed to arrive shortly thereafter. Through testing, eventually she discovered he could sense the evil hoaxcrock up to approximately one thousand paces away.

Around that same time, Harry had an idea. He said, "We should look for haystacks in India."

Hermione asked him, "Why India?"

"Because Oldyfart May has two signed posters in his entrance foyer – posters for M. Night Shyamalan movies, signed by the director. Since he's an Indian film-maker, the Fart Lord must have gone to India to get them signed."

Hermione said, "Not a bad thought. However, M. Night Shyamalan is an American film-maker of Indian ethnicity. He's from Philadelphia. So, using your logic, Oldyfart May would have gone to Pennsylvania to get his posters signed. Wouldn't that mean we should search the City of Brotherly Love for a haystack?"

Chapter 15

Harry frowned and said, "I doubt there are any haystacks in a big city like that. But maybe, the Fart Lord went to Hollywood and we should check the Hollywood warehouses and back lots for a haystack."

"Actually, Shyamalan has done most of his filming near his home in Eastern Pennsylvania. I'm not aware of any haystacks in his pictures, but then again, I haven't watched any of them."

"So, can you abberate us to Pennsylvania and we can take a look for haystacks."

"No, but I can abberate us to New York City. I know a spot at the Bronx Zoo – the place where my parents and I ate lunch while we were on holiday there five years ago. We'd have to take a bus or a train from there to Eastern Pennsylvania."

Harry asked, "So, do you think it's worth a try?"

Hermione answered, "Well, honestly, it's not much to go on. But perhaps we could do some further research and find out if there were any haystacks in Shyamalan's movies or find out about some of his film locations."

On the Internet, Hermione found out that Shyamalan's movie, *The Village,* was filmed almost entirely on a village set built in Chadd's Ford, Pennsylvania. She also found out that the production crew destroyed the set afterward, returning the film location to its original state – an empty farm field. She also had a few other rural locations, but none seemed quite so promising.

Shortly after, Hermione abberated them to the Bronx Zoo. From there they made their way into Manhattan and took an Amtrak train to Philadelphia and a bus to Chadd's Ford. They walked to Cossart Road and saw the farm fields with their haystacks.

Ron whispered, "It's here."

Hermione took her wand out and said the magic words, "Hess Premium Gasoline, needle."

A moment later the diabolical needle had painfully transfixed her palm. She cried out, "Ow, that was just mean!"

Two nights later, they broke into the home of Samuel L. Jackson, one of the stars of the M. Night Shyamalan movie, *Unbreakable.* They absconded with a single unbreakable comb from his huge unbreakable comb collection.

They also brought the stainless steel kitchen sink to the London Steel Tube Mills in Upper Edmonton. They watched as two of the workers there tossed it in the blast furnace.

And two weeks later Ellis Island disappeared forever in the middle of the night. It was one of the most baffling mysteries of all time. There were dozens of theories and conspiracy theories. Everything suspicious was blamed, from the Loch Ness Monster to Alien Island Abduction to Elvis Pressley's ghost.

However, what really happened was the three friends had used the pile of gold galleys to purchase a whole crate of antimatter toothpaste from Fred and George's joke shop. It took weeks for the young Cheesley men to produce such a large order.

In the gloom of early morning on the day before they destroyed Ellis Island, Hermione abberated them to the Statue of Liberty. She had visited Liberty Island on a holiday vacation five years ago. From there, Ron confirmed Ellis Island was indeed a hoaxcrock. The Fart Lord had not lied about it.

Next, they took the Liberty Island ferry to Jersey City. There they booked a midnight fishing excursion. They paid Captain Chumley handsomely to ensure there were no other guests aboard the *Three Sheets to the Wind* that night. Hermione memorized a nearby spot on the docks to abberate to later.

Then they were ready to pull off the crime of the millennium. Hermione abberated everyone back to their camp and they rested until it was time to go.

Ron, Harry, and Hermione arrived on the Jersey City dock at eleven o'clock at night with their supplies. They magically convinced Captain Chumley to moor at the Ellis Island Ferry dock. Then they stupidified him, took his clothing and possessions, tied him up, and blindfolded him. That night, they did the same to all the muddle guards on the island, putting them aboard the chartered fishing boat.

Chapter 15

Afterward, they used magically-enlarged anti-antimatter toothbrushes and massive amounts of antimatter toothpaste to literally brush the island off the map. They finished up in the gloom of early morning from the back of the fishing boat with only six tubes of toothpaste left over.

When they were ready to go, Harry and Hermione stupidified Captain Chumley again, untied him and put his bottle of rum in his hand. Hermione magically altered his memory, so that he believed the ghost of Elvis Pressley had visited him that night. Meanwhile, Ron left a note on the vessel's steering wheel. It read:

You should have renamed it Elvis Island like I asked!
Thank you very much,
The King

Then, Hermione abberated everyone back to their camp in the unnamed woods, where it was late morning. They celebrated by making brunch – a full English breakfast of tea, scrambled eggs, sausage, black pudding, bacon, baked beans, hash browns, and tomatoes.

While they were eating, suddenly Harry has a vision of Moldyfart accompanied by extreme pain. It was worse than ever, Harry thought he was going to pass out again. He fell to the floor and curled up in a fetal position. He barely held on to consciousness.

Of course, for several days it was big headline news around the world: Ellis Island Disappears Overnight! Ellis Island Gone! Ellis Island Mysteriously Vanishes!

When Moldyfart heard the news, he went ballistic. His rage was apoplectic. He was holding a meeting with his Fungus Eaters. They were gathered around a large boardroom table. Harry did not know where they were, however, it seemed likely to be at the Ministry of Magic. He recognized many of the faces he saw, including his ex-roommate, Shameonus Finnigan, and Bobby the Elf.

The Fart Lord immediately killed two of his Fungus Eaters, Crabby, Sr. and Foil, Sr. They were the only two that were standing. Harry thought perhaps they had been the bearers of the bad news. Putter felt his pain subside a bit. Killing the two helped to lessen the Fart Lord's rage, however, he was still an angry wizard. He decided to kill Osama Bin Ladin and Yahtzee, too. The pain lessened again.

After that, Moldyfart ranted and raved at the rest of the gathered Fungus Eaters for nearly an hour. During his tirade, his movie buddy, Shameonus, had a smug relaxed air about him even while the Fart Lord shouted. The disrespectful teenager remained leaning far back in his chair, with his hands behind his head and his feet up on the executive boardroom table. By comparison, the others looked very uptight and afraid.

Shameonus, finally asked, "Did you ever think that maybe you shouldn't have made a Master List? Or at least, hidden it somewhere better than under your mattress? That was really dumb of you, mate!"

A moment later, there is nothing left of Shameonus Finnigan but ashes and his smoking sneakers, still on the table.

Vermintail complained, "Master, you just killed one of the few hoaxcrocks left. That's like cutting off your nose to spite your face!"

Harry felt a knife of pain stab into his brain.

Moldyfart was shaking with rage.

Vermintail apologized, "Oh. Uh, sorry, poor choice of words."

Moldyfart obliterated Vermintail. The rest of the Fungus Eaters wisely and fearfully kept silent.

Over the next hour, The Fart Lord's anger slowly subsided as he tried to work out exactly how many hoaxcrocks were left. Harry's pain lessened proportionally and his vision faded.

Each time Moldyfart watched an M. Night Shyamalan movie and made a new hoaxcrock, he experienced a profound emptiness inside him. He felt suddenly vulnerable afterwards and usually held Snakey for an hour or so until he felt better and fell asleep.

However, when a hoaxcrock was destroyed, even though a piece of his soul slipped away forever, the Fart Lord felt nothing at all. The fragments of his soul were already no longer attached to him. And so, he did not know when any of his hoaxcrocks were destroyed. Nor did he know how many were left.

Chapter 15

He thought, "All the ones at home are gone. Those evil teenagers broke into my very mansion. They are ruthless!"

He considered it a personal violation. He was a victim of their foul play.

He continued to think to himself, "Snakey and I are obviously both still good. The Declaration of Independence and *The Moaning Lisa* are also still good. They would be big news. Like Ellis Island, if Putter somehow managed to get a hold of them, I would hear about it."

However, he was thoroughly shaken that the one hoaxcrock he thought was totally indestructible was now gone.

"It was impossible! Even a nuclear bomb couldn't do it. It would kill millions, everyone in New York City, but the land would still be there and so my soul would have survived. It was my best hoaxcrock idea ever. Yet, somehow that nerdy hooligan managed to do the impossible. It's just not fair! The teenage hoodlum must have found some new source of dark magic. It had to be black magic of the worst kind! Magic, I've never even heard of. Perhaps, I have underestimated my enemy."

He suddenly wished Snakey were there to hold, however, the loveable anaconda was at home.

"And if Putter could do that, none of the others hoaxcrocks are safe! Not *The Moaning Lisa* in the Louvre. Not the Declaration of Independence in Washington DC. Not even the Holy Grail, hidden in … What was it? What did Shameonus call it? The Temple of the Sun in the Canyon of the Crescent Moon? Or was it the Temple of the Crescent Moon in the Canyon of the Sun? Oh, whatever! It wasn't safe and none of the others – if there were still others – were safe either.

Worst still, I can't even find the flipping television remote. So I can't make any more. Not that I could really risk it anyway. After that last one, I'd never felt so empty before. One more and I'll wind up inside a hoaxcrock, while my body lies dead and soulless. Besides, with Shameonus gone now, there'd be no one to watch a movie with, and what fun is that? Hmm, maybe I'll put Shameonus's soul inside a cuddly iguana. I could make a pet out of him and call him Iggy. Then we could watch movies together again, just like old times.

But I digress. What was I thinking about? Ah, yes, hoaxcrocks. None of them are safe from Putter. If I don't do something, pretty soon he'll come after me and my beloved pet, Snakey.

The problem is he knows exactly where to find the Declaration of Independence and *The Moaning Lisa*. We've got to get to them first and then hide them. Ah, yes, that's it. We'll hide them somewhere where he'll never find them. But where? Hmmm. Where? Ah, yes, I know! My sock drawer. Just the place."

The Fart Lord began giving orders to his Fungus Eaters.

"Bobby, fetch me The Unbreakable Comb!"

Bobby the elf said, "Why? You don't need a comb. You don't have any hair."

Moldyfart blurted out, "Neither does Samuel L. Jackson! Just do what I say!"

He continued, "Bellatrix and Rodolphius, I want you to steal the Declaration of Independence. Get on it.

Yahtzee and Luscious bring me *The Moaning Lisa* and make it snappy.

Gramps Foil and Grandpappy Shabby, go to the Temple of the Sun in the Canyon of the Crescent Moon and bring back the Holy Grail pronto.

Trollores Underbridge, Narcissistic, be on call and ready, in case I remember anything else.

The rest of you, I am sick of your lame excuses. Find Putter! That's it. Get to work."

With those orders, all the Fungus Eaters knew that their half-sane boss had completely lost his marbles. They stood and began to talk to each other in whispers.

Gramps Foil, however, cried out loudly, "Wait. The Temple of the Sun in the Canyon of the Crescent Moon? Where the hell is that?"

Moldyfart answered, "Oh, uh, maybe I said it backwards? Is it the Temple of the Crescent Moon in the Canyon of the Sun?"

The old man replied, "How the heck should I know?"

The Fart Lord said, "Oh, just figure it out! If a nitwit like Shameonus could do it, an incompetent boob like you can, too."

Chapter 15

Chapter 16 – All's Fair in Louvre and War

Hermione hated the French. She hated everything about them. However, her hatred was complete bias and not founded on reason. She had never actually been to France and she never wanted to go. Unfortunately, that was the location of the next hoaxcrock – *The Moaning Lisa*. And more unfortunately, since she was not familiar with Paris, she could not abberate directly there. The three teenagers purchased one-way plane tickets at the airport for the next flight to the City of Love. (Even that term annoyed Hermione. It implied the conceited French had invented love.)

Ron was afraid to fly because he remembered the light-up sneaker's words. The deep malevolent voice had threatened, "On the next plane ride you take, I'll make the movie be *Maximum Overdrive*! And you'll be so bored that you'll watch the whole thing without sound." Despite Harry and Hermione's efforts to encourage him, he had misgivings. In his heart, he believed it was going to happen and he worried fretfully.

Shortly after boarding the plane, Harry put earphones on and started to listen to music. Hermione was reading a French to English, English to French dictionary.

Chapter 16

Ron asked the flight attendant nervously, "Will there be a movie on this flight?"

With a thick French accent, the woman replied, "Would you like to request something?"

Ron pleaded, "Anything but *Maximum Overdrive*."

"I'll see what I can do."

Cheesley felt a bit relieved.

When the attendant returned, she handed Ron a set of headphones and said, "You will be pleased to know that we have achieved *Maximum Overdrive*. Enjoy your flight."

Ron laughed nervously and was too embarrassed to ask her for a different movie. He wasn't sure it would help anyway. He plugged his headphones in, however, when the movie started, there was no sound.

Ron groaned and kicked himself. He had just made something awful happen while trying to prevent it. He asked Hermione if she had anything he could do instead of watching the movie without sound. She offered him a Three Musketeers candy bar and a juice box.

He groaned again.

After the plane had landed, and they were at the taxi stand, Hermione called out for a taxi and asked in terribly butchered French for a ride to the Louvre. Ron and Harry were less than impressed.

They spent the afternoon scouting the museum and becoming familiar with the layout, especially of the Salle des États, the Room of the States, where *The Moaning Lisa* was displayed. Afterward, they went to a cafe where the waiter ignored them for several hours, during which they discussed their plan. They procured a hotel room and rested until it was time for the big heist. At 1:00 AM they returned to the Louvre. At 1:15 AM Hermione pulled C4 explosives from Santa's bag.

Powerful protection spells were setup nightly, so they could not abberate in or out of the museum. Instead, they blew a hole in the side of the building – a little trick they had learned in Defense Against the Fine Arts.

Hermione casually quoted the principle, "Well, sometimes the best defense is a good offense."

They entered the museum and were surprised nobody was there yet. They expected guards.

Ron asked, "So why haven't the alarms gone off? Are they silent alarms?"

Hermione said, "They probably are on a direct line to the police station. Don't worry, we'll handle it when security and the police show up."

They walked to the front desk with their wands out. However, no one was around.

Hermione said, "Hmm. I guess the guard must be in the bathroom or something."

Just as they were walking by, they heard a deep voice. It called out Ron's name.

The three teenagers stopped.

Ron heard his name again. It was coming from the telephone on the desk. This made him feel quite afraid, for he had just watched a movie earlier that day about machines that came to life.

Hermione nudged Ron toward the desk and said, "Answer the phone, Ron. It's obviously for you."

Ron nervously picked up the receiver and quietly asked, "H-Hello?"

The deep malevolent voice on the phone replied, "You can have *The Moaning Lisa*..... but you can never leave! Muhuhaha."

Ron, forgetting the big hole in the wall, yelped when he heard the click of the nearby doors locking, shutting him in. He started to run for his life, the lights above flickered and a nearby vacuum cleaner turned itself on and began to chase him. Overhead lights began dropping in front of him hurling down with loud crashes and broken glass. They sent him veering in a new direction. Ron started shooting spells at the vacuum cleaner as he ran away from it. Suddenly, he noticed Harry in front of him with a video camera filming him.

He shouted, "Harry look out," and slapped the camera out of his friend's hands.

Hermione turned the vacuum cleaner off and told Ron to calm down. They were just messing with him.

Ron got angry and said, "I knew that."

Chapter 16

Harry was upset that Cheesley broke his camera. He wanted to post the video on his Facebook page.

Ron and Harry followed Hermione toward the Room of the States. As they made their way, an alarm sounded. They heard the loud fast footfall of running guards echoing in the hallway behind them. They quickly ducked into a broom closet until the footsteps passed. Then they snuck out of the closet again.

As they approached the Room of the States, they heard strange noises. They could see someone was lying on the ground. Suddenly, a man in a hooded sweatshirt ran out of the room with a painting under one arm and a magic wand in his other hand.

The painting called out, "Help! Help! I'm being kidnapped!" The kidnapper was running straight toward them with a security guard right behind. The guard quickly dove and grabbed the man's foot, tackling him and sending the painting sliding across the floor. Hermione noticed a tattoo of a mushroom on the thief's forearm.

She shouted, "Fungus Eater!"

Harry and Ron got a glimpse of the painting. It was *The Moaning Lisa*.

The work of art called out, "Are you crazy? You can't treat a masterpiece like this!"

Ron quickly dashed to pick it up. However, the man in the hooded sweatshirt shouted the words, "Hess Premium Gasoline, painting."

Harry thought that voice was familiar but couldn't quite place it.

The painting instantly flew back toward the wizard, knocking Ron over on his butt. There was a distinct crack.

Ron said, "Ow, I think I broke something!"

Another man, wearing a ski mask, arrived. The masked man stunned the security guard with a spell.

Hermione shouted, "Stupidify." Her spell shot forth toward the man holding the painting and he barely managed to roll aside and avoid it. The two men realized they weren't the only wizard there. Their eyes went wide.

Ron got up and said, "Phew. I'm alright, everyone. It was only my wand." He was holding one end of the snapped magic item, the other end dangled from it by a fiber of wood.

All's Fair in Louvre and War

Suddenly, the museum hall erupted in a wizard battle with spells shooting back and forth between Harry, Hermione, and the two thieves. Without his wand to protect himself, Ron began running around like a chicken without his head.

On both sides of the hallway artwork was being damaged in the course of the fight. Muddle guards arrived at the scene and were equally stunned by the destruction as by the bewildering magic.

One of Hermione's spells hit the man with the painting square in the chest and he toppled backwards.

Harry shouted, "Hess Premium Gasoline, painting." *The Moaning Lisa* flew from his grasp, through the air, to Harry.

The masked Fungus Eater and one of the muddle guards ran toward Putter. Harry stunned the guard and tossed the painting to Hermione just as the masked thief tackled him. Ron pulled out Excalibur and rapped the Fungus Eater's forehead with the sword's handle.

The thief cried out in pain, clutching his head.

Hermione ran, she rounded the corner and put the painting into Saint Nick's bag. Then she pulled it back out again as a wrapped present. Just as she did, the man in the hooded sweatshirt stunned her with a Stupidify spell. He pointed his wand at the present in her hand and said, "Hess Premium Gasoline, painting." The gift-wrapped painting flew out of her hands and into his. He looked at the present strangely for a moment, shrugged and laughed, "Thanks for gift wrapping it!"

Then the man made a run for a nearby window dodging spells from Ron and Harry.

He smashed through the window and abberated in mid air. Ron and Harry both thought that was pretty cool.

Harry said, "Ooh, we've got to have that in the movie, only we'll make it from the third floor instead of the ground."

Ron said, "Oh, man. That's going to be awesome." He gave Harry a high five.

Hermione yelled, "Stop wasting time, you idiots!"

They were in the Denon Wing among the Michelangelo sculptures. Suddenly, one of Michelangelo's Slaves grew an additional belly button. Less than a second after, Ron, Harry, and Hermione heard the loud report

Chapter 16

of a gun. One of the armed guards was shooting. They could also hear the whine of approaching police sirens, and gates were dropping, sealing off the Denon Wing. The building was going into lockdown. They needed to move fast.

Hermione pulled out three festively wrapped packages and handed one to Ron and another to Harry. The boys immediately realized from the size and shape that they were hoverboards. They didn't bother to unwrap them. They simply threw the boards to the ground and started pushing.

Several armed guards were shooting at them now. To escape they flew under one of the dropping gates, ducking very low to speed through in the nick of time. They turned left and went down the hallway.

There was a large window at the end of the hall and seeing it, they decided they would have to jump, smash through it, and have Hermione abberate them out in mid air.

Harry said, "Alright, steady, steady, and … GO!"

Ron and Harry both smashed through the window. Hermione was right behind. They each left an ape-shaped hole in the glass. Ron and Harry both fell into a bush below. Hermione landed heavily on top of them. Luckily, they were there to break her fall.

They were still groaning after she abberated them back to their campsite. Later, Ron and Harry agreed it had been a pretty cool getaway until that part at the very end. They both blamed Hermione because she had failed to abberate them in mid air.

Hermione ignored them and pulled out a gift-wrapped package. She ripped it open to reveal *The Moaning Lisa*. The teenagers admired the beautiful hoaxcrock for a minute. Then they built up a campfire and threw the screaming painting into the flames. They roasted marshmallows over it, and everyone agreed they were the most beautiful marshmallows they had ever seen.

Meanwhile, Yahtzee and Luscious were at Moldyfart's castle. Yahtzee pulled back the hood of his sweatshirt. He joyfully laughed and called up the marble staircase, "Yo, Master! C'm 'ere, I've got a present for you!"

Luscious pulled off his black ski mask. He had a lump the size of an egg in the middle of his forehead. He asked, "I've got a present? Don't you mean, we've got a present?"

Yahtzee scoffed, "Pffft. If it weren't for me, those meddling kids would have you cursing, 'Drat, foiled again!' You're lucky I've saved your butt, Maldoy."

Maldoy was about to reply when the Fart Lord arrived at the top of the stairs. Their boss asked, "Did you get it?"

Yahtzee smugly answered, "Not only that, but I had it gift-wrapped for you!"

Moldyfart was thrilled. He floated down the stairs in eager anticipation. He laughed and said, "I love presents!"

Yahtzee stepped forward and said, "My gift to you, Master." He stuck his tongue out at Maldoy.

Maldoy scowled.

The Fart Lord tore the paper from the framed painting, as he prematurely said, "Well done, Luscious. Good job, Yahtzee."

Luscious stuck his tongue out at Yahtzee and answered, "It is a pleasure to be of service…to…"

He knew something was terribly wrong. His master's face was not at all right. The smile vanished. The scowl appeared. The incontrollable angry twitch began in his left eye. His wand was now in his hand. Yahtzee was suddenly gone in an intense burst of flames. Yes, these were all signs of inconceivable displeasure.

Luscious asked, "What?"

Moldyfart sneered and the pain came abruptly and disappeared quickly, as the nerves crying out were mercifully obliterated along with the rest of Luscious Maldoy.

The following day, the Fart Lord hung the painting, *Velvet Elvis*, in his entertainment room.

Chapter 16

Chapter 17 – The Holy Grail of Hoaxcrocks

Ron said, "What do you mean there aren't any more of my wands left? I thought it was Santa's sack? I thought we could pull whatever we wanted out of it?"

Hermione said, "Sorry, Ron. It doesn't work that way, the only thing in the sack are the things I packed. I brought a box of five spare wands. I thought that would be enough."

Ron said, "That's usually good for about three or four months, but we've been camping out for let's see … uh, …" He started to count months on his fingers.

Hermione said, "I see your point, Ron. And you've done very well too. You've only broken six wands in the past six months. Would you like me to send a text to your Mum and ask her to send some more right away?"

Ron sighed, "Don't be silly, Mum would be worried if you wrote her. She'd wonder if something happened to me so that I couldn't write. I'll take care of it."

"You should probably do it right away, so you don't forget."

"Good idea," Ron agreed. He took out his phone and sent the text message:

Mum, please send more wands - Love, Ron

Chapter 17

Meanwhile, Harry was glad they were making progress on their quest. However, he felt like his contributions of late were still lacking. Hermione had been nothing short of amazing. Ron was doing his part with the evil hoaxcrock detecting. Harry wanted to contribute. After all, it was his quest to destroy Lord Moldyfart.

Hermione had told him to research the Holy Grail, so, he had given up playing video games and was doing what she asked. However, it did seem a bit unfair of her. That one seemed like it would be the hardest of all to find and obtain.

There were so many legends regarding the sacred vessel. However, Harry chose to give precedence to the work *Le Morte d'Arthur* by Sir Thomas Malory, after all, that one was mentioned in Grumblesnore's last will, in reference to the description of Excalibur.

And so, Harry read a book – no, not a comic book – a real book. It had been a very long time.

Le Morte d'Arthur told of a "Dolorous Stroke" by rash Sir Balin upon the Fisher King, Pellas, guardian of the Holy Grail. Calamity befalls Sir Balin and three kingdoms from that attack. Years after, the Knights of the Round Table took up the quest to find Castle Carbonek, heal King Pellas, and obtain the Holy Grail. However, the Grail "appeareth not to sinners." Gwain, Bors, Lancelot, Robin, Bedevere, and Percival fail in the quest due to their worldly sins. Galahad, who is pure, succeeds. He heals King Pellas and obtains the Holy Grail.

Harry wondered, "So the grail is a good object that cannot be seen or touched by … well, any of us. If none but the pure can obtain it, how on earth could Moldyfart have gotten his clutches on the Holy Grail and turned it into a hoaxcrock? And where would the sacred vessel be in modern times? Or had the Fart Lord used his flux capacitor to travel back in time to get it?

He reasoned to himself, "It's impossible. If the many good Knights of the Round Table were unable to attain the grail, there is no way that evil Kitten Killer or any of his wicked Death Eaters would be capable of it.

Furthermore, could an object so holy be turned into a hoaxcrock? An object of evil? Would God allow it? It was laughable.

So if Moldyfart thinks he turned a 'Holy Grail' into a hoaxcrock, then it must not be the real Holy Grail. It must be something that he mistakenly thinks is the sacred chalice. Perhaps, he ordered one of his Fungus Eaters to find it and they provided him with a fake."

And so, Harry came to believe the theory that Moldyfart only thinks he turned the Holy Grail into a hoaxcrock.

However, the idea didn't help much. Trying to find a fake Holy Grail was possibly even worse than trying to locate the real one. To find the real one, Harry could try and locate Castle Carbonek and search it for clues. However, a fake could be just about anything shaped like a cup and it could be anywhere in the world. Harry wondered, "Where do I even start?"

He started by making sure there was no relationship between the Holy Grail and any of Shyamalan's movies. He spent two hours on the Internet and came to a conclusion. As he thought, there was no connection.

Next, he remembered one of their dinner guests from months ago, Sir Robin. He was one of the Knights of the Round Table. He was one of the knights who had taken up the quest for the grail. He was on the run from the Fart Lord among an eclectic group of celebrities. With him was a fellow Gryffindor student, Spleen Thomas.

Harry texted Spleen Thomas, "How R U? R U still with Sir Robin?"

He received a text back, "No worries, mate. We hangin poolside, Rembrandt Hotel. ☺"

He replied, "Is Sir Robin w/U?"

"Yes."

"I'd like 2 speak 2 him. Can U 2 meet me in an hour?"

"Where?"

"The Rembrandt. The one in Knightsbridge?"

"Yeah, Rm 309."

The three teenagers went together. Hermione abberated them to a tube station in South Kensington, and they walked from there. An hour later Harry was knocking on the door of room 309. Spleen Thomas let them all into his luxurious hotel guest room.

Spleen said, "What up, Dudes?"

Sir Robin, who was lying on one of the beds, laughed and stiffly repeated, "What up, Dudes? I love it. What up, Dudes?"

Chapter 17

Sir Robin was small, thin, and pasty white. His eye sockets were sunken in, while his eyes were bulging out. He had a droopy mustache and orange hair. He was wearing his bathing suit and sandals. His sunglasses were high on his forehead.

Harry said, "Good Sir Robin, I'm so glad you're here. I really need to talk to you about the Quest for the Holy Grail."

Sir Robin replied, "Cheers, mate. Fancy a little rabbit about the rabbit then? Take a load off your plates, laddie."

Ron and Hermione took the two nearby chairs. Harry sat down on the bed opposite the knight. He began, "Sir Robin, would you please be so kind as to tell us about the Holy Grail?"

"No frets, mate." Brave Sir Robin asked, "What do you want to know about it?"

"Have you seen it?"

"Well… no."

Harry asked with surprise evident in his voice, "No?"

The knight who was not as brave as Sir Lancelot replied, "Crikey, don't get your knickers all in a twist. I fell in the Gorge of Eternal Peril. Sir Galahad's the Todd who found it."

"But I thought it appeared to you in a vision?"

"Sort of."

"Sort of?"

"Well, it could have, but when the skies opened up and God revealed the Holy Grail to us, I, umm, humbly averted my minces."

"Averted your eyes?"

"Aye, I was, ahem, making certain that no one was hiding in the shrubbery nearby, waiting to ambush us."

"So you never saw either the grail or a vision of the grail?"

"No. That was Galahad and the others."

"Drat. I was hoping you'd be able to describe it to me."

"Sorry, mate. But maybe I can put you in touch with some of the others who saw it."

"What about Sir Galahad?"

"Oh, no. I didn't mean him."

"No, I meant where did Sir Galahad put it?"

Sir Robin said, "What do you mean? Heaven?"

The Holy Grail of Hoaxcrocks

Harry said, "Then it's not in Castle Carbonek?"

"He didn't put it anywhere. Sir Galahad was the knightly embodiment of perfection. Galahad was always known as "Sir Perfect." He was "Sir Perfect" in courage, gentleness, courtesy, and chivalry. He used to monitor the hallways in knight school. Anyway, after he obtained the grail and completed his quest, his purpose here on earth was fulfilled. And so, he shed this mortal coil. He was raised bodily unto the heavens by a multitude of angels. Enough to make you sick, isn't it? You know, I could of done it! I was about to. He just happened to get there first."

"Then the Grail could still be in Castle Carbonek?"

"What do you mean?"

"If Sir Galahad saw the grail but didn't take it, then it must still be there, right?"

"You really don't get it. It's got nothing to do with a trophy cup, a wine cup, a sacred vessel, or a golden chalice. That part's all symbolic. The grail is the quest for perfection. And since, that's already been done, there's no sense in trying to do it again. What'd be the point? God doesn't give out trophy cups for second place."

"So, you don't think that the grail exists physically?"

"Now, you've got it, laddie."

Harry sighed.

"I'm in bits," Spleen Thomas asked, "What's all this grail stuff all about anyway?"

Harry answered, "Spleen, we have a list of the Fart Lord's hoaxcrocks and the Holy Grail is on the list."

Spleen laughed, "Where'd you get a list from?"

"From under his mattress."

Spleen and Sir Robin both laughed at this. Afterward, Spleen said, "Well, I think it's quite an obvious lie. There's no way an evil blighter like him got a hold of the Holy Grail. If God wouldn't allow a great guy like Sir Robin to see it, He wouldn't let a wanker like Pull-Me-Finger have a go at it. Ol' Farthead's pullin' your chain, mate."

"Well, I actually thought about that. However, I've good reason to believe he's not."

"How's that?"

Chapter 17

"Everything else on the list is valid, including some items I thought might be hoax hoaxcrocks. However, what also occurred to me was that perhaps one of the Fungus Eaters gave Moldy…err, Oldyfart May, a fake Holy Grail."

Spleen Thomas gasped. He said, "Wait a minute!"

Everyone stared at him waiting.

Spleen was working something out in his head. Several times he gasped, "Oh!"

Finally, he said, "It was Shameonus Finnigan! I had forgotten all about it. One evening he was going off to see his chum and before he left, he took Harry's Dribble Goblet of Fire. He said he was going to prank his movie buddy with it. Harry wasn't around to ask, so he borrowed it. When he got back, he tucked it back in Harry's trunk. I didn't think anything of it at the time, as I'm sure Harry wouldn't have minded.

However, now that everyone knows Shameonus Finnigan is a Fungus Eater and his movie buddy is Mr. Buttpuffer, well? What d'you think? He probably brought the goblet all lit up in flames and told his pal it was the Holy Grail. That stupid wanker would of fallen for it for sure. Then for fun, the scallywag planted the hoaxcrock back where he got it – right under Harry's nose."

Harry said, "Heck, we can check that right now! Hermione?"

His friend pulled a present out of Santa's sack and handed it to Harry.

Before Harry had even unwrapped it, Ron exclaimed, "Oh my God! It is a hoaxcrock!"

Harry gritted his teeth and seethed, "Shameonus Finnigan must die! I'm gonna kill that son of a …"

Hermione interrupted, "Harry, remember? He's already dead."

Harry answered, "Darn it! I forgot."

Spleen Thomas said, "Dudes, have you heard the latest? There a panic going on at Hogwashes. There's a fiendish devil cat roaming the dungeons. It's even killed two students – Shabby and Foil. And after it rends them to death with its sharp claws, it leaves a hairball behind on each of its victims. Kinda like the Joker in Batman leaving his calling card at the scene of the crime."

Hermione exclaimed, "Oh, no!"

Ron commiserated, "How terrible."

The Holy Grail of Hoaxcrocks

Harry was simply stunned. He thought, "The Death Cat is real?"

Meanwhile, a man was prowling the dungeon level corridors of Hogwashes.

Since the deaths of Shabby and Foil, the students feared and dreaded the dark and dismal lower levels of the school. News circulated of a feral animal roaming the dungeons. Rumors about that creature ran rife. Some scoffed that it was only an ordinary cat, which had merely passed through the scene of the boys' murders after the fact, leaving its paw prints behind. However, others whispered of a fierce creature with glowing eyes that could pierce the complete darkness of the unlit corridors. Tales of a devil cat, a feline demon, a vampires bat, and of werewolves and other shape-shifters abound. False sightings were imagined, leading to screams of terror, fleeing students, class disruptions, and general chaos.

The headmaster, Carnivorous Ape, had instructed the students to avoid the area, when possible. However, the PRK student's facilities, including dorm rooms and their common room, were in the dungeon. There was no way to relocate them, so the PRKs had no choice but to risk their lives in their daily routines. They grouped together and never wandered. They moved rapidly in twos and threes. And their eyes were always nervously searching the poorly-lit corridors as they came and went.

However, one man braved the unlit lowest levels of Hogwashes daily. He carried a lantern to light his way. As he roamed the dungeon corridors, he did so calmly and without the trepidation of the students.

He knew the murders weren't so mysterious. The wizard coroner had confirmed what the teachers already knew. With no sign of visible trauma, no symptoms of poisoning, and no obvious other biological reason for death, it was the Death Curse. Clearly, In-a-Godda-Da-Vida was the cause. Someone in the school was a cold-blooded killer.

However, to ease the student's nerves and to end the panic and the rumors, the Headmaster had given him the task of capturing the cat. The man assigned this task was Cubious Hasbeen, the keeper of the Hogwashes Magical Creatures Petting Zoo and the teacher of Magical Beast Biology.

Hasbeen did not search the dungeons unprepared. He knew exactly what he was looking for. He could recognize the footprints of the

Chapter 17

creature. It was a cat. And it wasn't some devil cat or a feline demon. He knew there was no such thing. It may be a wild feral cat or a domestic one, but it was cat of the ordinary variety – Felis Catus.

Hasbeen joked, "Unless it has learned how to speak and cast spells!"

The big man had seen many typical signs of its presence. Such as, scratch marks toward the bottom of the wooden dungeon doors, where it had sharpened its claws, and the remains of mice and rats. The poor creature even had digestive problems and had left several hairballs behind.

Unfortunately, it had coincidentally left them at the two murder sites. In the case of Belch, the hairball was pinched between his fingers, indicating that the man had picked up the hairball just before he was attacked. In the case of the boys, they were on forehead and neck. It was clear the cat was there at their murders, because one of the hairballs had been soaked by splashed dye. That couldn't have happened afterward.

Two weeks ago, Hasbeen had set two traps – box-shaped cages with sides that dropped into place once their trigger was tripped. He baited one with dry cat food and the other with catnip. Yet the infernal feline had not been caught. He sighed when he saw the second cage was still empty.

However, he noticed something in the dark corridor ahead. Reflecting the light of the lantern was a pair of eyes – cat's eyes. He raised the lantern and peered into the darkness. He thought he saw the outline of the cat lighter than the dark stone floor.

He made kissing noises and said, "Here kitty, kitty." However, the cat turned away. He lumbered after it and caught a glimpse of it turn the corner ahead. He followed.

Though he was by no means even close to the agility of a cat and knew he'd never catch it by chasing it, he hoped that he might get the feline to come to him by being friendly to it.

However, when he turned the corner, he saw the cat was cornered, backed up against a heavy wooden door.

He laughed to himself, "Unless you've learned how to open doors."

The following morning, Cubious Hasbeen was not at class. He was not in his cabin by the edge of the Forbidden Forest of Sure Death. Later that afternoon, his body was found in the deepest level of Hogwashes. There was a hairball at the bridge of his nose, right between his unblinking eyes.

Chapter 18 – Irrational Treasure

The next morning, while eating breakfast, Harry pulled out the list of hoaxcrocks and crossed off the Holy Grail.

Chapter 18

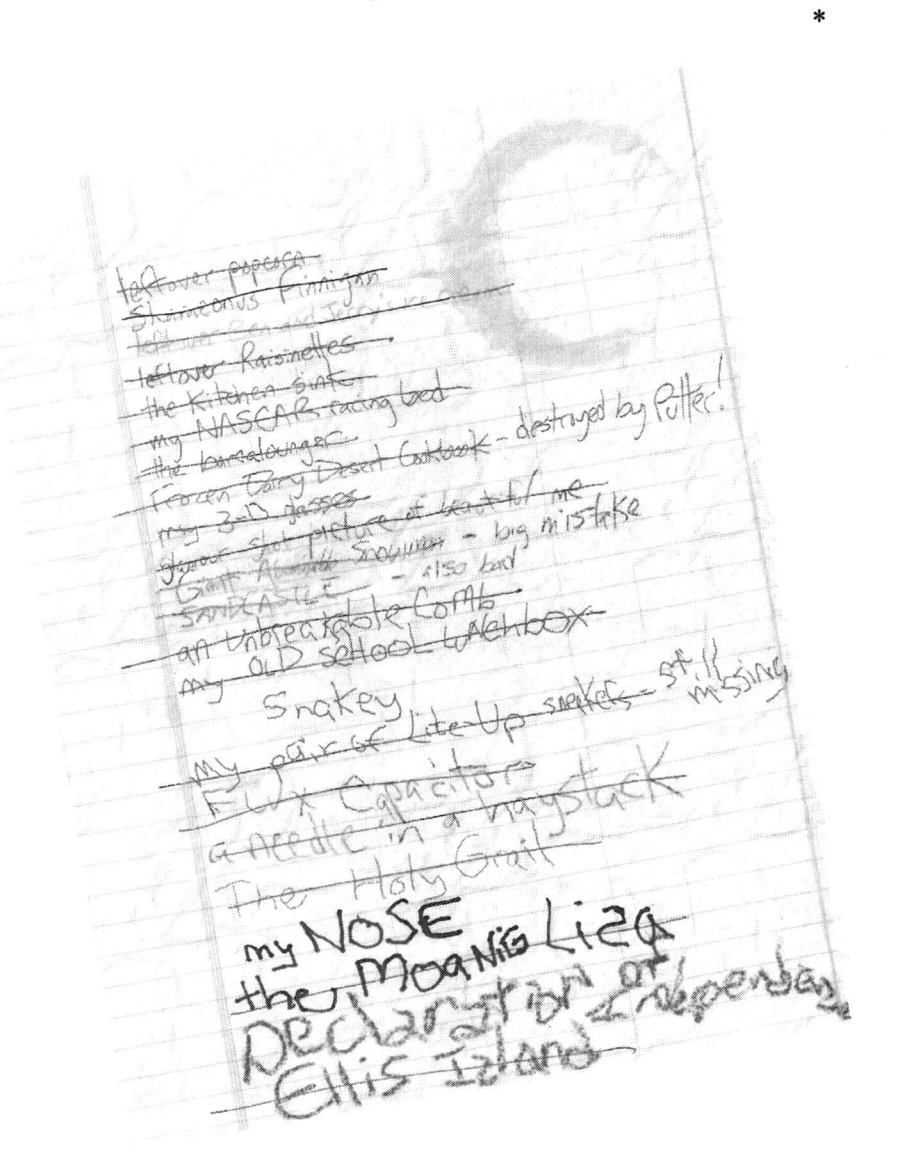

Handwritten list on lined paper (items crossed out except as noted):

- ~~leftover popcorn~~
- ~~Shannon's Finnigan~~
- ~~leftover Raisinettes~~
- ~~the kitchen sink~~
- ~~my NASCAR racing bed~~
- ~~the Lazy Lounger~~
- ~~Frozen Berry Desert Cookbook~~ — destroyed by Potter!
- ~~my 3-D glasses~~
- ~~a picture of beautiful me~~ — big mistake
- ~~Grant Abominable Snowman~~ — also bad
- ~~Sandcastle~~
- ~~an unbreakable comb~~
- ~~OLD SCHOOL LUNCHBOX~~
- ~~my Snakey Lite-Up Sneakers~~ — still missing
- ~~my pair of~~
- ~~Flux Capacitor~~
- ~~a needle in a haystack~~
- ~~The Holy Grail~~
- ~~my NOSE~~
- ~~the Moaning Lisa~~
- Declaration of Independence
- ~~Ellis Island~~

Ron asked, "So what do we need to destroy next?"

"The Declaration of Independence," Hermione replied. "And it's probably going to be the hardest one yet. The historic document is going to be heavily guarded."

"Well, *The Moaning Lisa* was guarded too, and that wasn't hard to get," argued Ron.

Irrational Treasure

Hermione explained, "Yes, but they were French guards, these will be Americans and they will be much harder to evade. But more importantly, I meant that it's guarded by stronger security systems."

Ron suggested, "What we should do is break in just like they did in that movie, what was it called? *National Treasure?*"

Hermione slapped her forehead and said, "Why didn't I think of that."

Ron said, "That's an awesome movie. Did you happen to pack it?"

Hermione sighed and said for the millionth time, "Of course, I packed it."

The three teenagers carefully watched the movie and took notes. As they watched, they realized they were going to need help. The Declaration of Independence was well-protected by a laser security detection system, surveillance cameras, and motion detectors, as well as by armed guards. And that was just to get to the area outside the door to the Preservation Room in the National Archive in Washington, DC. If these were the only measures, help would not be necessary.

However, to get into the Preservation Room, they needed to have the password to the electronic cipher lock. Hermione was good with computers, a computer nerd of sorts. She had packed the right equipment including a sophisticated password-cracking software tool. Yet, none of them would be able to extrapolate for the duplication of key strokes, the way Cage did in the movie. They were going to need a genius at guessing the right password.

Nicholas Cage was famous world-wide as an Academy Award winning actor. More so, he was well-known within the wizard community as a sorcerer. In fact, he is best known as a master at altering memories. He uses this ability mostly on casting directors, in order to make them forget about his performances in two bombs in particular – *Bangkok Dangerous* and *The Wicker Man*.

The teenagers decided to pay a call on Butthilda Bigshot, hoping that her husband, Benny Bigshot, could use his Hollywood connections to put them in touch with the famous actor. They told Butthilda about all their progress in destroying the hoaxcrocks. She was delighted to hear how well it was going. She introduced them to her husband and made sure that Benny gave them the contact information they needed.

Eleven minutes later, they were in Nicholas Cage's living room waiting

Chapter 18

for the actor to come home.

At 6:30 PM Cage arrived. He was holding a box the size of a shoe box and a DVD.

He said, "Oh, hey, guys. I was expecting you."

The three teenagers all said, "Hey."

Hermione asked, "You were expecting us?"

Cage replied, "Well, of course, I was expecting you. Do you really think I would eat a dozen donuts by myself while watching the movie, *Finding Nemo*?"

Cage actually had not been expecting anyone in his living room when he got home. He had been planning on spending Friday night in his usual manner – eating twelve Boston Crème donuts while watching a Pixar movie. However, the actor also liked to play it cool, particularly when something unexpected did occur. And he did not anticipate that he might have to share his donuts.

When the movie was over, Cage had eaten nine of the twelve donuts. He said, "Great story, wonderful character development, however, the voice acting of Albert Brooks in his portrayal of Marlin, the father, was a little weak. They probably should have brought in a professional."

The three teenagers thoroughly agreed.

Nick said, "Anyway, so, what do you cats want to do next? We could go get some hot dogs? Or I know this roller skating rink where Wednesday night is Michael Jackson night. I know it's not Wednesday, but it'd probably still be pretty good. What do you say?"

Hermione said, "Actually, we're here to ask you for your help."

Cage replied, "I knew that."

Of course, Cage really did not know that.

He continued, "So what's your project and how may I be of assistance?"

She answered, "Well, you see, we're on a hoaxcrock destroying mission. And…"

The actor joked, "Is that anything like a mission from God? *Blues Brothers*, 1980."

"No, well, maybe… I don't know. Basically, we're trying to kill this horribly evil, half-insane wizard."

Irrational Treasure

Cage asked, "And his name is Hoaxcrock?"

Hermione answered, "Err, no. A hoaxcrock is a physical repository that this wizard has put a part of his evil soul into."

Cage shook his head, "Sorry, I can't help you. Your movie is too much like *Child's Play*, 1988."

Hermione bit her lip and said, "Sorry, I don't get the reference."

Cage said, "Sure, you do. Remember, Chucky, the doll from hell? This horribly evil, half-insane wizard is dying, so he uses a Voodoo ritual to put his soul into the Chucky doll."

Hermione said, "Oh, uh, yes. Like that, only our evil wizard splits his soul into a whole mess of objects, but no dolls."

Cage answered, "It's still not unique enough. What else have you cats got? Got anything with kicking superheroes that we can turn into a 3-D CGI animation spectacular? Preferably with a male lead character, but not necessarily. If need be, I can do women's roles too."

Hermione said, "But we're not pitching a mov…"

Harry clamped his hand over Hermione's mouth. He nervously said, "Mr. Cage probably wouldn't understand your crazy sense of humor, Hermione. Of course, we're pitching a movie, and we have Benny Bigshot as our producer!"

Cage said, "I knew that. Why else would you be here?"

Harry said, "No other reason. We're here to pitch our big movie. Did I mention it's a Benny Bigshot Production?"

The actor replied, "Yes, you did. What's the working title?"

Harry said, *"The Quest to Destroy Lord M…"*

Hermione clamped her hand over Harry's mouth. She said, *The Quest to Destroy the Fart Lord.*

Cage said, "The Fart Lord? Hey! You're Harry Put… wait, I knew that. But that means, you don't have the script finished yet. Moldyfart's not dead. He's taken over the Ministry."

Harry said, "Hey, don't worry about the script! We'll take care of that. We have a team of writers working on the ending. They can't wait for the Final Battle to find out how it all turns out. In the meanwhile, we need your help to destroy one of the hoaxcrocks – The Declaration of Independence."

Nicholas said, "But, that's already been done before! C'mon, you cats

Chapter 18

have to have seen *National Treasure*. I played Benjamin Gates, the lead role in that one."

Ron piped in, "Of course, that's why I thought of you in the first place."

Cage asked, "Hey, where'd you come from?"

Ron didn't understand. He asked, "Who me?"

The actor said, "Yeah, you."

Ron answered, "I've been here the whole time. I even ate a donut."

Cage said, "I knew that. I was just messing with you. You have a very forgettable face, and I'm not just saying that to be mean. I know, I'm an actor."

Harry said, "So, what do you say? Will you help us? Please?"

Cage replied, "I've got one condition. I get to play the lead role in the movie."

Harry answered, "Oh, no. Not the lead. I think that's much better suited to Brad Pitt or Matt Damon. How about we cast you as the main villain?"

The actor scoffed, "Good one! Ha ha! But seriously, I have more draw than those two cats combined! I even make more movies than those two put together. Plus I won the Academy Awards for best actor. There's no way, I take back seat to either one of them. And the villain? What level of talent does that take? That's a role for a guy without skills."

Hermione tittered nervously, "Good one, Harry. You do realize that if Mr. Cage doesn't help us, no one's going to make a movie about you?"

Cage said, "Don't look so disappointed, kid. If you really wanted Matt Damon, you can always cast him in the gritty reboot. Besides, it will give him a chance to work on his skills in the meantime."

Harry had no choice but to concede.

Fortunately, the National Archives was hosting a gala event later that week. They decided it would be the perfect time to stage their heist. Hermione would be the computer expert operating in the back of the van waiting outside. She would hack into the security system. Harry and Cage would crash the party, infiltrate the access-restricted areas of the building, perform the robbery, and escape with the document. Ron would be the getaway driver.

Irrational Treasure

Cheesley was not happy about it. He wanted to go in with Harry and Cage and make a real contribution to the team. However, he didn't have any magic wands left. He had even texted his mother a second time requesting them. In reply, she told him there weren't any left at the Boil either, and that she would pick up a box of them when she got a chance.

All week long, Ron kept watching for the family goat, Pigwedgie, to arrive with the package. He grew grumpier as the day of the heist drew closer.

Furthermore, Cage was annoying. He kept calling Ron names, like butterfingers, klutz, and spastic dope.

Ron argued, "I'm clutch. When it's important, I always come through. In fact, the more dire the situation, the more likely I am to pull off the incredible catch, or save, or whatever else is needed."

Hermione stuck up for him, "It's true. Sometimes I'm in awe at some of the things Ron does. Err, in an incredible sort of way."

Cage said, "But, you don't have a wand. What we truly need is an incredible getaway driver. That's a crucial job. There's likely to be all kinds of heat on us by the time we get back to the van. Seconds can be the difference between success and failure Think you can handle the job?"

Ron sulked, without his wand, he had no choice. He dejectedly said, "Yeah."

Hermione conducted the preliminary work of installing a rogue wireless router in the National Archives computer network. She collected communications until she captured a logon sequence. Then she offloaded the information and ran her password cracking software against it. She used special hardware for this step – four video accelerators to quickly handle the extensive mathematical computations involved. Two days later, she had the logon credentials she would need in order to access the security surveillance system when she arrived.

In the meanwhile, Nicholas Cage was working on some surefire disguises so that they could get past the guards and into the National Archives building.

Harry, however, was distracted with thoughts of the upcoming Final Battle. He was worried about the Fart Lord's army. While Harry was

Chapter 18

busy destroying hoaxcrocks, Moldyfart was out recruiting. Where was Harry going to find help against the Fart Lord's minions?

He also wondered about what Spleen Thomas had told them. 'The Death Cat' was real. And that meant the drunken tale of Beadie the Blowhard, "The Three Bad Kittens," was a true story. And that meant the light-up sneakers were once Death's sneakers. And it also meant, somewhere out there, there's a magic hat – one that can be used to fake your own death. And Harry thought he knew where it might be.

Everything was set. When Ron pulled the rented van up to the front of the National Archives building, Hermione went into action. Earlier in the week, she had craftily left the wireless router in monitor mode. Now she sent the router a knock sequence to activate it, and then used it for wireless access to the system from her laptop while she sat in the back of the vehicle.

Once Harry and Cage took the elevator down to the basement level, cell phone communication would not be possible. And so, they came prepared with shortwave radio equipment. Before Harry and Cage went in, they tested it to make sure it was working properly. Hermione would be able to inform them of the guards' movements as she saw them over the video surveillance system.

Cage and Harry were both in disguise, which was necessary to get past the guards and into the building, but also so no one would recognize the famous actor. And so, Harry and Cage left the rented van and went inside. Their stern librarian disguises were Hollywood caliber. The guards barely noticed them and hardly glanced at their fake IDs. They were such plain-looking women, no one took a second look at them as they navigated through the crowd attending the party.

They made their way to the service elevator. Cage inserted the key and turned the lock in the elevator so they could use it to access the basement, the restricted area where the Preservation Room was located.

Harry asked, "Where'd you get the key?"

Cage said, "It's the copy from when we were filming *National Treasure*."

"And they didn't change the lock?"

"Why would they? Anyone would have to be insane to try and actually steal the Declaration of Independence!"

As the elevator brought them to their destination, Cage checked in with their computer expert. He said, "Hermione, we're in the elevator heading down. What's the guard status looking like?"

Hermione answered, "You're clear, and I already have a feed looping on security monitors displaying the basement. They won't be able to see you on the surveillance system. Currently the coast is clear. I'll let you know if anything comes up."

Cage said, "Roger that." He turned to Harry and said, "So far, so good."

In the meanwhile, Pigwedgie arrived outside the National Archives with a package for Ron. The old goat put its front hooves up against the service van's driver side door and nearly scared Ron to death. Ron exclaimed, "Pigwedgie! Oh, wow, this is so great!" He got out of the van and led the family goat around to the side door of the rented vehicle. He opened it and let the family mail-carrier inside the back area.

Hermione exclaimed, "Ron! What are you doing? Keep the door shut! You want someone to become suspicious?"

Ron said, "Fine!" He slid the door closed, walked around to the driver's side, and climbed back in.

Hermione was peeved. She angrily asked, "What the hell is your goat doing here while we're running a delicate mission?"

Ron answered, "He was delivering a package. My wands are finally here. Isn't that great? I can go in and catch up with Harry and Nick. They might need my help."

He was hastily opening his package.

Hermione said, "Um, Ron. You're not dressed for it."

Ron realized it was true and said, "Darn it." He sighed, slumped down in the driver's seat to sulk, and set the package down in the seat beside him.

From his slumped position, when he looked out the window again, he saw in the side mirror a black SUV had pulled up behind him. He noticed the vehicle had a vanity plate –

ƎℲIꞀ ⅁UHT

Chapter 18

He took a while working it out, "Life Guth? Guth Life? TH-U-G Life. THU-G Life. THUG LIFE. Holy Crap! That's the Fart Lord behind us. Hermione! The Fart Lord's behind us! That's his black SUV, the license plate says, 'THUG LIFE!'"

Hermione asked, "Are you sure?"

Ron answered, "Yeah, I'm positive. Remember the night we brought Harry to the Boil? He said he was attacked by Oldyfart May in a black SUV with spinning rims and a license plate that read, 'THUG LIFE.'"

"Let me see." She took off her headset, placed it on the laptop and had to nearly climb into the passenger seat to see into the side mirror at an angle that she could read the license plate. After she verified the plate, she said, "I've got to warn Harry."

Hermione returned to the back of the van. She yelled, "No, Pigwedgie! No!"

The old goat was busily chewing on her headset. She tried to take it from the animal, but the stubborn creature wouldn't let go. He gave her a shove with his head and short horns, which knocked her over. She accidentally pushed the laptop off the back bench and onto the floor of the van with a crash.

"Ron, do something about this stupid goat!"

Ron chastised Pigwedgie, "Stop it, Wedgie! Give me that! Bad goat! Bad!" He retrieved the headset from the animal, however, it was in an obvious state of disrepair. Loose wires were hanging out of the goat's mouth.

Hermione said, "Oh, great! Now how are we going to warn Harry and Nick?"

She tried the cell phone, but got no answer. She left a message, though she never-the-less knew it was unlikely that Harry would get it in time to matter.

She asked, "Ron, what are we going to do?"

Harry and Cage were in the Preservation Room with the Declaration of Independence. They were busy trying to unlock the bulletproof case that held the historic document, when they heard someone keying in the password. The cipher lock beeped with each button depressed. They quickly hid. Nick dropped under a desk. Harry crawled under a large work table.

Suddenly, Harry saw the legs of a goat standing next to the table. He heard the animal bleat. He peeked out from under the table and said aloud, "Funny, that old goat looks familiar. Almost like, Pigwedgie."

He looked around but didn't see anyone else, and so he crawled back out from under the table. He took the folded note out of the animal's mouth. The outside of the paper read, "Harry."

He opened the note and read it:

Hurry up, the Fart Lord just arrived, Ron and Hermione

Harry said aloud, "What the heck? Why would they send a goat?"

Nick came out of his hiding spot. Harry showed him the note and said, "Look what they sent."

The actor asked, "The goat delivered this? How'd it manage to do that?"

Harry said, "I don't know! How'd he get by the invisible laser grid without setting off the alarms?"

"Well, we don't know for sure that he didn't. It may be a silent alarm. What I meant was, how did it manage to guess the 'Valley Forge' password, key it in on the touchpad, and open the cipher-locked door? Personally, I feel like this goat is trying to belittle my skills and accomplishments."

Harry consoled, "Don't worry, Nick, a goat could never replace you."

The actor said, "Thanks. As for why they sent the goat in the first place, well, perhaps our prior radio signals were compromised. Based on this communication, we'll have to assume radio silence. Hopefully not, and I hate to say it, but our friends may have been captured. We won't know until…"

Just then, they heard a huge explosion that shook the floor and set off the alarms. A brash bell began to loudly and incessantly clang.

Harry said, "Uh oh, we'd better get out of here quick."

Cage hefted the bulky bulletproof case that held the Declaration of Independence. He called out, "Grab the door!"

Chapter 18

With the alarm already blaring, they ran through the invisible laser field. Halfway through, they heard an angry voice shout, "In-a-Godda-Da-Vida, Honey!"

Cage turned and blocked the spell with the display case. It reflected off the bulletproof glass and a Fungus Eater ducked to avoid the returning bolt of energy.

Cage yelled, "Grab the elevator!"

Harry ran ahead of the actor and pushed the button to call the elevator. Pigwedgie followed. Cage worked his way backwards, using the historic document's protective spell-proof container as a shield to block numerous death curses.

As they waited impatiently for the elevator to arrive, Harry took cover behind Cage's bulky shield. He began firing spells back at Moldyfart and his Fungus Eaters.

When the elevator doors opened, they quickly got on. Harry tapped furiously at the 'close door' button. In the meanwhile, they continued to defend themselves until the door finally and thankfully slid closed.

As they traveled upward, Cage worked open the clasp on the Declaration's display case. He removed the historic document.

Harry said, "Quick, we gotta destroy it!"

Cage said, "How? We can't light it on fire in the elevator, we'll get stuck between floors."

Pigwedgie knew how to destroy it. He began to eat the Declaration of Independence.

Harry and Cage were shocked for a moment. Then they began to call their encouragement, "Chew, Pigwedgie! Chew!"

Cage said, "Faster, Goat. Eat faster."

However, the animal couldn't eat the whole document before the elevator arrived at the first floor. The goat was only a third of the way finished when the doors opened.

Several of the party guests looked over and saw the open elevator door. Inside, the empty bulletproof display case leaned against the back wall. In front of it, a goat was chewing up the celebrated written foundation of the United States of America, the most important document in the National Archive, the reason for the evening's gala event. Their jaws dropped.

Cage stepped out of the elevator. Harry tapped a button for the top floor as he exited. Everyone watched Pigwedgie continue to eat the cherished symbol of liberty until the doors closed. Harry knew he could count on Pigwedgie to finish destroying the evil document.

They quickly pushed through the crowded party. Cage had his wand out. He kept saying the magic words, "Don't forget to brush with Colgate Toothpaste." The actor was a master with that spell. The guests closest to them made their way to the bathrooms to brush their teeth, before they realized they didn't have their toothbrushes with them. They each felt a bit foolish, however, the two librarians and the goat were completely erased from their minds. The same spell sent the guards at the front door scurrying towards the men's room.

The two librarians hurried from the National Archive building to the waiting white van. As they ran, Fungus Eaters jumped out of Moldyfart's black SUV. They began casting unforgettable curses. Harry and Nick countered their attacks with their own spells. Meanwhile, Hermione slid the van's side door wide open and got out of the way. The disguised men leapt into the back of the vehicle.

The van surged forward as Ron took off, before they had even closed the door behind them. In the side mirror, Ron watched the black SUV. A moment later, Moldyfart's vehicle sped after them. Ron turned the corner sharply.

Hermione said, "Thank God, you're alright! I was so worried. Were you able to get it?"

Harry teased, "Nick had it in his hands for one second, but then it was snatched right from his grasp."

"No!" exclaimed Hermione, "So the Fungus Eater's have it?"

Harry answered, "Nope."

Hermione asked, "Who then? Not the guards?"

Harry said, "At this moment, the Declaration of Independence is in the stomach of an old goat!"

Ron exclaimed, "Oh my God, not Pigwedgie?"

"Sorry," said Harry, "but, yeah, Pigwedgie."

Ron cried out, "Arggh, that's the fourth historic document he's eaten."

Harry added, "And the old goat sure seemed to know what he was about. Right when we needed to destroy the declaration, the beast didn't hesitate to take matter into his own hands, err, hooves ... I mean, in his

Chapter 18

own mouth. He also seemed to know, he was going to take the blame, while giving us a chance to escape. It looks like your family's scapegoat is going to be in the news quite extensively for the next few days."

Ron cried out, "Poor Wedgie. Hold tight everyone, sharp turn."

The getaway driver slammed the brakes and skidded halfway through the turn. He then gunned it, accelerating through the other half, picking up speed on the straightaway. The passengers were momentarily pressed up against the side of the van.

Ron said, "The SUV's on our tail. I'm gonna have to shake off our pursuit. You'd best buckle-up."

As Harry fastened his safety belt, he said, "Well, we certainly didn't plan on Pigwedgie being there, however, sometimes things work out for the best."

Ron said, "I just hope he doesn't get sick."

Hermione said, "Don't worry, Ron, he's got the stomach of a goat."

Harry added, "And after the Fungus Eaters set off that explosion, I'm sure they won't blame Pigwedgie. They'll likely think someone got away with stealing it."

Ron said, "Hang on, everyone." He took another sharp turn and headed down a narrow alley, running over two garbage cans. The alley funneled them onto a one-way street. The one-way street took them into an enclosed parking lot.

Ron said, "Crap! I went the wrong way!"

Cage complained, "We give you one simple job, and you mess it up."

Ron said, "Hold on everyone, I'm gonna back us out of this."

He put the van into reverse and floored the gas pedal. He was looking in his side mirrors to steer. He said, "Oh, crap, the Fart Lord's right behind us. We're gonna crash!"

Hermione abberated, taking Ron, Harry, and Nick with her. I moment later their four bodies flew through the inside of the tent in the unnamed woods. They hit the wall and the tent collapsed with the loud tearing of canvas.

In addition to his own aches and pains from a hard landing, Harry immediately felt the Fart Lord's anger. He had a vision of Moldyfart.

The rear end of the empty white van collided with the Black SUV with glass-shattering, airbag-deploying force. The Fart Lord stumbled out of the vehicle holding his neck. He shouted, "Grandpappy Shabby, you are an even worse driver than Vermintail! And that's saying a lot!"

Gramps Foil sniggered.

Moldyfart continued, "What I ought to do is leave you here to take the blame for this whole fiasco! The FBI would probe every crevice of your body searching for The Declaration. And you'd have a fine time answering all their questions for the rest of your miserable life."

Bellatrix Le Deranged urged, "Let's just get out of here, before there are any more witnesses."

Harry's vision abruptly disappeared.

Chapter 18

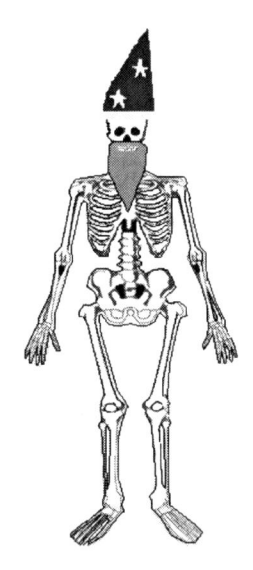

Chapter 19 – Calling Elvis

    Harry crossed the Declaration of Independence off the Master List. The last hoaxcrock, other than Snakey and the Fart Lord himself, was Moldyfart's nose. He didn't know where it was. He didn't have any clues. About the only thing he knew about it was that, according to Ron, it was not at Moldyfart's mansion. However, even as he crossed the Declaration of Independence off the list his thoughts were distracted.

    He was thinking, "Somewhere out there, there's a magic hat – one that can be used to fake your own death. And I think I know where it is."

    He announced to Ron, Hermione, and Nicholas Cage, "Get ready. We're going to Hogwashes."

    Nicholas Cage put on a pair of dark sunglasses, grabbed his leather jacket, and said, "Awesome, it'll give me a chance to get a good feel for the set."

    Hermione ignored the actor and asked Harry, "Why?"

    Harry answered, "I want to find out if Grumblesnore is really dead."

    Hermione said, "Oh c'mon, Harry. The hat he always used to wear is just a hat. It doesn't look anything like the hat from the story. Just because Elvis Presley faked his own death years ago to get away from all

Chapter 19

the public scrutiny of being a superstar, and started a new life as Elvis Grumblesnore, doesn't mean he used the hat to do it."

Harry said, "That's true, but it doesn't mean he doesn't have the hat. And let's face it, he did such a great job of fooling almost everyone the first time he supposedly died. Just maybe he had – oh, a little extra help? And just maybe, he's done it again? After all, how many people do you know that have faked their own death?"

Hermione said, "Harry, that's just dumb. If they fake their own death, I would think they were really gone. How would I know otherwise? You're not being logical."

Harry snorted, "I'm not logical? What about you? You're the one who was all like, the story is real. Well, you were right."

Hermione sniffed and said, "As usual."

Nicholas Cage interrupted, "Hold on, here. Harry's the main character. You're just a side-kick. The hero's always right. I say we follow Harry's lead."

Hermione said, "This is real life. I'm a real person, not a supporting role."

Cage gasped, "Oh, I see. Character immersion. Yes. You're doing great. Keep it up."

Hermione said sarcastically, "Thanks, I was born to play this role, I've been doing it my whole life."

Nick replied, "Sorry for the interruption." The actor began to mimic Harry's posture and mannerisms. It was pretty annoying.

Harry said, "Don't worry about it. As I was saying, now that we both know the story's real, why wouldn't The Hat be around here somewhere?"

Hermione answered, "Because it could be anywhere. And it's dangerous to go to Hogwashes looking for it. Everyone will recognize us, and the ones that are Fungus Eaters, like Maldoy, will text the Fart Lord that you're there."

Harry scoffed, "We'll be in and out. All we have to do is check Grumblesnore's Tomb and that's in the dungeon. With the Death Cat scaring everyone away, there won't be anyone down there to even notice us."

"And just what about the Death Cat? Do you want to become her next victim?"

"Her? What makes you think it's a she?"

"In the story the female cat killed her two brothers."

Harry admitted, "Oh, that's right. I forgot. Well, I suppose she is a bit of a risk. But there's three, err, four of us. If we keep a sharp eye out for her, one of us should be able to spot her and zap her before she can get us."

Hermione said, "I'll be sure to put that on your tombstone. We'll bury you right next to your uncle. Remember his famous last words, 'What's the worst that could happen?'"

Harry stuck his tongue out and said, "If I'm dead, you'll be dead too."

Hermione scoffed, "Not likely, Putter!"

Harry returned, "Right back at you, Stranger!"

Hermione sighed, "Fine, but can we wait until after curfew. That way we won't bump into anyone."

Harry said, "Great! It will be like old times – us sneaking around Hogwashes after hours."

"Only with Nicholas Cage, Academy Award winning movie superstar," added Nick.

At midnight, Hermione tried to abberate. A moment later she said, "I'm blocked out of Hogwashes. I guess they've updated the protection spells. Since I'm no longer a student there, I can't get directly in."

Harry suggested, "Well, how about the Whopping Willow tree? We can use the secret passage there."

Hermione said, "Yeah, I can do that."

Moments later, they were there. From the Whopping Willow tree, they followed the secret passage through the woods. They pushed their way through coats draped over hangers and entered Hogwashes through the Wardrobe of Requirements. They were in a room of old, unwanted, unused, and broken furniture on the third floor of the castle's main keep.

Ron whispered, "It's here."

Harry asked, "What, the hat?"

Ron said, "No. There's a hoaxcrock here. I can sense it."

Harry asked, "What here in this room?"

Ron answered, "No, I mean here at the school."

Chapter 19

Harry and Hermione became worried. There were only three hoaxcrocks left: Moldyfart, Snakey, and Moldyfart's nose. It seemed unlikely for any of them to be at the school. However, it seemed very unlikely that either the Fart Lord or his pet would be visiting Hogwashes, especially at this hour. And that left only one other choice – his nose. It must be.

Yet, if his nose was here, could the Fart Lord and his Fungus Eaters be far behind? Their efforts of late were obvious. They were trying to get their hands on the hoaxcrocks before Harry could. They might arrive at any moment.

Hermione reasoned, "Harry, we have to find the hoaxcrock first."

Harry said, "Darn it. I knew you were going to say that. Fine. Let's go."

Hermione said furtively, "Shhh, someone's coming!"

When she stopped talking, Nicholas Cage, Harry, and Ron heard it too – footsteps in the hallway outside. Someone else was up late at night. They waited while the late night curfew-breaker walked by quickly. The footsteps receded.

Ron was about to peek into the hallway to see if it was clear, when they heard the voices of two students as they came and went.

Harry said, "There seem to be a lot of people up past curfew tonight."

They heard a pair of sneakers slapping and squeaking as someone ran down the hallway.

Hermione asked, "What's going on here, anyway?"

Harry shrugged and said, "Let's find out."

Ron opened the door.

A moment later, they bumped into Professor McGooglesnot. She said, "My goodness. Nicholas Cage! What on earth are you doing here? May I have your autograph?"

Despite the actor's dark sunglasses, the teacher had recognized him. It happened all the time. The actor said, "Sure, why not?"

Minerva tittered like a school girl.

Hermione interrupted, "Mrs. McG, we're trying to find the last hoaxcrock – Moldy, err, the Fart Lord's nose. We're kind of in a hurry."

Calling Elvis

Minerva replied, "Oh, hello, Hermione ... Ron ... Harry. Don't worry, this will only take a sec. I have a pen right here. And you can sign my...oh dear." She began to rummage through her pockets for something the Academy Award winning actor could sign.

Hermione said, "Have you seen a nose anywhere?"

McGooglesnot answered absent-mindedly, "I'm sure you'll find it, dear. Oh, I know, my bra! Oh, wait, even better. Here, you can sign my walking stick."

She held her cane up for Cage to sign and thanked him when he finished.

Hermione persisted, "Mrs. McG, we need to find the last hoaxcrock. It's important."

Mrs. McGooglesnot did not take her eyes from the actor. She brushed aside the question by suggesting, "Why don't you try behind the couch cushions? I absolutely adored you in *Moonstruck*."

Nicholas Cage tried, "Thank you, Ma'am. But, if you would be so kind, we really need to find the Fart Lord's nose. Have you seen it?"

Minerva blinked and asked, "Here? Why on earth would it be here? Is that what the Fungus Eaters want?"

Hermione asked, "Fungus Eaters? Are they here?"

Their old teacher was more herself now and replied, "Yes, they're outside demanding that we let them in. Ape has refused them and they are furious. They say they have the place surrounded and will force their way in, if necessary. Ape laughed in their faces. It is a castle after all, built to withstand the siege of an army, let alone a few wizards with hugely inflated egos. Yet, they insist that we let them in and threaten that if Ape doesn't open the door, they will destroy the school and everyone in it. We're preparing to defend ourselves."

Harry said, "They're after the last hoaxcrock too. We have to find it quickly. Have you seen a nose anywhere?"

McGooglesnot answered, "A nose? No, but I'll gather the Nerds and we'll help Mr. Cage search for it."

The actor said, "That would be great."

She added, "I'll ask if any of them have seen a nose lying around anywhere." She headed toward the Nerd quarters.

Harry called after her, "Fabulous. Thanks, Mrs. McG."

Chapter 19

In the meanwhile, they began their search. Ron led the way. However, knowing the general direction of a hoaxcrock and finding it were two different things. He got confused at times. First he thought it was on one floor, but as they got closer, he realized it was below them on a lower floor. That meant backtracking to a stairwell and going down a level. Afterwards, they discovered Ron was wrong. It was actually two floors below them, not one. They had to backtrack again, which greatly annoyed Nick.

All the while, as they made their way, they discovered that the whole school was roused already. And their fellow students and friends impeded their progress. Everyone wanted to know what Nicholas Cage was doing there and there simply wasn't time to explain. They answered, "We're here to help. Talk to you later."

As Ron led them, they ran into more difficulty. The hallways sometimes seemed to be the right way to go, yet eventually veered away from their target, forcing them to backtrack and try a different corridor.

Eventually, they found themselves heading toward the preschool area. He announced, "We're getting close now."

Cage muttered, "About time."

However, just then, they noticed a child skipping happily toward them. It was a preschooler – a boy. When he reached them, he said, "Hi!"

They all returned the greeting wondering what the child wanted.

The boy said, "I'm Reginald Hosepiper. Who are you?"

They introduced themselves.

Reginald suddenly said, "Move it, Tubby!"

He brushed past Ron, turned the light on and entered the room they were about to go in. It was the preschool center. They watched him skip over to a shelf and grab a toy set. It was a Mr. Potato Head. He opened Mr. Potato Head's back-spud compartment. He shook the small parts out onto the table.

While everyone was watching Hosepiper, they saw a giant anaconda slither out of the preschool area bathroom behind him. Snakey was heading right for the child.

They let out a collective gasp of surprise and called out to Hosepiper.

Calling Elvis

Hermione cried, "Watch out, Reginald," as she reached into her robe pocket for her wand.

Cage called, "Come here, boy!" He waved his arms frantically, trying to get Hosepiper's attention.

As he fumbled for his wand, Harry shouted, "Get away from there!"

Ron shrieked, "Ahh. It's Snakey! Oh, wait, I have a sword!"

Mrs. McGooglesnot arrived slightly breathless. When she saw the anaconda, she gasped, clutched at her heart, and exclaimed, "Holy Crap!"

Unaware of his own imminent danger, Hosepiper exclaimed, "Here it is!" And he picked up the nose as Snakey loomed over his head from behind. However, the snake with lightning reflexes ducked back down to avoid the spells coursing at its head. It slithered away quickly, much faster than anyone suspected it could go. More spells missed, as Snakey weaved to and fro propelling its long body back into the bathroom.

Ron gave chase, waving Excalibur as he ran after it. He arrived only in time to see the tail end of the giant anaconda slither into a broken grate. Snakey escaped.

Ron returned and said dejectedly, "It got away."

Reginald called out, "Mrs. McGooglesnot! I've got it! I've got it!"
He ran to her and handed her the nose.

Mrs. McGooglesnot held it up. She said, "Well done, Hosepiper! That's one hundred points for the Nerd house."

Ron complained, "Eww, Gross! I remember playing with that."

Hermione replied, "Don't worry about that, Ron. It can't have been here long or else it would have decayed by now. I'm sure it wasn't there back when you were in preschool."

Ron looked uncomfortable as he said, "Right, that's what I meant. Preschool. Right."

Hermione stated, "That was a close one. We arrived just in the nick of time. As a matter of fact, I'll bet that's why Ron had so much trouble locating the nose. He was probably following the snake as it moved through the walls and pipes."

Mrs. McGooglesnot asserted, "Allow me to do the honors." She put the nose on the table, pulled a basilisk fang from her robe pocket, and

Chapter 19

jabbed it into the small lump of flesh. Black venom oozed from the hole she made in the hoaxcrock. The nose shriveled up before their eyes until it was the size of a small black pea.

Hermione said, "Wow, we usually just burn them."

The old teacher answered, "Where's the fun in that?" She flicked what was left of the nose off the table expertly, as though it were a booger.

Cage said, "Thanks for your help, Mrs. McG."

Minerva tittered and replied, "It was my pleasure."

A student ran in and said, "Mrs. McGooglesnot. There you are! Professor Ape wants you to come to the Astronomy Tower quickly."

The teacher sighed and excused herself, "It was so nice to meet you, Mr. Cage. Thank you again for the autograph."

"The pleasure was all mine," Nick replied dashingly.

Minerva said, "Oh, and good to see you three too. I'm glad we were able to help you in your mission. Kill 'em, Harry. We're all counting on you."

Hermione asked, "What should we do now? Someone has to have told the Fungus Eaters we're here. Should we stay to help the teachers fight them off?"

Ron said, "I think we should try and find that snake. It's still in the school somewhere. And we need to kill it."

Hermione disagreed, "That's likely to be a wild goose chase, Ron. The snake slithered in here somehow. It will probably leave the way it came, especially since we prevented it from getting to the hoaxcrock. It won't stay here. And it obviously can travel places you can't go."

Harry said, "I think we should stay and help fight. The Fungus Eaters aren't going to take Ape's 'no' for an answer. And this might be a good opportunity to kill some of them off before we have to face Oldyfart May."

Hermione said, "I wonder what makes them think they can force their way in? The students must have them outnumbered forty to one – perhaps more. They must have been pretty desperate to get the last hoaxcrock."

Harry explained, "Well, the Fart Lord did kill a bunch of them already. I'd be afraid if I were one of them too."

Ron asked, "Won't they just go away? We already got the nose. They're too late."

Hermione mused, "Hmm. I wonder. That would all depend on whether they somehow know we got it. Snakey was obviously after the hoaxcrock, that seems very intelligent for a snake. So it must have some way of communicating with the Fart Lord. And it's got a piece of Fartypant's soul in it. And that could mean just about anything. For all we know, the Fart Lord already knows about it."

She concluded, "It would probably be best if we stay a while to help if we are needed. And if the Fungus Eaters go away, we can leave too."

Harry said, "Well, anyway, before we do anything else, I want to check out Grumblesnore's Tomb first. Follow me."

They made their way downward. Harry was leading the way now, as they headed toward the dungeon levels. When they arrived, Faco Maldoy was walking by and texting at the same time. As he passed them, he muttered with derision, "Putter."

Harry replied with equal venom, "Maldoy."

Cage whispered in the same derisive tone, "Maldoy."

Faco suddenly realized that hadn't happened in a long while. He turned and said, "Whoa. Putter? What the hell are you doing here, loser? I thought you dropped out and heard you were planning to shovel horse manure for a living."

Harry said, "Maybe I'll get some practice by shoveling your brain!"

Faco sneered, "Oh yeah? Well, be prepared for a lot of work, Putter, because my brain is a huge pile of…D'oh!"

Harry pumped his fist and said, "Oh, yeah! Owned!"

Nicholas Cage pumped his fist too, imitating Harry.

Hermione nudged Harry forward. She said, "C'mon, let's go."

Maldoy asked, "Wait. Is that Nicholas Cage?"

Harry bragged "That's right, our friend, Nicholas Cage. He's an actor, you know?"

Maldoy declared, "I must be dreaming. This is too bizarre."

Harry said, "So's your face!"

Cage mimicked Harry.

Chapter 19

Maldoy called after them, "Oh, yeah? Well, you know that's just, like, your opinion."

Cage laughed, "Wow, he has even worse comebacks than Ron!"

Ron retorted, "Oh yeah? Well, you starred in *The Wicker Man*!"

Harry said, "Owned!"

"Hey! I was not! That movie wasn't THAT bad!"

Ron cried out, "Oh, no! Not the bees! Not the bees! Ahh!"

Cage sighed and admitted, "All right, enough already. I was owned."

They opened the door to the headmaster's mausoleum. Inside was an unadorned stone sarcophagus.

Harry said the magic incantation, "Wigwamia Levi-straussa!" He pointed his wand at the heavy stone lid. It levitated upward revealing the contents of Grumblesnore's tomb. Inside was the decomposing body of Elvis Grumblesnore.

Hermione said, "See, he's still there."

Harry said, "Oh, yeah. Look again!" He removed Grumblesnore's hat and the body became a mannequin, not a real corpse. It was Grumblesnore's old Elvis mannequin. It looked like young Elvis Presley. However, it had been severely abused over the years.

The hat Harry was holding also changed. It was no longer the headmaster's wizard's cap. It was a flat wide-brimmed hat with goat tassels dangling from its brim.

Harry tried it on.

Ron asked, "How do you feel?"

Harry replied, "Not any different."

A moment later, his head exploded and bits of his brain flew everywhere spattering the walls and his friends.

Nick, Hermione, and Ron were all shocked. Harry's headless body plopped to the floor. The hat floated down and landed beside it.

Harry immediately popped back up, his head was intact and the hat was upon it again. He said, "Seems to work as described. What did you think? Did I look dead?"

Ron cried out, "That was bloody brilliant!"

Cage exclaimed, "Spectacular special effects. This movie is going to be so awesome! I'm in it, you know?"

Calling Elvis

Hermione sniffed and said, "That was just gross, Harry."

Harry proudly replied, "Thanks. You guys should have seen the look on your ..."

Hermione interrupted, "Really, Harry, we should be upstairs helping to fight the Fungus Eaters. Let's hurry and get to the Astronomy Tower."

Harry asked, "Oh, man. Please tell me you can abberate us to the top."

Hermione said, "Unfortunately, no. Even though we're already inside the protection spells and I shouldn't be blocked, there are too many students and teachers up and about. Likely there are a lot of people at the top of the tower keeping watch on the Fungus Eaters. It wouldn't be safe to abberate into a crowd."

Harry said, "Oh, crap."

They made their way out of the dungeon and into the keep. When they reached the Great Eatery, the school's dining hall, there was a crowd of students gathered. The children were watching as a long column of knights in full armor riding on horseback filed into the Great Eatery.

Upon seeing Harry, Ron, and Hermione, one of the knights, who had a fowl emblazoned upon his shield, lifted his visor, laughed, and called out, "What up, dudes?"

Harry exclaimed, "Sir Robin! What are you doing here?"

"I'm with the Knights of the Round Table, Harry. We have been summoned and are here for the Final Battle. We're going to help you defeat Lord Pull-Me-Finger."

"That's great." Harry asked, "Who summoned all of you?"

Sir Robin replied, "The King. Long live the King." A cheer from the students and knights rang out, "Long live the King. Long live the King."

Meanwhile, Sir Robin urged his horse into the Great Eatery.

Hermione turned to Ron and Harry. She asked, "The King? Who does he mean?"

Ron shrugged and said, "Beats me."

Harry answered, "This is so awesome. He must mean Elvis! You know – The King. Elvis faked his own death and has been out gathering our army for the Final Battle."

Ron said, "That seems logical."

Chapter 19

Hermione pointed and said, "Look, Ron. Your family's here."

Coming up the keep steps from the main entrance were Mr. and Mrs. Cheesley and their numerous orange-haired offspring. Arthur was leading Pigwedgie on a short tether.

Mrs. Cheesley hugged Ron and said, "Thank goodness you're still alive. Where are Suzanne and Ginny?"

"Hello, Mum," Ron said, "I'm sure they're around here somewhere."

She let out a snort, "I would think you'd care a little more about your younger sisters. Well, let me tell you, you'd better defend them well, Ronald. You'll regret it the rest of your life if something happens to them. I mean it."

Ron rolled his eyes and replied, "Yes, Mum."

She called to her children, "Everyone, split up and find Ginny and Suzanne. Meet back here at the Great Eatery in twenty minutes. Ron, you too! Harry, we're all here to support you, but Ron has to attend to his family first. He will see you later."

Harry said, "No problem, Mrs. C."

The frumpy housewife added, "And, young man, we're all counting on you to do the right thing when the time comes. I hope you've taken some time to think about what I said before. Make us proud, Harry."

Harry swallowed and said, "I will."

As they left, Arthur was overhead saying, "I think that man in the sunglasses was Nicholas Cage."

Mrs. Cheesley answered, "Don't be ridiculous. What would he be doing here?"

Nick, Hermione, and Harry made their way into the courtyard. Across the way the front gate was open. Harry thought for a moment, "Oh, no! Arthur left the gates open by mistake!" However, he then realized the gates were open because a military honor guard was marshalling into the castle.

A man wearing a tan military coat and a navy blue and red hat embroidered with fancy gold plumes all around it was leading the way. He was heading directly toward the front door to the keep, directly toward Nick, Harry, and Hermione.

Calling Elvis

The military man stopped before Harry and saluted with his right hand palm facing toward the teenager. He kissed Harry on each of his cheeks and said, "Mon Ami, Harry Putter. I am General Blownapart of the Armée de Terre – the French Army – the longest standing permanent army. It is the third largest militia in the world – though it is second to none. The full might of the unstoppable force that is the French Military is just outside the gate and is at your service. Victory will be ours!"

Hermione rolled her eyes and said sarcastically, "Great."

Standing behind Harry, Cage muttered, "Weak-kneed surrender monkeys."

Harry said loudly, "Wow! Grumblesnore's really outdid himself now! That's wonderful. By all means, do what you do best."

General Blownapart replied, "Then I will order the men to prepare. We will begin fortifying our position in anticipation of the forthcoming Final Battle."

Harry answered, "That would be really smashing."

The military man saluted again, turned crisply, and began ordering his military guard in French.

The three made their way to the Astronomy Tower. As they crossed the courtyard, Harry peered up at the dark and cloudy night sky. It looked like a trite storm was approaching, the tired old harbinger of clash encounters had also arrived for the Final Battle. His eyes then fell upon the defenders on the outer wall. Some were students. Others were diminutive. Harry tried to make them out in the gloom. They seemed to be very small men in camouflage raingear and army fatigues.

Harry stopped, pointed, and asked, "Are those elves, there, on the battlements looking over the gate?"

Hermione wondered too. Then she too pointed and said, "They are. Look, there's Father Christmas!"

Saint Nick was on one the battlements. His beard and the white fringe of his outfit stood out in the darkness. He seemed to be directing the efforts of his elves.

Harry laughed and said, "Well, you know Santa. He loves a good fight."

Hermione replied, "Yes, he's quite the brawler."

Chapter 19

Cage agreed, "He is one tough cat."
Harry said, "C'mon, let's get going."

At the entrance to the Astronomy Tower they bumped into Fabulous Butterpants. He said, "Oh, hey, guys! You excited about the upcoming battle? I'm psyched! I can't wait to whoop some Fungus Eater's butt."

Harry said, "Butterpants. I'm surprised to see you. I thought after the way Loopin and the rest of us treated you that night, you'd be the last person to come help."

Fabulous replied, "Hey, that's all water under the bridge. Loopin was man enough to apologize about the misunderstanding. So, it's all good. And I'm happy to be here to do my part. The rest of the guys are here too."

Harry asked, "The Fan Club is here already?"

Butterpants said, "Of course. We wouldn't miss this. It's going to be epic. Someone ought to get Madman and Butterball to do a play by play commentary while it's going on. Too bad we'll all be too busy fighting to take time to admire it."

Harry replied, "Don't worry about that. It's going to be a big summer blockbuster movie one day. It'll be even better watching it on the big screen."

Butterpants laughed, "Hey, that's a good one. Do you think they'll let me play myself? Which side do you think is my good side?"

Cage answered, "You don't have one. Trust me, I'm an actor."

Harry laughed nervously in embarrassment. He said, "Hey, uh, wouldn't you rather someone professional do your role, maybe, say… George Clooney?"

Fabulous said, "Gee, I'm not sure he could do justice to my character. But thanks anyhow. Hey, do any of you guys need something from the Best One? Coffee? Tea?"

The two teenagers declined.

Nick answered, "Yes, I'll have a tall half-skinny half half-n'-half extra hot split quad-shot latte with whip. And ask them to put a maraschino cherry on top. Thanks."

Fabulous replied, "Wait, let me write that down."

Calling Elvis

It took nearly ten minutes for Fabulous to take Nick's order. Then he said, "Alrighty then, I'll catch up to you later."

The three climbed the long staircase to the Astronomy Tower. As they reached the upper floors, they heard the raised voices of Ape's head and Professor McGooglesnot.

Ape was ranting, "I will not allow this school to take sides in a wizard war. I am responsible for the safety of our students. I want that gate opened and everyone who doesn't belong here out! They can fight their war somewhere else."

McGooglesnot answered, "It's too late, Ape. You've already pissed the Fungus Eaters off. If you wanted to stay neutral, you should have let them in."

Ape's head shouted, "I do not have to capitulate to anyone's bullying demands. I offered to make an early morning appointment. They refused to wait until then. However, I did not invite Father Christmas and a division of heavily-armed elves to set up artillery in our courtyard. How did they even get in? I thought the protection spells would have blocked him."

McGooglesnot replied, "First of all, Saint Nick is on the explicitly allowed list. No one blocks Santa. Besides, he arrived in his typical conveyance, and you, of all people, know protection spells don't block reindeer or any other physical mode of access. All they stop are aberration spells."

Ape cried out, "Well who let him take control of the gates? I don't want him letting in any more unwanted guests. I want those gates kept closed! I did not invite the Knights of the Round Table to use the Great Eatery as a stable for their horses. And I did not invite the French Army to park itself outside our walls. The next thing you know, Putter will show up with all his weird friends, thinking they can use our school as their army headquarters. Well, I'm putting my foot down. Putter is not coming inside Hogwashes. You know, he tried to kill me the last time he was here?"

McGooglesnot said, "Yes, if I recall, you fled out the window on your hoverboard."

Chapter 19

Ape's head growled, "That boy is a menace. He was trying to blame me for that stupid fortune in that stupid fortune cookie. How am I responsible? I didn't put it there. And I can't help it that Tom Riddly went crazy because of it. Yet, you should have seen the murderous look on Putter's face. I've tried my best with that boy, but he's simply beyond control. He's as insane as the Fart Lord. Both are hell bent on destruction. Well, let the two of them take their wizard war somewhere else. I didn't let the Fungus Eaters in, and Putter's not getting in here either."

Harry chose that moment to make his entrance. He stepped into the high-level tower room. Hermione and Cage were right behind.
Ape's eyes went wide. He said, "Holy Crap! It's Putter." He turned his hoverboard to make a quick exit out the window. However, in his haste, the hoverboard struck the stone window sill. The jar containing Ape's Head flew through the window. Without means of flight, the glass jar plummeted.
Harry stuck his head out the window and looked down, but it was too dark to see anything so far below.
Hermione gasped, "Is he? Is he dead?"
Harry answered, "I can't tell."

Had Ape acted quickly, he could have cast a levitation spell to save himself. However, the terror of falling made him scream. He plummeted eleven stories to his death.

✷✶   School of Hard Knocks   ✶✷
✶   ✶

Chapter 20 – School of Hard Knocks

The Knights of the Round Table had their horses stabled in the Great Eatery under such guard as could be spared – a few of their squires. They had taken position upon the battlements along with many of the students, Santa's elves, and the members of the Order of the Harry Putter Fan Club.

Santa ordered his hard-working elves to prepare for battle. They were hastily filling up sandbags and arranging them to give further protection to machine gun and artillery positions. However, most of Santa's elves were already manning the Outer Wall and its towers, waiting between crenulations, upon parapets, and behind narrow castle windows. Santa and his second in command Herbie the Dentist arrayed most of their strength near the front gate, for here the enemy was expected to attack hardest, trying to force their entrance. If the Fart Lord's assault were determined and in great strength, they might break down the heavy wooden doors and iron portcullis and force the defenders to retreat to the main keep or into the dungeons of Hogwashes. And they would hold out there as long as possible, retreating to the Astronomy Tower, which was directly attached to the Keep, as a last line of defense.

The Outer Wall was twenty feet high. It had a stout embankment, wide enough that four elves could walk abreast along the top, sheltered by a parapet meant for humans. Only a tall elf could look over it. Many of

Chapter 20

them were standing on sandbags to get the extra height they needed to aim a machine gun over the wall. Others were stationed in clefts in the stone through which the elves could shoot.

The elves were all wearing camouflaged rain ponchos with hoods tucked inside broad rimmed army helmets. They were prepared for the inevitable rain. And should the upcoming battle become desperate, they were prepared to shed their raingear too, evoking the beast within. If things got ugly, they could unleash a whole lot of ugly.

For a moment Santa stood leaning against the breastwork upon the wall, his shotgun on his shoulder. Herbie the Elven Dentist sat above on the parapet itself, fingering his XM8 Carbine with the 40mm grenade launcher attached. He was peering out into the gloom.

"This is more to my liking," said jolly St. Nick. "Ever my heart rises as battle draws near. Sure beats being cooped up in the workshop, making toys, checking lists, and especially, checking them twice."

"Without a doubt," agreed Herbie the Elven Dentist. "I get tired of all the cavities and root canals. Sometimes you just want to blow stuff up. But, I wish there were more of us elves around. Better still, I'd give up eggnog for a hundred Tomahawk missiles. We sure could use 'em. I suppose the Knights of the Round Table will be useful in their own way, but there are too few of us elves here, far too few."

"It'll have to do," said Santa. "After all, it's not like the Knights of the Round Table are gonna help us catch up on all the toy-making afterward."

Time passed slowly as everyone waited for their enemies with anticipation and wonder. None knew what to expect. It was said the Fart Lord's army was vast. Far away in the valley scattered fires were burning. It was the first sign of the approaching enemy. Scout began arriving with reports. And rumors spread along the wall. A Panzer Tank Unit was advancing along the road leading Moldyfart's huge army of men, ogres, trolls, and giants. Burning torches, flashlights, and floodlights could be seen winding up the road in many lines.

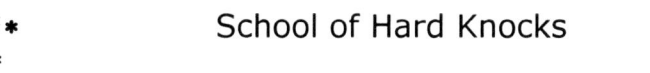

Suddenly from the trenches below came yells and shouts in French, "Sacré Bleu! Sacré Bleu! Les allemands, les Nazis! Nous sommes destines! Capitule. Capitule!"

Screams and the distant fierce battle-cries of men broke out. And then the sharp cracks of gunfire. A small group of men came galloping back over the quibbage field and up the ramp to the gate of the castle. It was the rearguard of the Knights of Camelot. They had conducted a stealthy ambush and were now driven back.

"The enemy is at hand!" they said. "From the darkness we loosed every arrow that we had, and littered the road with Nazis. But it will not slow them for long. Already they are overrunning the trenches. And the French will only slow them down for as long as it takes the Germans to accept their submission. General Blownapart has ordered a full surrender. They are already laying down their arms."

Santa sneered with disgust, "Sounds like the Knights are at least more useful to us than the French."

Moldyfart was in a pavilion three kilometers away – his field headquarters. When one of his own scouts arrived, he eagerly asked, "What news is there?"

The Nazi messenger saluted and was pleased to inform his Lordship, "Heil Lord Moldyvart. Der französische army hast surrendered!"

The Fart Lord scoffed, "News? You call that news? That was a foregone conclusion. Why do you think I went and got you Nazis! Has the battle started yet? I thought I heard some gunfire."

"Nein, mien Vart Lord. Heardst du a minor skirmish. Der Schutzstaffel, der SS, hast driven der enemy rear guard zu der castle."

"Tell Field Marshall Von Küchler to get his head out of his butt and commence with the attack."

"Ja, mein Vart Lord."

Chapter 20

It was now three in the morning. Harry, Hermione, and Nicholas Cage were at the top of the Astronomy Tower. They observed as the surrendered French military had vacated the field of battle.

Harry muttered, "The full might of the unstoppable force that is the French Military, is just outside the gate and is at your service. Victory will be ours! My fat butt!"

Nicholas Cage said, "I tried to tell your butt's big."

Hermione agreed, "No question about it."

Meanwhile, Moldyfart's army had extinguished their lights and was maneuvering into position for the night time assault. The heavily-clouded sky was utterly dark and foreboding. Lightning suddenly flashed, rolling across the sky and striking down upon the distant hills. The defenders upon the walls and castle turrets saw all the space between them and the trenches lit with white light. Arrayed in an arc in front were dozens of Panzer Tanks. Behind them was a seething, boiling mass of black shapes. Mostly they were of human form, Nazis. However, among them were oversized terrible creatures. There were giants and ogres with massive spiked clubs and tall, grim trolls wearing battle armor and carrying war hammers. Hundreds upon hundreds were still pouring over the trenches. Like an ocean tide the army flowed up toward the castle filling the entire battle field between the steep walled cliffs. A clap of thunder followed. And the clouds opened sending rain lashing down.

With a sudden roar of the Panzer tanks' cannons, the assault on Hogwashes began. The barrage shook the stone walls, however, no sound of reply or exchange of fire was heard from within the castle. A deathly silence foiled the attackers as the canon roar reverberated from the stones of the castle and the steep cliffs. It was as though the stronghold was empty, yet the walls still defied them. This enraged Moldyfart's army.

The lightning flashed, and emblazoned upon every helm the ghastly swastika was seen. There was a battle cry. The Nazis screamed, the Giants stomped their feet, the ogres bellowed, the trolls growled. The defenders ducked back down as the crack of Nazi rifles began. The German gunners shot at the battlements and into the clefts between the stones.

After a minute of shooting, they stopped firing again, listening to the echoes of their guns. Their attack again met no resistance. Yet they were no closer to overrunning the castle. The passive defenders were infuriating to the attackers.

And then a trumpet sounded in the ensuing silence. Hogwashes erupted in return fire. The elven battery of guns lay down a deathly artillery barrage among their foes. And machine gun positions roared sending a hail of bullets into the Nazi ranks. Students sent spells coursing downward to stun and scorch their adversaries. The knights and their men sent arrows arching over the walls to fall among the enemy.

At first, the Fungus Eaters tried to counter some of the student's spells, however, they were so severely outnumbered their efforts were largely ineffective. Furthermore, they became targets. For every spell they cast, a hundred came raining down from the walls to stupidify them and those nearest to them. After the stun spells eventually wore off, the Fungus Eaters withdrew to the rear of the battlefield to observe.

Moldyfart's army surged forward, some against the Outer Wall, others ran towards the causeway that led up to the main gates. There, many of the hugest creatures were gathered – crazed giants, wild ogres, and terrible trolls. These enemies knew no fear and did not hesitate even from the bite of bullets. They strode forward determined to destroy the gates with spiked clubs and war hammers wielded with brutal strength. They reached the causeway and strode towards the gates. And there they met with a barrage of elven launched grenades. Several died from the explosion-hurled shrapnel. The rest discovered fear. They wavered, broke, and fled back.

Next, the Germans sent a Panzer tank. It fired its main gun at the gate as it rumbled forward. Meanwhile, behind the armored vehicle, Nazi

Chapter 20

riflemen and machine gunners crowded on the causeway, sending a hail of bullets against the defenders on the walls. The tank rammed the gates with a rending boom. The armored Panzer withstood a barrage of elven launched grenades. Again and again the Panzer crashed into the gates weakening the stout timbers and iron bars.

Ron stood with his family on the Keep Wall. They were casting small bolts of electricity down upon the Nazis. They heard the thudding of the German tank as it rammed the front gates; and in a sudden flash of light they beheld the damaged entrance from within.

"Mum," said Ron. "I'm needed! The grenades aren't enough to stop them from battering down the doors!"

His mother asked, "And just what do you think you're going to do?"

However, Ron did not stay to listen or to answer.

He drew Excalibur and it glowed brightly with white fire. He ran quickly along the battlements atop the wall.

His mother called out, "Don't you run with a sword, young man! It's not safe!"

Her words fell on deaf ears. As Ron ran he commanded a handful of elves to accompany him. And a few of the Knights of the Round Table were drawn by the flaming sword and followed too. The smaller creatures ran as fast as they could, but toting heavy automatic weapons, they lagged behind. The armored men struggled too, as Ron flew down the steps, out the keep door, and passed into the courtyard. He paused as the nearby elven artillery installation roared, launching another barrage.

There was a small man-sized door within the main gate. As Ron waited for the others, he watched from within as the tank collided with the giant doors and he saw the wood splinter and iron bars bend inward. The gate held but was quickly weakening.

He ordered the elves into position, "When the door opens, dash through and take out the Nazi soldiers, leave the tank to me! Get READY."

School of Hard Knocks

Ron waited for the next crash of the Panzer into the gate. There was another spray of splinters and cracking of wooden beams. He could hear the iron bars groan as they bent inward and held.

He called out, "NOW!"

A burly knight yanked open the small door within the gate. The elves streamed out the door. They ran past the tank and began strafing bullets into the Nazi soldiers upon the causeway. The elves were mowing them down.

Meanwhile, Ron smote a heavy blow with Excalibur upon the tank's treads. The magic sword was made to cut steel. It clove through the treads, the wheels, and the mechanisms that turned them as though they were made of cardboard. The Panzer, which was backing up for another ram at the gates, slued. Ron moved forward and sliced through the other side of the tank's continuous track propulsion system, completely disabling its movement. He leapt upon the hull of the Panzer and with another heavy stroke, lopped the main gun from the turret.

He commanded the elves, "Fall back!"

While the elves backed their way into the castle Ron, with a series of three strokes, cut a large triangular hole in the side of the tank's turret. Standing aside of the hole, he called to a nearby elf for a hand grenade. Herbie the Dentist lobbed one to him. Ron snagged it out of the air and pulled the ring with his teeth. He tossed it through the hole inside the tank and jumped back down from the hull.

Herbie yelled, "Look out!"

An ogre was right behind Ron as he was running for the door. With Ron in the way, Herbie couldn't fire at the ogre. And then, there was a small explosion as the grenade went off, followed immediately by a tremendous explosion as the tank's magazine and fuel exploded. Herbie ducked behind the doorway as the blast hurled flames, shrapnel, and debris.

There was a huge cheer from the defenders upon the walls. When Herbie looked back through the doorway, he saw the black shell of the

Chapter 20

Panzer in flames and smoke. He saw the ogre lying dead but no sign of Ron.

Herbie ordered the small contingent of elves back out the door. They took position and began providing covering fire, strafing more Nazis on the causeway. Meanwhile, Al Roker arrived and said, "Wigwamia Levi-straussa!" He pointed his wand and levitated the huge ogre's body, placing it to the side. Ron was underneath the massive corpse.

He groaned and said, "Ouch."

Sir Percival arrived and helped Al Roker to lift Ron up and quickly usher him back inside. The elves followed and the small door within the gate was closed and made fast.

Ron was a hero and many people congratulated him. However, the gate's great hinges and iron bars were wrenched and bent; many of their timbers were cracked.

He said, "Thanks, Mr. Roker and everyone, for rescuing me."

Herbie called out, "Elves, quickly, we are needed upon the walls." They returned to their positions.

Al Roker said, "The rest of us must see what we can do to reinforce these gates. We can pile stones and brace them with beams from within."

Sir Percival said, "We can help you with that. I will gather a few of the knights."

Ron volunteered, "I'll help too."

Meanwhile, at the top of the Astronomy Tower, Nicholas Cage was holding his latte and had whipped cream on his upper lip. He said, "C'mon, Harry. You're supposed to be the hero of the movie. You should do something, well, heroic."

Harry asked, "Like what?"

Cage replied, "How should I know? I'm just an actor. All I know is that this is a huge climactic moment of the story and you've just been sitting on top of the highest tower, the safest location in the castle."

Harry answered, "What do mean? I've been casting spells down at the enemy this whole time."

"Yeah, but so has 'Crybaby Peepants' Jones, over there."

Harry glanced at the Nerd, Jones, then said, "Crap, you're right. I can't just sit here. I've got to do something."

Hermione reasoned, "Don't listen to him, Harry. You're waiting for the Fart Lord to show up, so you can battle him in a wizard's duel. In the meantime, you don't need to get yourself shot."

Cage disagreed, "In the meantime, he could do some kicking-cool stunts. Audiences eat that stuff up. I should know, I'm an actor."

Hermione rolled her eyes and said, "Yes, we all know you're an actor."

Harry pleaded, "Hermione, can you abberate us down?"

She snorted and said, "You're like the laziest blockbuster movie hero ever!"

Harry wheedled, "C'mon, please?"

She sighed and said, "If you're in such a hurry to get yourself killed, you can just run down all those stairs. Don't trip on the way."

Cage and Harry made their way down the Tower stairs to the Keep Wall.

Meanwhile, there was a small reprieve in the attack, during which the rain slowed and eventually stopped. The foreboding storm had done its duty and moved on, leaving clouds in the sky that were thinner now. The waning quarter moon peeked out between them. However, the dim light brought little hope to the defenders at Hogwashes. The enemy was rallying for another assault and their number seemed to have grown rather than diminished.

Al Roker, Ron, and the Knights of the Round Table braced the gates with stout beams of wood and piled stone. They were dismantling the goat stables to provide the necessary materials. Even as they worked, the assault on Hogwashes was renewed.

Chapter 20

Against the Outer Wall the Panzer Tank Unit's canons thundered. Their shells made the stout stone battlements shake. Nazis and ogres swarmed about its feet from end to end. Ropes with grappling hooks were hurled over the parapet faster than defenders could cut them. Hundreds of tall wooden ladders were lifted up. Many were cast down in ruin, but many more replaced them, and Nazi soldiers sprang up them like madmen. Though few in number the elves decimated their enemies. Along the Outer Wall's foot the dead were piling up in hideous mounds, and still the enemy advanced.

The students at Hogwashes grew weary. Their magic power was already spent. Then a clamor arose behind the school, where only a few defenders were posted to watch and protect the rear gate. There was a monstrous scream that rent the air. It was louder than the noise of battle.

Those posted at the rear gate pointed to Lake Iwannabealifeguard. A tremendous creature was wading through the lake as though it were a pond. It was heading toward them. The defenders pointed and cried out, "Godzilla! Godzilla!"

One of the students, Yu Rang, groaned similarly in dismay.

Even as they watched, the giant squid, Nemoy, began to wrap his tentacles around Godzilla and a battle of giant monsters began. Nemoy's ten tentacles kept Godzilla struggling to free himself. Godzilla's radiation blast made Nemoy grow even larger and more powerful. Godzilla tried to use his atomic breath, however, the squid countered with a huge spray of water.

Meanwhile, as the assault above was at its peak, the Nazis attempted to take advantage of the castle's drainage culvert. They had noticed water pouring out of it when it had been raining earlier. Now they crept like rats through the cement runoff and attached a grappling hook and line to the iron bars protecting access to the castle through the drain. The giants pulled the rope and wrenched the iron bars out. Then Nazi soldiers crawled through and into a narrow passageway that led into the courtyard.

The first few waited there until they gathered strength of numbers and then they issued forth shooting at the elves, students, and knights on the battlements from inside the courtyard.

    Down from the Outer Wall leapt Santa with a fierce cry that echoed in the cliffs, "Ho, Ho, Ho!" He blasted one Nazi with his shotgun and used the butt of his weapon to smash the face of another. He shouted. "Bad boys are behind the wall! Ho! Come, Herbie! Men are needed in the courtyard below. Ho, ho, ho!"

    Arthur Cheesley, and his oldest son, Bill, ran to help, along with Hogwashes students, Charlie Cartuffle and Michael Coronary. Behind them were Harrison Ford, Sir Bedevere, Sir Bors, and a small contingent of armored men. They ran to Santa's aid and began battling the Nazis in the courtyard in close combat.

    Fabulous Butterpants looked down from the Keep Wall, hearing the deep voice of jolly St. Nick above all the tumult. "The Nazis are in the courtyard!" he cried. "To me, Fan Club!" he shouted.

    Nick Cage said, "Hold on there, Short Stuff! Putter's the lead role in this picture and it's his Fan Club. Step aside and let Harry lead the way."

    Fabulous stepped aside and let Harry go first. The teenager leapt down the stair and through the keep gate with his many friends at his back, including Butterpants and Cage.

    The Fan Club's onset was fierce and sudden, and the Nazis gave way before them. Before long they were hemmed in the narrows of the passageway, and all were slain. However, they had caused many deaths to the defenders between those who were taken unaware, and those who arrived earliest to fight them off. Fred and George Cheesley were among those who had been killed upon the battlements. Arthur and Bill Cheesley were among those who died in combat. However, there was no time for anyone to mourn.

    Cage said, "Not too bad, Harry, but I think your fans deserve better. Let's see what else you got."

Chapter 20

Harry was still sucking wind. He answered, "I don't know. Maybe the screenwriter can embellish things."

The actor said, "Well, yeah. I was already taking that into account."

Ron arrived at that moment coming from bracing the Main Gate. He said, "Hey, Harry. I'm …"

Nicholas Cage interrupted, "Now, this cat is awesome."

Nick was being nice to him? Ron warily said, "Thanks."

"Did you see the way he took out that tank, Harry? That's the kind of heroic stuff I'm talking about. Maybe you could do something to take out some Panzers?"

Harry said, "I don't know. I don't have a magic sword like Ron."

"In the meantime, we'd better stop up this rat-hole," said Fabulous Butterpants.

Cage replied, "That's work for stage hands. Let's go up on the Outer Wall. That's where all the action is. There should be plenty of opportunities to kill off some of these extras."

Harry ran for the stairway. Nicholas Cage followed.

Fabulous said, "Stage hands? Extras? Does he think they're just movie extras? He must be crazy. He's going to get Harry killed."

Ron called after Harry, "Be careful, Harry!"

Soon after, Ron Cheesley and the Knights began blocking the inner end of the culvert with more of the stones from the goat stable. The goats and Saint Nick's reindeer were no longer confined and were now wandering in the courtyard.

Afterward, Ron climbed the stairway to the battlements to see how the fight was going. Away on the left the crash and clamor of the battle rose loud again. Giants, ogres, and trolls were smashing at the gates with their clubs and war hammers. Though the gates were almost in ruin, Roker, Ron, and the Knights had erected a formidable barrier of beams and stones, and so as of yet, no enemy had made it past.

School of Hard Knocks

Ron looked up at the dark sky, the thin gray clouds, and the pale stars and dim moon peeking through. "Will this night ever end?" he asked. "How long is it until morning?"

"Dawn isn't far off," said Neville Largebottom. He and Looney Luvnoodle were standing nearby, defending the battlements.

Looney replied, "But the morning isn't going to help much, I fear. Sure, the trolls will quail at the sun, but ogres and giants won't."

Neville added, "And neither will the Germans Do you hear them?"

"Yes," said Ron, "but I don't speak their language."

Fabulous Butterpants, who was standing nearby said excitedly, "I do! Did you know, it's one of the more ancient speeches of men. And it was once spoken in many Eastern states in the US, particularly Pennsylvania. The Germans hate us, these guys are still mad about World War I. Can you believe it? Anyway, they seem to think they've got the upper hand on us this time. Go figure. They're calling out, "Death to Harry Putter. Death to the Order of his Fan Club! Death to the English Knights! Death to the North Pole elves! Surrender, like the French or we will kill your women and abuse your dog." They have not forgotten their grievances against the English from World War I, when the British used magic against them to foil their conquest of the world. Moldyfart has inflamed their hatred for us. They won't give up until Harry Putter is taken, or they themselves are slain."

"None-the-less, I'd feel a lot better if it was morning and I could see what we're up against. It's dismal fighting in the darkness." complained Ron.

Even as they spoke there was a large explosion accompanied by a ball of flame and smoke. A gaping hole was blasted in the Outer Wall. A host of dark shapes began pouring in.

"Holy crap!" cried Ron. "Those tricky Nazi bastards must have crept into the culvert again. While we were talking, they must have packed it with explosives."

Chapter 20

At that moment, the Nazis raised a hundred ladders against the battlements. Over the wall and through the gaping hole the enemy assault came sweeping onto the battlements and into the courtyard. The defense was driven back. The exhausted students were routed. Further and further into the courtyard, they fell back, fighting as they gave way, step by step, towards the dungeons. Others made their way towards the keep door or the Astronomy Tower.

Harry made his way to the broad stairway that climbed from the courtyard to the Astronomy Tower. He decided here was a heroic place to make a stand. From here, he could defend the stairway while the others made it to safety. However, Cage had already become separated from Putter in the ensuing chaos.

One by one the defenders retreated into the tower, as Putter cast spells, sending crackling electricity into the Nazis pouring into the courtyard. Behind him, on the upper steps knelt Herbie the Elven Dentist. His gun was smoking as he provided covering fire, sweeping the Nazis from the battlements.

The Nazis, however, were not even trying to shoot Harry. They were either leaving him for the Fart Lord to handle, or they were secretly members of the Harry Putter Fan Club and according to by-laws were not allowed to shoot their idol.

Finally, Herbie called out, "That's everyone, Harry. Come, get inside!"

Harry slowly backed up the stairs fending off the press of Nazis. He shot balls of fire out of the tip of his wand, incinerating the German soldiers.

And then Herbie saw a giant approaching. He called, "Run, Harry. Run!"

Harry turned and ran, and Herbie lobbed a grenade at the Nazis at the bottom of the stairs, clearing them out and delaying their pursuit. He opened fire on several more as Harry ran up the steps. However, the giant was coming fast. He swatted Germans out of his way and bound up the stairs after the teenager. He didn't appear to be a fan of Harry's. Herbie poured bullets into the huge creature, but they were like the bite of flies to the roaring giant.

The North Pole elf fired until his last bullet was gone. The giant was nearly upon Harry when Hermione levitated and dropped a great boulder from the top of the Astronomy Tower. It crashed down behind her friend. It hurled into the giant, dashing his brains and knocking him from the stairway. Harry gained the door and swiftly closed it with a clang, leaving Herbie outside to pound on it and scream, "Ahh! Open the door, Harry!"

A moment later, Harry realized his haste and quickly pulled the elf inside to safety, slamming the door behind him and locking it fast.

"Man, I thought I was a goner for sure," said Herbie.

"Sorry about that," Harry said, breathing heavily and wiping the sweat from his brow with the sleeve of his robe.

Herbie, asked, "Did either of you happen to see if Santa made it in all right?"

"I don't think he did," answered Ron. "I saw him fighting in the courtyard, but the enemy swept us apart."

"Crap, more bad news," said Herbie. "Mrs. C. will never forgive me if anything happens to the fat man."

"Don't worry about my Mum. With Fred and George…" Ron started to feel all choked up, but managed to finish. "Well, she has other things to worry about besides next Christmas."

Herbie said, "Nah, not your mom, knucklehead. I meant Mrs. Claus."

Ron replied, "Oh. Well in that case, let's hope Santa made it safely into the dungeons."

"Jesus Christmas!" exclaimed Herbie. "You do know there's a Death Cat in there, don't you?"

Ron said, "Oh, yeah. I forgot."

The Elven Dentist sarcastically asked. "You're good at making someone feel better when things aren't going so well, aren't you?"

"Sorry."

Chapter 20

"Aw, forget it. I gotta find some more ammunition," muttered Herbie as he walked away.

Harry asked Ron, "Did you see if Cage made it in all right?"

Ron turned to Harry and said, "I'm glad you're alright, Harry. That was a close one for you. You need to be more careful. We need you to fight the Fart Lord whenever he gets here."

Harry said, "Yeah, you're right. I'll play it safer from here on."

Ron replied, "Good. And I think Cage got caught up in the crowd heading for the dungeons."

Chapter 21 – The Final Battle Rages On

In the dungeons at Hogwashes, Neville said to Looney, "Things aren't going too well. They've taken the Outer Wall. Our first line of defense is gone."

Before Looney could answer, Cage replied, "Don't be such a downer, man. We're the good guys and the good guys always win."

Neville sighed and said, "If you say so."

The actor said, "I do. It's just good cinema to have the bad guys appear to be doing well at first. What we really need is for a certain 'best friend' character to die, so the hero can exact his revenge. Then the good guys step it up, you know, turn the tide of battle? Plus, we've already had some fantastic explosions, and audiences always love explosions. Really, who doesn't?"

Neville asked, "You do know this is real life and not a movie?"

Cage indignantly said, "With good writing and editing everything's a movie. I'm just putting things in an actor's perspective. I am an actor, you know."

"I was aware of that."

Nicholas said, "Anyway, Harry is about to turn the tide of this battle, aren't you, Harry?"

Chapter 21

Standing nearby, Santa laughed and said, "I think I saw Putter heading for the Astronomy Tower."

Cage slapped his forehead and sighed, "Probably playing it safe again. Hey, is there a bathroom anywhere down here?"

Ron slowly dragged himself up the long stairway to the Astronomy Tower. He was hoping to find Hermione. In the highest chamber Sir Lancelot was looking out of a narrow window upon the battle.

The brave knight asked, "What is the news, King Ron?"

Ron was surprised to hear the knight call him King Ron. He wondered, "Lancelot thinks I'm a king? Where did he get that from?" However, he did not correct the knight for fear that if he did, the Knights of the Round Table would abandon the castle's defense.

He sullenly answered, "Unfortunately, the Outer Wall is taken, Sir. The defense was swept from the courtyard, and now we must defend the keep and the Tower."

"And did Santa make it in?"

"No, Sir. But many of your men retreated into the dungeons; and I believe Father Christmas was among them. In the narrow corridors they may hold back the enemy for a long while and they may find provisions in the Great Eatery."

Sir Lancelot answered, "Yes, and that is more than we have here. There are no provisions within the Tower. I fear things will go poorly if the siege does not end within the day."

"The way their Panzer tanks blast at the tower walls and make the stones shake, I doubt it will come to that. But for now, let's turn our thoughts to preventing them."

"Unfortunately, I feel helpless to contribute, confined as I am in this prison tower," said Sir Lancelot. "I serve little purpose here. If only I could set my lance in the crook of my arm and ride forth before my men upon the field of battle, then the Nazis would know fear!"

The Final Battle Rages On

"I don't know. With their guns, I'm thinking that's probably not the best of ideas," said Ron.

"Hmm. Yes, their guns are formidable. However, Saint Nicholas's elves have superior modern weaponry. It is only the sheer number of our enemy that is such a 'kill buzzard.'"

Ron laughed, "Kill buzzard?"

Sir Lancelot replied, "Oh, dear. I thought that was how Sir Robin said it."

Ron laughed and corrected him, "You mean a buzzkill. Yeah, the Nazis are such a buzzkill."

The knight laughed and said, "That's it. Verily, the Nazis are such a 'buzzkill.'"

Ron laughed and asked, "I was looking for Hermione, have you seen her?"

Lancelot answered, "She is upon the battlements just above us."

"Thanks, and if you will excuse me…"

The Knight of the Round Table said, "Your Majesty, I will not stay here in this tower until it falls. The horses are in the Great Eatery. When dawn comes, my men and I will mount. We will sound the horns and ride forth. Then the Nazis will know fear! Will you ride with me then, King Ron? Perhaps we shall cleave a road, or make such an end as will be worthy of a song – if any of Sir Robin's minstrels are left to sing of us hereafter. Your presence would greatly encourage the men."

Ron swallowed and said, "I will ride with you. We'll go out in a blaze of glory."

"That's the spirit, Your Majesty."

Taking his leave of Sir Lancelot, Ron climbed the stairs to the battlements. However, Hermione had abberated down to the Keep Wall.

The courtyard below was teeming with enemies. Among them there were three Panzers. They were the only ones left. The elves had taken the others out with heavy artillery barrages from the big guns, which were just

Chapter 21

outside the Keep Wall. However, now that the enemy was within the courtyard, the artillery installation had to be abandoned. There was nothing to stop the three Panzers. The German tank's main canons roared and the blasts shook the stones.

While Harry contemplated how to destroy the remaining tanks, grappling-hooks were hurled and ladders were raised. Again and again the Nazis gained the summit of the Keep Wall, and the defenders cast them down to their deaths.

Harry looked forth and saw the eastern sky growing paler. Dawn was coming. The trolls were already abandoning the battle. Yet, the defenders needed further encouragement. They needed another small victory. They needed to destroy the remaining three tanks. But how? And then Harry had an idea, which he put in motion.

The first thing Harry did was find Herbie. Then Harry, Herbie, Hermione, Harrison Ford, Al Roker, and Yu Rang spent the next hour modifying six of Herbie's grenades. For safety, they modified his supply of smoke grenades. It was a good thing, too. Al Roker accidentally set his off and filled one of the floors of the Astronomy Tower with smoke. They had to move down a level to finish what they were doing.

Meanwhile, Ron came down the stairs coughing from all the smoke. Hermione ran to him, hugged him, and kissed him. She said, "I saw what you did! You were magnificent!"

Harry agreed, "You were really amazing, Ron."

Ron didn't answer. His lips puckered a little.

Harry groaned and said, "What did you do that for? You kissed him. Now, he'll be good for nothing the rest of the night!"

Hermione said, "Oh, dear. I forgot all about that."

Then she yelled, "Snap out of it, Ron!" As she did, she gave Ron a heavy-handed slap to the face. There was a loud smack and his whole head turned from it.

The Final Battle Rages On

He stared at her for a moment with angry smoldering eyes and then he embraced her and gave her a huge kiss. When he disengaged from her, she staggered dizzily.

Ron announced, "I have work to do!" He dashed off.

Hermione said, "Wow, what a man!"

Meanwhile, Cage found himself alone in a dungeon bathroom battling a giant anaconda with his bare hands. The snake had bitten his wrist and that made him drop his wand. It had rolled under one of the toilet stalls.

Neville had led the actor to the men's room. However, when the teenager opened the door for Cage and saw Snakey, the young man immediately went into cardiac arrest, clutched at his heart, and fell.

Cage said, "If you don't mind, I'll give you my autograph later. I'm kind of in a hurry."

It was so dark, Cage didn't even see the snake until he lifted up his sunglasses. When he did, he said, "Oh, … my bad."

He managed to pull his wand out of the pocket of his leather jacket, but before he could do anything more, the giant snake latched onto his wrist with a mouth full of dozens of sharp teeth. The snake yanked him into the bathroom. Nicholas promptly tripped over Neville and his wand rolled away out of reach. The huge snake was tossing him about as though he was a salad. As it did, it wound its way around his legs and waist.

Fortunately, Cage carried a Swiss Army knife. He pulled it from his jacket pocket and proceeded to locate his nail file, his can opener, corkscrew, screw driver, and mini saw blade. By the time he located the knife, the snake had wrapped itself around his chest and began squeezing.

Cage plunged the knife into one of the snake's coils. The reaction was painful. The snake constricted harder and his chest ached from it. The knife was his only chance to live. He stabbed it again. The snake's coils tightened. He could barely breathe. His breath came in quick shallow gasps. He stabbed again and the constriction became so tight he could no longer breathe. His heart was pounding in his chest. He could feel his

Chapter 21

pulse throbbing in his temples. He thought his head would explode if his heart didn't.

Then he remembered Harry's magic hat and wished he was wearing it instead of Putter. He could fake his own death and the dumb snake would never know. Then he remembered. He was an Oscar-winning actor. He didn't need a stinking hat to fake his own death. He decided to give the performance of his life.

His body tensed. His back arched. Every muscle in his body became rigid. Then he died. His taut body became limp and lifeless.

A moment later, when the snake unwound itself from the actor's dead body, Cage breathed a huge lungful of air, and as he did, he attacked. He jumped on the snake's back and began stabbing it frantically. His lungs were heaving.

Snakey was in trouble now. The small knife wounds had already taken their toll. He felt weak – too weak to fight back. He tried to escape. However, the man's weight kept him pinned to the floor. Pain kept piercing his body, each time in a new spot. Snakey slowly bled to death.

An hour later, Harry and Herbie were ready. As they unwound the fire hose in the Astronomy Tower, Nicholas Cage arrived. He had a giant anaconda draped over his neck. The tail and head were dragging behind him and he struggled with his enormous burden.

Harry shouted with glee, "You killed Snakey!"

Cage answered, "Well, I *am* awesome, you know!"

He hefted his load off his shoulders and put the giant dead snake down with its head hanging over the Keep Wall.

Harry said, "Me too. Just watch this."

They brought the end of the fire hose out to the Keep Wall. Next Herbie fired the modified grenades at the three Panzers, two at each. The effect was less than spectacular. The Fan Club and other curious onlookers were greatly disappointed. Cage was less than impressed.

The Final Battle Rages On

Nick scoffed, "Sorry, Harry, but you just don't seem to get it at all. Audiences want big explosions. That was a pathetic little popping noise. I barely heard it over the rest of the shooting. Plus, it was Herbie doing all the grenade launching. You just stood there in that stupid-looking sombrero."

However, Harry said, "Wait for it."

Putter yelled for the water to be turned on. A moment later, he aimed a jet of water as it arched over the battlement across the courtyard and struck one of the Panzers, then the second, and then the third. When the water struck the anti-matter toothpaste, which was splattered upon the tanks, it foamed and ate gaping holes in the tank's hulls and turrets. The main guns on two of the Panzer were immediately destroyed. The third could no longer move, but its turret was still functional. It required an explosive grenade to be launched. Herbie did the honors. The grenade bounced into a huge hole in the tank's hull. When it exploded, it set off the ammunition supply. The resultant explosion sent a ball of fire and smoke coursing into the dawn sky. It was a lovely explosion enhanced by the background colors of the rising sun.

Nick called out, "Yeah! Now, that's what I'm talking about!"

There was a huge cheer from the defenders on the walls. The enemy was unnerved by this new defeat. All their tanks were gone. And curse the English, with their black magic again!

Harrison Ford congratulated Harry, "Well done, Putter. Hey, keep me in mind for lead role when they turn this baby into a movie."

Cage cried out, "Too late, Ford, the role's already taken!"

Ford leaned nonchalantly against the parapet and said, "This guy? C'mon, Harry, he's second string. He's the one who ends up with half the roles I turn down."

Cage scoffed, "You mean the roles that are too tough for you to handle."

Ford laughed, "Pffft, I loved your work in *Bangkok Dangerous*."

Chapter 21

"Likewise, you were great in *Hollywood Homicides*."

"*Sorcerer's Apprentice.*"

"*Crystal Skull*"

"*Ghost Rider.*"

"*Six Days, Seven Nights.*"

"*Weatherman.*"

"*Temple of Doom.*"

"What's wrong with *Temple of Doom*? In its day it was the tenth highest grossing film of all time."

"Nothing, if you like cheese."

"You want cheese? How about *The Wicker Man*?"

Cage gritted his teeth. *The Wicker Man* again! It was his weak spot. In fact, in order to get any roles after that bomb, he had to constantly alter casting director's memories to forget about it. Cage knew he should have never started this. He was always outmatched when it came to terrible performances, and *The Wicker Man*, was like the Godzilla of bad acting.

Cage put his nose in the air and said, "Harry wants an Academy Award winning actor playing his role."

Cage pulled no punches. He knew Ford's weak spot too. With all his success the man had never achieved the coveted Oscar.

Ford swallowed and said, "Hey, if Harry wants to take a fifty-fifty chance on his movie, that's all right with me. But if you decide you want the number one actor in the 'Top 100 Movie Stars of All Time,' the actor that's been in three of the top five box-office hits of all time, an actor that brings in billions, not millions, BILLIONS; give me a call."

Harrison handed Harry his business card.

Cage said, "For Pete's sake, Ford. You're a seventy year old man and he's a teenager. You're too old for the role."

Ford said, "I'm not dead yet."

"Your career is."

The Final Battle Rages On

The argument had attracted a small crowd of onlookers. When Cage said this, they cried out, "Ooh!" That last attack was like a boxer hitting below the belt. Everyone knew it was blatantly uncalled for.

Harrison Ford did not answer. He simply stared at Nicholas Cage with an icy glare until the man turned and cowardly fled into the Astronomy Tower.

Harry applied the Resounderous spell to his throat, amplifying his voice, and said, "Attention shoppers, we have a special this morning for those of you who realize that we've whipped your butts all night. Surrender now and live. Don't wait for your friends, be the first to survive."

As Harry spoke, the fighting died down and came to a halt.

Several Nazis yelled and jeered in English, "Commen zee down! If you wish to speak mit us, commen zee down! Ve are the Schutzstaffel, der SS. Ve will fetch you from your dungeon rat hole and burn you stinkink vitches and varlocks at the stake."

"Oh come on already. You guys don't have a prayer now that your tanks are all destroyed."

"That vat you think, Putter. Look at der greatness of our army. Ve are the SS, the lighting war, der blizkreig! We are not dee französische. Ve do not surrender. Ve are not afraid. Ve do not stop the fight for night or day, for fair veather or for storm. Ve come to kill."

Harry said, "Then you do not see that the tide of battle has turned! Surrender now before it is too late."

"Commen zee down or ve will shoot you from the wall," they cried. "This is no parley. You have nothing to offer."

"I have still this to say," answered Harry. "Surrender or I will not spare even one of you. None will be left alive to take back tidings to the Fart Lord. You do not know your own peril."

As Harry stood there upon the battlements before the host of his enemies, many of the SS paused, and looked over their shoulders

Chapter 21

wondering if some doom might be approaching, and some looked up doubtfully at the sky and the rising sun for signs of more tricky wizardry. But other Nazis laughed with loud voices; and a hail of bullets whistled and ricocheted along the wall, as Harry ducked his head back down.

Suddenly, there was a roar of an explosion. The massive keep doors, the archway above them, and the section of the battlements atop, all crumbled and crashed in smoke and dust. Many defenders had gathered there upon the Keep Wall. They plummeted to their deaths. Elves, including Henry the Kitchen Elf and Knights, including Sir Bors and Sir Gwain died. Several of Harry's teachers and fellow students fell, including Humphrey the Wise and Mystical, Ms. Smooch, Ernie Mackelroy, Lavatory Brown, Justin Flinch-Retchedly, and Tabithaa Stevens. And several Cheesleys died including Perky, Greg, Marsha, Jan, Cindy, and Ginny. And among the Fan Club, Wrestlemania Trunks and Rhomulus Loopin were lost.
    Mrs. Cheesley almost died too. However, Kingsley Shuckthecorn quickly cast a levitation spell upon her and saved her life.
    Harry cursed. Those sneaky Nazi bastards used the lull in combat to rig up explosives.

But even as the school's front gate fell, and the Nazis in the courtyard yelled, preparing to charge, a murmur arose behind them. At first it sounded like the rustle of a distant wind, but it grew to a clamor of many German voices crying out in dismay. Harry did not know German but he knew something was not going well for his enemies. The Nazis in the courtyard, heard the rumors, wavered, and looked back.
    And then, sudden and brash, from the Astronomy Tower above, the sound of the great horns of the Knights of Camelot rang out. It was a sound that made everyone who heard it, friend or foe, tremble. Many of the Nazis immediately cast their rifles down and their hands in the air. The echoes rang off the cliffs. And those still upon the Keep Walls looked up, listening with wonder; for the echoes did not fade. The horn blasts rang back from the distant hills of the valley, nearer now and louder they

The Final Battle Rages On

answered one another. It was eerie and chilling. The enemy worried that they had been outflanked and surrounded.

"To Arms! To Arms!" the Knights shouted. "Make ready to charge. For the King. For Sir Bors. For Sir Gwain. Make ready to charge!"

And with that command the Knights of the Round Table came upon their white horses. Their armor and shields gleamed in the morning sun. Their long lances held upward. In front was brave Sir Lancelot. To his right hand was Ron. Behind them rode Sir Balin, Sir Percival, and all the other knights of the Round Table and their retinue of men.

Lancelot called, "Forward, Charge!" With a cry and a great noise they spurred their steeds and lowered their lances. Down from the keep they rode shouting their battle cry as they came. Over the causeway they swept, and they drove through the petrified Nazis as the hot air blows from Beadie the Blowhard. Behind them from the dungeon came the war cry of Saint Nick leading the students, rallying forth to engage the enemy. And the other defenders ran to join them in the attack. The shouting of their voices drowned out the echoes of the horn blasts in the hills.

On they rode, the Knight of the Round Table and their companion Ron. German Captains and Lieutenants fell or fled before them. With their leaders abandoning them, their troops turned and ran for their lives. Ogres and giants did not fully understand, but ran anyway. All enemies had their backs to the lances and their faces to the valley. Though they still outnumbered the defenders, their morale was utterly broken. They cried out and wailed in their fear.

So the Knight of the Round Table and Ron rode from the castle ruins and clove a wide path among the fleeing Nazis to the foot of the great hill. There the company halted to briefly rest. The light of day was bright around them. Shafts of sunlight streamed through the white clouds and glimmered on their armor and lances. But they sat silent on their horses, and they gazed upward along the road.

Only two kilometers lay between them and the crest of the hills. There the proud army of Moldyfart cowered in disarray. In terror they kept their

Chapter 21

distance from the Knight of the Round Table and fled from the students of Hogwashes. They streamed down from the school until all the Quibbage Field was empty of them. Above it, they were packed like swarming insects. They pushed each other and trampled each other, trying to escape. Vainly the Nazis crawled and clambered about the sheer cliff walls of the valley, seeking to get away.

Then suddenly upon the crest of the great hill a rider appeared before them, clad in a white robe, shining bright in the rising sun. Ron recognized the white-robed wizard immediately. It was Grumblesnore and behind him, hastening over the ridge and down the long slope of the great hill poured a thousand men on foot; with swords in their hands. Amid them strode a magnificent steed, tall and strong. Upon its back, a knight in gleaming armor. Upon his shield and banners, a black field with a white tree. As he came to the valley's brink, he set to his lips a great black horn and blew a deep blast.

"What crest be that? A white tree?" Sir Lancelot asked confused. One of the squires answered, "Sir, 'tis the mark of Gondor. The army of Gondor approacheth."

"Alright! Yes! The good guys win!" cried Ron joyously, pumping his fist high in the air. "Grumblesnore has come back! With such a big army, and with the Germans in disarray, victory is ours! Whoopie!"

The Nazis roared, swaying this way and that, turning from one fright to another. Hemmed in by cliff walls and now escape cut off by enemies on both sides! Again the horn sounded from the tower signaling the charge. Down charged the newly arrived army led by their fearsome warrior king and Elvis Grumblesnore. Thousands of fierce swordsmen ran down from the crest of the hills and more followed. Grumblesnore, the White Rider was upon them, and the terror of his coming filled the enemy with madness. The wild ogres fell on their faces before him. The Nazis reeled and screamed and cast aside both rifles and lugers, their hands held high in

The Final Battle Rages On

surrender. Others ran wildly, not knowing which way to turn. Wailing they passed by the knights of Camelot, fleeing the massive army which still poured down from the hilltop crest.

And as the King of Gondor and Grumblesnore approached, the knights of Camelot waited to greet them – to joyfully clasp hands in solidarity of purpose and call out, "Well met!"

Ron shouted to his old Headmaster, "Wow, you came just in time!"

And Grumblesnore laughed as his army drove down from the hill and crashed into the Knights of the Round Table in a surprise attack! Many valiant knights were pulled from their horses. Those behind, turned their steeds and made a hasty retreat. With Excalibur in hand, Ron was able to carve an escape. The small retinue was driven from the field of battle by the vast Army of Gondor.

Trumpets blared once more, only this time sounding a hasty retreat. The students of Hogwashes turned and ran back to their school grounds, back to the Astronomy Tower.

Grumblesnore yelled, "Death to Harry Putter!"

King Aragorm, Son of Arathorm, shouted, "Death to Harry Putter!"

Chapter 21

Chapter 22 – The Deathly Hairballs

The Nazis, having been reinforced by the Army of Gondor, began to pick up their weapons and regroup. As they did, Moldyfart arrived.

The Fart Lord pointed his wand to his throat and cast the Resounderous spell. His loud voice echoed off the cliffs and castle walls as he said, "Putter, I'm giving you one hour to surrender. And if you don't, we will renew the battle and I will personally join in the fight. Every one of your friends will die. I will not spare anyone in the school."

Harry was horrified at the toll of death this wizard's war had already inflicted. He was more horrified that Moldyfart would kill all the students. No one else should have to die.

Harry used his magic to amplify his own voice. He replied, "And I challenge you to meet me in the courtyard in a Wizard's Duel to the Death."

Moldyfart was pleased with that idea. He longed for such an opportunity to annihilate Harry Putter, the cheating scumweasel.

Harry added, "That is unless you're chicken?"

The Fart Lord called out, "Chicken? You're on, Putter! I'll destroy you! No, wait! First, I'm going to make you eat your words. Nobody calls me chicken, especially a… a big 'fraidy cat like you. No wait! First,

Chapter 22

I'll make you eat your words, then I'll mock you some more, and then I'll destroy you."

Harry said, "Alright. But I have one condition! If I choose to meet you in the courtyard for a wizard's duel to the death, you have to spare everyone else's lives – all the students and teachers, all the elves and knights, – everyone here."

The Fart Lord considered this and replied, "Certainly not! I'll spare everyone but Neville Largebottom, he… killed my Snakey! He's going to pay for it with his life!"

Harry did not correct Moldyfart. Nicholas Cage had killed Snakey. And since Neville was already dead, let him think that the student killed the giant anaconda.

Harry simply told the Fart Lord, "Neville's already dead."

The Fart Lord yelled, "Then have Nurse Pomfrite raise him back to life, so I can kill him!"

Harry said, "Nurse Pomfrite's dead too."

Moldyfart yelled, "D'oh! You're next, Putter! And if I find out you're lying to me, I'll have Nurse Pomfrite resurrect you, just so I can have the satisfaction of killing you twice! You have one hour to meet me for a duel to the death."

Considering everything, it was a very generous offer. The situation was grim for the defenders, who had already lost many of their friends in battle. Harry informed everyone that he would duel Lord Moldyfart.

The young man's plan was simple. He would use the magic hat to fake his own death, and while the Fart Lord was celebrating his victory, he'd conduct a surprise attack. He'd fling the snow globe at the back of Moldyfart's head and kill him with the Deathly Hairball.

It was a beautiful early morning that promised a wonderful day of warmth and sunshine. Under a white flag of truce, Harry left the Astronomy Tower. His friends carried the flags and led him out into the courtyard. They formed half of the large circle in which the two combatants would duel. Among those in the front row were: Harry's good friends, Ron and Hermione; celebrities Nicholas Cage, Harrison Ford, and Al Roker; Fan Club members Fabulous Butterpants, Kingsley Shuckthecorn, and Molly Cheesley; Santa and Herbie; Spleen Thomas and

Sir Robin; teachers Minerva McGooglesnot, Mrs. Tickwick, Mrs. Fatfree, and the centaur, Frenzy; and several students such as Yu Rang, Colin Creepy, and 'Crybaby Peepants' Jones. Behind them were many of the other castle defenders.

On the other side of the circle, the Fart Lord's allies stood. There were Fungus Eaters; Bellatrix and Rodolphius Le Deranged, Narcissistic Vain Maldoy and her son, Faco; Grandpappy Shabby and Gramps Foil; the venerable Great Grandpappy Shabby and the revered Great Gramps Foil; Trollores Underbridge, and other enemies of Harry's such as Bobby the Elf, King Aragorm, and Elvis Grumblesnore. There were even a few of the students such as Panties Pimpleton, Ophelia Quirkey, and Perverti Pickle. Behind them were Nazi soldiers with their rifles slung over their shoulders, the men of Gondor, and several ogres.

Many of those in back tried to find a way to see over those in front and so tried to find an advantage to do so. Many lined the battlements overhead. Others stood upon the debris of battle – fallen stones and the wreckage of tanks. The Knights of the Round Table and their followers gazed down from the back of their steeds.

Mrs. Smooch took the center of the circle and with a magically amplified voice, she said, "This is a wizard's duel to the death. The contest is between the two combatants only. Combat will not begin until I throw this white handkerchief. When the handkerchief touches the ground, the two combatants will …"

Just then a beautiful woman arrived on horseback, richly beseen. She cried, "Hold!"

Upon her bidding the crowd parted and let her handsome steed through to the inner circle, where she saluted King Putter. Then and there she asked him a gift that he promised her when she gave him the sword. The beautiful damsel was the Lady of the Pond.

"Now?" asked Harry.

The Lady of the Pond answered, "Verily, I see my time and have come to you anon."

Harry asked, "What sword do you mean?"

Chapter 22

The damsel said, "The sword, Excalibur! That is as much to say as Cut-steel."

Harry slyly said, "But I didn't take the sword. Ron did."

The beautiful woman pouted and was even more lovely to behold. She said, "You were the one who made a promise that day! Is that not so? And has the sword not served you well, bringing you enough men and armies to forge a kingdom?"

A murmur arose from somewhere in the crowd.

Harry sighed. He said, "It is true, a gift I promised you, I mean ye. Ask what ye will and ye shall have it, and it lie in my power to give it."

"Well," said the lady, "I ask the hat upon thy head!"

Harry answered, "Err, I'm a little busy at the moment, can't it wait until after this?"

"What is that, your girlfriend, Putter?" Moldyfart razzed. The Fungus Eaters all laughed. However, they each thought the joke dumb, as the woman was so very beautiful.

The Lady of the Pond replied icily, "You promised, and it is well within your power to hand me the hat."

The knights of Camelot began to whisper most agitatedly among themselves. One among them spurred forward upon his steed, pushing through the crowd.

Harry coolly replied, "But then my head shall be bare. Ask what else ye will, and I shall fulfill your desire."

"I will ask none other thing," said the lady.

Moldyfart teased, "I haven't got all day for you to say your last goodbyes to your girlfriend, Putter." The Fungus Eaters laughed on cue.

The Lady of the Pond asked, "Are you a man of your word? Or aren't you? Are you a King? Or are you a cheating, welching scumweasel?"

Meanwhile, the knights continued to converse in agitation. The one knight, Sir Balin, continued to advance through the crowd and into the circle and as he did, he drew forth his sword.

Harry scowled, "Fine! There! Take it." He thrust the hat out to her.

The Lady of the Pond placed the hat on her head. A mere second later, Sir Balin's sword cut through her graceful neck. Both her head and the hat fell to the ground and a moment later, her body slumped from her mount.

Moldyfart laughed, "Cool, looks like your girlfriend's bought the farm, Putter." The Fungus Eaters all laughed punctually.

Harry turned to Sir Balin and said, "We are under truce and none should die but the Fart Lord or I. For shame! Why have ye done so?"

"Sir," said Balin, "me forthinketh of your displeasure, for this same lady was the untruest lady living, and by enchantment and sorcery she hath been the destroyer of many good knights, and she was causer that my mother was burnt at the stake, through her falsehood and treachery."

Harry replied, "What cause so ever ye had, ye should have forborne her in truce and kept peace in lieu of war. Therefore, withdraw you from the field of battle in all haste ye may, and repent thy dishonor."

Sir Balin was sorry he had displeased Harry and dishonored the truce. He answered, "Forgive me, Sir." He withdrew to his squire, and so they rode forth from the field of battle.

Moldyfart growled, "Can we get on with this?"

When Sir Balin was gone, the Lady of the Pond popped back up. In reality she had ducked the blade, and so despite earlier appearances, she was alive as could be, thanks to the Hat of Imaginary Death. She said, "Not a moment too soon, Sir! Thank you for thy gift."

Moldyfart angrily shouted, "What treachery is this? The woman was dead a second ago and now she lives and is thanking Harry for saving her! How did you do that, Putter? I didn't see you cast any spells. You didn't even raise your wand."

Harry said nonchalantly, "Don't worry about it. It was just a parlor trick – smoke and mirrors."

Moldyfart chewed his lip. He was about to duel his most formidable enemy, and just beforehand, his adversary displays new and powerful magic, – powerful enough to instantly raise the dead. On top of it all, his nemesis claims it to be a parlor trick and tells him not to worry about it.

Furthermore, his archenemy had somehow managed to destroy Ellis Island, which was impossible. He was not aware of any magic that could destroy a whole island. Putter must have used some new and very strong magic to have accomplished that.

Moldyfart was feeling quite vulnerable. His beloved pet was dead and, as far as he knew, there weren't any hoaxcrocks left. All his attempts to

Chapter 22

recover them had been foiled by those meddling teenagers. Plus he hadn't had a chance to make any more Hoaxcrocks because he couldn't find the television remote.

And what was the young man holding? Some sort of glass or crystal shining in the sun. No doubt it was a magic weapon of some kind. Perhaps he had used it to destroy Ellis Island.

Oh, Moldyfart was worried about it alright. He wiped the sweat from his forehead on the sleeve of his dark brown robe. He felt hot.

He stalled, "Confound it, Putter. The sun's up now and that's not good for a man of my complexion."

Harry said, "Well, you are a rather sickly hue. A little sun would probably be good for you."

Moldyfart yelled, "Oh, shut up! I haven't had my breakfast yet and I'm starting to feel a bit irritable. I don't like to duel on an empty stomach. Why don't we all come back in about an hour and a half?"

Harry said, "That's crazy, this will all be over in a minute or two. Let's just get on with it."

The Fart Lord made another terrible excuse, "I just remembered, I have an appointment this morning with my chiropractor and he hates it when I'm late. How does your schedule look for tomorrow morning?"

Harry scoffed, "Oh My God! You're chickening out! You're chicken little!"

"Am not! You're the one who's a… you're a big chicken weasel! Chicken Weasel!"

Grumblesnore yelled impatiently, "Oh, just get on with it already! Smooch, get this thing under way!"

Smooch said, "Are you two ready?"

Harry answered, "Yes."

Moldyfart said, "No. The sun is in my eyes. It's not a fair fight if the sun is in my eyes."

Harry and the Fart Lord shifted so the sun was not in either of their eyes.

Mrs. Smooch called out, "Alright, ready?"

Harry said, "Yes."

Moldyfart answered, "Just a moment."

The Deathly Hairballs

The Fart Lord wiped the sweat from his forehead again. As he did, Harry noticed a terrible smell. It was putrid. Many in the crowd smelled it too and began complaining and trying to back up away from the stench. Several of those downwind passed out. Other's scrambled to find fresh air.

Moldyfart said, "Alright, let's get this over with!"

Smooch said, "When the handkerchief hits the ground, fight. Ready …Set…" She threw the weighted handkerchief arching in the air between the two combatants.

As the cloth fell, Harry held his wand ready and raised his arm overhead, prepared to throw the Elvis Snow globe. If there was ever a time when he needed his aim to be true, this was it. He thought, "Lord, please, let this work!"

He gauged the distance to his enemy, putting all his concentration into his target. And so, he did not notice that Molly Cheesley was running forward into the circle.

He watched the handkerchief ruffle as it arched downward. He concentrated on its decent. He knew the Fart Lord would cast a spell the moment it struck the ground. Yet spells took concentration, energy, and magic words. While his enemy was casting, he would not be able to duck or dodge the snow globe. And so, all Harry needed to do was aim precisely where Moldyfart stood.

When the handkerchief struck the ground, Harry threw the snow globe directly at the Fart Lord. Moldyfart, shouted, "In-a-Godda-Da-Vida!" His wand stabbed forward and the Death Curse shot out of the tip. The green bolt of light coursed through the air toward his nemesis.

Harry dove to the side and avoided the spell. Bellatrix Le Deranged was standing behind him and was not so lucky. She fell down dead.

Harry raised himself to one knee, already casting a spell to counter. However, he stopped. Mrs. Cheesley was lying on the ground in front of Moldyfart.

Ron absolutely snapped. He shrieked insanely, "You killed my mother! I can't believe it! YOU KILLED MY MOTHER! I can't believe it! You just killed MY MOTHER! You freaking killed my MOTHER! OH MY GOD! You just …Wait. Is she dead?"

Chapter 22

The Fart Lord shrugged. He didn't know what the hell just happened, other than Bellatrix was certainly dead.

What had happened was Molly Cheesley ran out into the dueling circle. She had already lost most of the members of her family. She couldn't bear to see the man, Tom Farisol Riddly die too. She loved him. Ever since she was a schoolgirl she had loved him. She had always had a big crush on Tom Farisol Riddly. She took a 'bullet' in the form of a Deathly Hairball in order to save his life.

The thrown snow globe flew directly at the Fart Lord. As it arched through the air, Molly leaped in front of her love. She tried to catch the snow globe, however, it sailed through her fingertips and struck her squarely in her forehead. The globe shattered sending a spray of water and shards of glass flying. She was dead before her body struck the ground. A soggy but Deathly Hairball clung to her forehead.

The duel paused as Ron rushed to his mother's side with tears in his eyes. Everyone watched him. As he ran forward, he said, "Mum, are you alright? Speak to me! Mum?" He knelt by her side and patted her face, saying "Mum? Please, don't be dead. Please, don't be dead."

He grabbed her wrist and tried to find a pulse. He couldn't feel anything. He said, "Come back, Mum! Don't go. Come back!"

Ron used his wand to flick the hairball from her forehead. He began to scream again, "She's dead! She's really dead! Oh God! She's really dead! I can't believe it! You just killed my mother! I can't believe it! You just FREAKING killed MY MOTHER!"

The bereft teenager stood and furiously yelled, "You're SO freaking dead for that, Putter!"

Moldyfart was feeling a bit braver now. He said, "You're gonna have to wait your turn, Cheesley!"

Ron turned his anger upon Moldyfart. His eyes glared with a venomous deadly look. If the Cheesley family had potent levels of magic power, the Fart Lord might have been worried at the look in the teenager's eyes. However, everyone knew the Cheesley's were laughingstocks in the wizard world. They didn't even have a house-elf. The boy was like one of those little yip dogs – all bark and no bite. The young man sure made a lot of noise, but there was no way he was going to kill Putter.

Ron growled, "Why do you get the first turn?"

Moldyfart shrugged and nonchalantly said, "Because I'm older than you, Cheesley."

Ron was so angry, he was visibly shaking. He unleashed his wrath upon the Fart Lord in the form of a giant ball of flame. When it struck the evil wizard, it exploded, blowing him away and leaving a small crater in the earth where Lord Moldyfart had been standing.

The furious teenager yelled, "Not anymore!"

The crowd cheered. The Fart Lord was dead. And he wasn't just dead for the time being. All his hoaxcrocks were destroyed. Moldyfart's entire soul was gone for good.

However, Ron was not satisfied. He turned to the young man who had killed his mother. He growled, "Prepare to die, Putter!"

Hermione pointed her wand and said, "Stupidify!" Ron was stunned when the spell struck him. She said, "Looks like we'll have to alter his memories a bit before he wakes up again."

Nicholas Cage said, "I can help with that." He pointed his wand and said, "Don't forget to brush your teeth with Colgate toothpaste!" He spent a minute rearranging Ron's memory so that Ron would believe that Moldyfart killed his mother and Harry's snow globe had killed Bellatrix Le Deranged.

In the meanwhile, Grumblesnore cast the Resounderous spell on his throat as he stepped onto one of the large stones in the middle of the circle. As he did, three hundred Nazi soldiers cocked the firing pins on their bolt-action rifles. And men by the thousands drew their swords. They had the much smaller group defending Hogwashes completely surrounded and had rifles leveled at their backs.

Grumblesnore said, "Surprise! Ha, Ha! I hope everyone likes surprises as much as I do! Now, throw down your weapons! Especially you, Putter!"

Chapter 22

The defenders of Hogwashes had no choice but to surrender. Resistance would be suicide. They threw down their weapons. The students dropped wands, the elves discarded their automatic machine guns and grenades, the knights abandoned their swords and daggers. Harry tossed his wand to the ground.

Grumblesnore laughed and said, "Looks like everything has gone according to my plan. I knew Harry would come through for me and destroy all the hoaxcrocks. And then it didn't matter who won the wizard's duel to the death. Either way, I'd be the winner! Thanks, Harry, oh, err, I mean, Ron, for conveniently getting Moldyfart out of my way. And since I'm the one with the biggest army in his pocket around here, I'm large and in charge! Who's the King? Me! The King is King! Ha, Ha! Thank you very much!

And as of this moment forward, I declare myself King! King of the Ministry of Magic, King of Hogwashes, King of Middle Earth, King of the Magic Kingdom, and King of France, but c'mon France is just a freebee.

Ron, who had recovered, said, "Not the Magic Kingdom! Take over Epcot, if you have to, but not the Magic Kingdom!"

Grumblesnore ignored Ron's comment. He continued, "But I must say, I'm glad you are the one left alive Putter. Killing Moldyfart would have been nice, but not nearly as satisfying as killing you is going to be! Ha, Ha!

And then, I will rule happily ever after without any diva-wizards to make my life miserable. And I must say, if anyone deserves to kill you Putter, it's me! Oh, I can't tell you how long I've dreamed of it. All those years of trying to run a school with you running amok! It was enough, well, to make me want to kill you. Seriously."

As Grumblesnore spoke, a tawny cat crept out from under a nearby pile of rubble. Unseen by the man addressing the crowd, it stretched its front paws upon the rock where Elvis was standing. The King continued his speech unaware.

He said, "For decades, I run a school peacefully and like clockwork, then Harry Putter shows up, and ever since his preschool year, it's been nothing but trouble! All my problems will be gone, once and for all, when I kill Harry Putter in a duel to the ..."

The Deathly Hairballs

At that moment, in one wracking cough, the cat cacked up a hairball upon Grumblesnore's boot. The old man's eyes rolled up in their sockets and he keeled over dead.

Harry laughed and shouted, "Long live the King!"

A chant ensued where everyone there joined in, shouting, "Long live the King! Long live the King!"

The defenders of Hogwashes ran forward and lifted Ron Cheesley upon their shoulders. They continued to shout, "Long live the King! Long live the King!"

Hermione picked up the tawny cat and said, "Who's a Good Girl! Yes, you are! Mommy missed you while she was gone."

Harry said, "Wait a sec! Croakshanks is the third bad kitten?"

Hermione answered, "Why do you think we named her Croakshanks?"

Chapter 22

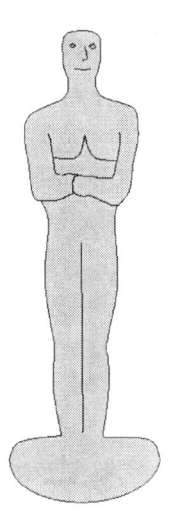

Chapter 23 – Epilogue: 19 Years Later

(Note to Readers – In order to experience this epilogue to its fullest potential, please wait until 19 years pass since you read the first 22 chapters.)

It was the first day of September, which happened to be the first day of preschool for young Pugsly Putter. Harry, his wife, Yu Rang-Putter, and Uncle Regular Smack the Mime were all there at Victoria Station on Platform π (Pi). Harry had ingeniously brought along a Hostess French Apple Pie and had his son, Pugsly, concentrate on it, while running into the illusionary brick wall between platforms three and four. It worked like a charm. And it was much easier than memorizing π to the tenth decimal. It was just a little trick he had learned – part of his life's experiences – and it sure beat beating your head against a brick wall.

For Harry, who was now 37 years old, being there was like taking a walk down memory lane. Memories of his many escapades at Hogwashes filled his thoughts. His school days had been the highlight of his life. The career of an Auditor was a lot more boring than Kingsley Shuckthecorn and Mad Dog Hooty made it seem. He spent his days toiling in relative anonymity and leading a very boring middle-aged life. Regardless of his

Chapter 23

chosen career, it would be hard to top his school years. After all, they did make a movie all about his former adventurous days.

And it was not just any movie – it was a Benny Bigshot production, so of course, it was a summer blockbuster when it first premiered seventeen years ago. The working title, *The Quest to Destroy Lord Moldyfart* was changed to *The Return of the King*. Audiences were mesmerized by the incredible story enhanced by a great script, superb acting, and amazing special effects.

The movie won a slew of awards, chief among them was the Oscar for Best Picture. Nicholas Cage won the Academy Award for Best Actor for his portrayal of Spanky Wu-Tang. (Harry Putter was not considered a worthy enough name for a Hollywood blockbuster hero.) Will Smith ran away with the Oscar for Best Supporting actor for his role as Ron Cheesley. Angelina Jolie swept up the Best Actress award for her rendition of Hermione Stranger. And though he didn't win an Academy Award, Toby McGuire received rave reviews for his portrayal of Soul Splitter, better known as Lord Moldyfart.

And incidentally, there was a sequel, *The Return of the King II: Kingdom of the Crystal Skull*. However, the sequel had nothing to do with any of Harry's real life adventures. Of the original cast, only Nicholas Cage was in it, and it consequently bombed at the box office and was trashed in all its reviews.

And so Harry sighed, as he often did, remembering fondly his school years. Yu Rang groaned. Obviously, she was reminiscing too.

The overweight auditor thought to himself, "It's too bad Ron and Hermione couldn't be here to see their son off to school too."

However, young Skippy (short for Skipper), was going to attend Oxford preschool. Harry couldn't really fault Ron and Hermione for it. They were in the public eye and Hogwashes didn't have quite the same reputation and prestige as Oxford, as though that should matter.

Shorty after the death of Lord Moldyfart, Ron Cheesley became King of France. It was determined that his lineage on his mother's side was

Epilogue: 19 Years Later

from a French Paladin of the surname De Fromage. However, more importantly his father was a direct descendent of Louis the Fourteenth. After the French Army had surrendered, their Prime Minister resigned in embarrassment. The French people became disgusted with the rest of the spineless, gutless, and sissified aristocracy that had pervaded the fifth Republic's assembly, senate, and other ministry positions.

The French people rose in revolt forming a giant ragtag army of civilians flocking to the sword of kings – Excalibur. In a needlessly bloody coup d'état, they overthrew the government that was already in disarray due to the unexpected resignation of the Prime Minister. The French army, of course, did not engage the French people in combat. Seeing how things were going, they joined sides with the citizens and helped them to overthrow the Fifth Republic. The people were only too glad to install a new regime and begin a new era.

That era began with optimism and hope in the Return of the King. The people stole the Crown of Louis XV from the Louvre Museum and used it in the coronation ceremony. They named Ron king, or more specifically, Roi Ronald Qui a Un Goût de Fromage, meaning King Ronald, who has a taste of cheese. In the same ceremony, they placed the Crown of Empress Eugenie, also stolen from the Louvre, upon the head of Hermione Stranger, his newly taken wife. They had lots of names for her, such as: disgusting harpy, tacky she-devil, repulsive wench, out-of-style shrew, stuck-up strumpet, tasteless tart, unfashionable snot, pouting know-it-all, and big-headed freak.

And so, Ron and Hermione wouldn't be there waiting for the Hogwashes Express to arrive. Unfortunately, Faco Maldoy showed up with his wife, Panties Pimpleton, and their son, Scrumptious Maldoy. The preschooler was holding the hand of a six-foot tall female android.

Harry groaned at their arrival.

Maldoy, his voice full of derision, said, "Putter."

Harry replied with detestation, "Maldoy."

Maldoy asked, "Still shoveling horse manure, Putter?"

Chapter 23

Harry asked, "You mean like you did in your book?"

Harry was referring to the bestseller Faco had written eighteen years earlier, *The Truth About Harry Putter: Secrets Only a Best Friend Would Know*. The blonde-haired swindler had cashed in on Putter's notoriety, dishing the dirt in a slamming exposé that shredded Putter's character or, depending on your perspective, lack thereof. In doing so, Maldoy had become filthy rich in a way Harry never managed for himself. Despite the success of the movie about his life, Putter neglected to sufficiently protect his rights to his own story, and so, did not profit overly from the blockbuster film.

Scrumptious said to Pugsly, "I'm bringing in my droid, I named her 'Optimus Prime.' What do you got for show and tell?"

Pugsly took out his show and tell from his little backpack. It was a *Return of the King* action figure of Nicholas Cage's character, Spanky Wu-Tang.

"Pffft," Scrumptious asked, "What's the matter with you, Putter? Don't you have any real toys?"

Pugsly stuck his tongue out at the obnoxious little boy. The preschool Maldoy returned the favor.

Harry sighed and thought to himself, "Memories are like kittens, reality is like a full grown cat."

Also by Timothy R. O'Donnell:
The Epic Erthelba Series

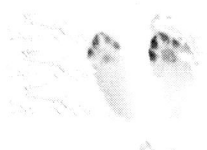

Iibrahiim introduces a post-apocalyptic earth of adapting life forms, some of which can use 'magic,' including man, who has evolved into five races. Iibrahiim explores rich and fascinating new cultures, philosophies, and religions, while telling the tale of one of its heroes, Quaagthook. Meanwhile, the over arching storyline examines the nature of reality and perception, and man's obligation to himself – to discover his life's purpose, and to fulfill the reason for his existence, if possible.

Nothing good ever comes from the darkness! The saga continues in Polydora, the second novel in the epic Erthelba series. Quaagthook encounters the soulless Umaanii, a warlike race, cruel and quick to fight. Meanwhile, his soul is trapped in Polydora's Abyss. He must match wits with the conniving goddess of evil, with not only his life, but his very soul at stake. How does a mere mortal defy and defeat an all-powerful goddess?

What destiny lies within the Goddess of Fate's control? The saga continues in Hgia Lucii, the third novel in the epic Erthelba series. Quaagthook discovers the dead do not always rest peacefully. In the Realm of Discord, a chaotic domain with aberrations hitherto unimagined – demons are unfathomably embodied as in no other realm. Here only the strangest of chances make survival possible. Here the Goddess, Hgia Lucii holds his soul in the palm of her hand. How will he win it back?

Quaagthook discovers the only commodity of value is his everlasting soul. Another god was even at that heartbeat endeavoring to obtain it. But the price, he would have to pay to save it is unbearably high. As difficult as his previous tests were, they pale by comparison to the temptation of the god of law. The saga continues in Athandoros, the final novel in the epic Erthelba series.

CPSIA information can be obtained at www.ICGtesting.com
265437BV00001B/2/P